CW01249996

# The Horus Heresy

Book 1 – HORUS RISING
Dan Abnett

Book 2 – FALSE GODS
Graham McNeill

Book 3 – GALAXY IN FLAMES
Ben Counter

Book 4 – THE FLIGHT OF THE EISENSTEIN
James Swallow

Book 5 – FULGRIM
Graham McNeill

Book 6 – DESCENT OF ANGELS
Mitchel Scanlon

Book 7 – LEGION
Dan Abnett

Book 8 – BATTLE FOR THE ABYSS
Ben Counter

Book 9 – MECHANICUM
Graham McNeill

Book 10 – TALES OF HERESY
edited by Nick Kyme and Lindsey Priestley

Book 11 – FALLEN ANGELS
Mike Lee

Book 12 – A THOUSAND SONS
Graham McNeill

Book 13 – NEMESIS
James Swallow

Book 14 – THE FIRST HERETIC
Aaron Dembski-Bowden

Book 15 – PROSPERO BURNS
Dan Abnett

Book 16 – AGE OF DARKNESS
edited by Christian Dunn

Book 17 – THE OUTCAST DEAD
Graham McNeill

Book 18 – DELIVERANCE LOST
Gav Thorpe

Book 19 – KNOW NO FEAR
Dan Abnett

Book 20 – THE PRIMARCHS
edited by Christian Dunn

Book 21 – FEAR TO TREAD
James Swallow

Book 22 – SHADOWS OF TREACHERY
edited by Christian Dunn and Nick Kyme

Book 23 – ANGEL EXTERMINATUS
Graham McNeill

Book 24 – BETRAYER
Aaron Dembski-Bowden

Book 25 – MARK OF CALTH
edited by Laurie Goulding

Book 26 – VULKAN LIVES
Nick Kyme

Book 27 – THE UNREMEMBERED EMPIRE
Dan Abnett

Book 28 – SCARS
Chris Wraight

Book 29 – VENGEFUL SPIRIT
Graham McNeill

Book 30 – THE DAMNATION OF PYTHOS
David Annandale

Book 31 – LEGACIES OF BETRAYAL
Various authors

Book 32 – DEATHFIRE
Nick Kyme

Book 33 – WAR WITHOUT END
Various authors

Book 34 – PHAROS
Guy Haley

Book 35 – EYE OF TERRA
Various authors

Book 36 – THE PATH OF HEAVEN
Chris Wraight

Book 37 – THE SILENT WAR
Various authors

*Other Novels and Novellas*

PROMETHEAN SUN
Nick Kyme

TALLARN: EXECUTIONER
John French

AURELIAN
Aaron Dembski-Bowden

SCORCHED EARTH
Nick Kyme

BROTHERHOOD OF THE STORM
Chris Wraight

THE PURGE
Anthony Reynolds

THE CRIMSON FIST
John French

THE HONOURED
Rob Sanders

PRINCE OF CROWS
Aaron Dembski-Bowden

THE UNBURDENED
David Annandale

DEATH AND DEFIANCE
Various authors

RAVENLORD
Gav Thorpe

*Many of these titles are also available as abridged and unabridged audiobooks.
Order the full range of Horus Heresy novels and audiobooks from*
blacklibrary.com

*Audio Dramas*

| | |
|---|---|
| THE DARK KING<br>Graham McNeill | CENSURE<br>Nick Kyme |
| THE LIGHTNING TOWER<br>Dan Abnett | WOLF HUNT<br>Graham McNeill |
| RAVEN'S FLIGHT<br>Gav Thorpe | HUNTER'S MOON<br>Guy Haley |
| GARRO: OATH OF MOMENT<br>James Swallow | THIEF OF REVELATIONS<br>Graham McNeill |
| GARRO: LEGION OF ONE<br>James Swallow | TEMPLAR<br>John French |
| BUTCHER'S NAILS<br>Aaron Dembski-Bowden | ECHOES OF RUIN<br>Various authors |
| GREY ANGEL<br>John French | MASTER OF THE FIRST<br>Gav Thorpe |
| GARRO: BURDEN OF DUTY<br>James Swallow | THE LONG NIGHT<br>Aaron Dembski-Bowden |
| GARRO: SWORD OF TRUTH<br>James Swallow | THE EAGLE'S TALON<br>John French |
| THE SIGILLITE<br>Chris Wraight | IRON CORPSES<br>David Annandale |
| HONOUR TO THE DEAD<br>Gav Thorpe | RAPTOR<br>Gav Thorpe |

*Download the full range of Horus Heresy audio dramas from*
blacklibrary.com

*Also available*

THE SCRIPTS: VOLUME I
edited by Christian Dunn

THE SCRIPTS: VOLUME II
edited by Laurie Goulding

VISIONS OF HERESY
Alan Merrett

MACRAGGE'S HONOUR
Dan Abnett and Neil Roberts

# THE HORUS HERESY®

*John French*

# TALLARN: IRONCLAD

*The darkness beneath…*

BLACK LIBRARY

*For Andy Smillie.*

**A BLACK LIBRARY PUBLICATION**

First published in Great Britain in 2015.
This edition published in 2016 by
Black Library,
Games Workshop Ltd.,
Willow Road,
Nottingham, NG7 2WS, UK.

10 9 8 7 6 5 4 3 2 1

Produced by Games Workshop in Nottingham.

Tallarn: Ironclad © Copyright Games Workshop Limited 2016. Tallarn: Ironclad, GW, Games Workshop, Black Library, The Horus Heresy, The Horus Heresy Eye logo, Space Marine, 40K, Warhammer, Warhammer 40,000, the 'Aquila' Double-headed Eagle logo, and all associated logos, illustrations, images, names, creatures, races, vehicles, locations, weapons, characters, and the distinctive likenesses thereof, are either ® or TM, and/or © Games Workshop Limited, variably registered around the world.
All Rights Reserved.

A CIP record for this book is available from the British Library.

ISBN13: 978 1 78496 135 0

Product code: 60040181199

No part of this publication may be reproduced, stored in a retrieval system, or transmitted in any form or by any means, electronic, mechanical, photocopying, recording or otherwise, without the prior permission of the publishers.

This is a work of fiction. All the characters and events portrayed in this book are fictional, and any resemblance to real people or incidents is purely coincidental.

See Black Library on the internet at
# blacklibrary.com

Find out more about Games Workshop
and the world of Warhammer 40,000 at
# games-workshop.com

Printed and bound in China.

# The Horus Heresy®
*It is a time of legend.*

The galaxy is in flames. The Emperor's glorious vision for humanity is in ruins. His favoured son, Horus, has turned from his father's light and embraced Chaos.

His armies, the mighty and redoubtable Space Marines, are locked in a brutal civil war. Once, these ultimate warriors fought side by side as brothers, protecting the galaxy and bringing mankind back into the Emperor's light.
Now they are divided.

Some remain loyal to the Emperor, whilst others have sided with the Warmaster. Pre-eminent amongst them, the leaders of their thousands-strong Legions are the primarchs. Magnificent, superhuman beings, they are the crowning achievement of the Emperor's genetic science. Thrust into battle against one another, victory is uncertain for either side.

Worlds are burning. At Isstvan V, Horus dealt a vicious blow and three loyal Legions were all but destroyed. War was begun, a conflict that will engulf all mankind in fire. Treachery and betrayal have usurped honour and nobility. Assassins lurk in every shadow. Armies are gathering.
All must choose a side or die.

Horus musters his armada, Terra itself the object of his wrath. Seated upon the Golden Throne, the Emperor waits for his wayward son to return. But his true enemy is Chaos, a primordial force that seeks to enslave mankind to its capricious whims.

The screams of the innocent, the pleas of the righteous resound to the cruel laughter of Dark Gods. Suffering and damnation await all should the Emperor fail and the war be lost.

The age of knowledge and enlightenment has ended.
The Age of Darkness has begun.

# ~ DRAMATIS PERSONAE ~

*Imperial Army*

| | |
|---|---|
| SILAS KORD | Colonel Commander, 001 Malcador assault tank *War Anvil*, officer commanding Tallarn 71st |
| MORI | Driver, 001 Malcador assault tank *War Anvil* |
| ZADE | 1st Gunner, 001 Malcador assault tank *War Anvil* |
| SACHA | 1st Loader, 001 Malcador assault tank *War Anvil* |
| SAUL | Forward Gunner, 001 Malcador assault tank *War Anvil* |
| KOGETSU | Sponson Gunner, 001 Malcador assault tank *War Anvil* |
| SHORNAL | Sponson Gunner, 001 Malcador assault tank *War Anvil* |
| | |
| ABBAS | Lieutenant, Vanquisher *Mourner*, commander No.1 Sqdn, Tallarn 71st |
| ZEKENILLA | Lieutenant, Executioner *Noon Star*, commander No.2 Sqdn, Tallarn 71st |
| ORIGO | Lieutenant, lead scout *Razor* |
| | |
| AUGUSTUS FASK | Colonel, Crescent Shelter command staff |
| ELO SUSSABARKA | Brigadier-Elite, commander of the Rachab fortress |

*Officio Assassinorum*

| | |
|---|---|
| IAEO | Unbound Infocyte, Omega Tabulation, Clade Vanus |

*Dark Mechanicum*

| | |
|---|---|
| SOTA-NUL | Disciple of Kelbor-Hal |

*Adeptus Astra Telepathica*

| | |
|---|---|
| PROPHESIUS | Metatron |

*Navigators*

| | |
|---|---|
| HES-THAL | Black Oculus Navigator |

*IV Legion 'Iron Warriors'*

| | |
|---|---|
| PERTURABO | Primarch of the Iron Warriors |
| FORRIX | 'The Breaker', First Captain, triarch |
| HREND | 'The Ironclad', Contemptor-class Dreadnought, commander of the 'Cyllaros' armoured assault group |
| JARVAK | Commander, Sicaran '78/5', lieutenant of 'Cyllaros' group |
| ORUN | Castraferrum-class Dreadnought – Mortis Pattern, 'Cyllaros' group |
| GORTUN | Contemptor-class Dreadnought, 'Cyllaros' group |
| VOLK | Commander of Sightless Warren – Core Reach I, Master of 786th Grand Flight armada |
| TALDAK | Warrior of the 17th Grand Battalion elite |

*X Legion 'Iron Hands'*

| | |
|---|---|
| MENOETIUS | Commander, Predator *Cretatogran* |

*XVI Legion 'Sons of Horus'*

| | |
|---|---|
| ARGONIS | 'The Unscarred', emissary of the Warmaster, Chieftain of the Isidis Flight |

*XX Legion 'Alpha Legion'*

| | |
|---|---|
| THETACRON | Commander, Harrow Group Arcadus |
| JALEN | Operative |

'Victory is a child of many parents. Defeat is an orphan.'
— ancient Terran aphorism, origin unknown

'To know war we should ask the dead how they ended, not the living how they endured.'
— General Zavier Gorn, recorded remarks

'To think that we know everything is a condition of the human mind. The animal within us cannot tolerate the possibility that knowledge is a matter of selection, judgement a matter of focus, clarity a consequence of exclusion.
There is not one truth.
Reality does not break along clean lines.'
— Precepts of the Vanus Temple, Officio Assassinorum

# PART ONE
# SEEKERS

*Night fell across the face of Tallarn, and the war machines followed the dying light. Dust rose in their wake as the drying ground powdered under their tracks. If any living thing could have stood on the surface of Tallarn and survived, they would have heard the approach of the machines long before they saw them. Spread out in long lines, or clustered together, they covered the dark ground in a carpet of armour. It was not an army. Such a name could not touch its nature.*

*It was a host.*

*They had come from dozens of the buried shelters across Tallarn, war machines bearing the scars of war like honours bestowed by great kings. Between them walked the automata of the Mechanicum, and above them the god machines of the Titan Legions strode. Signals crackled between them, swarming invisibly through the air.*

*Far behind the advancing host, men and women waited in small rooms filled with the voices that scratched from speaker grilles. Few spoke, most simply waited and listened. There was nothing they could do now. All the weeks of planning, preparation and coordination were unfolding across the dead land above. Some twitched with nervousness. Others simply stared into space with the dead eyes of people who were trying not to feel anything. A few slept, slumped over their consoles, in spite of the power of the moment. No one woke them. Sleep would be banished soon enough.*

*In the time since the first loyalist forces had reached Tallarn there had been two attempts to do what they now were trying to do again. This night would be the third attempt to break the Iron Warriors foothold on the surface of Tallarn, and bring the battle to an end.*

# ONE

**Waking
Arrival
Sight**

'War Anvil, confirm *unit status*.' The voice from the vox filled Kord's ears.

'Closing on waypoint,' he replied, keeping his eyes on the auspex screen. 'No enemy sighted.'

*'Attack pattern one, confirmed.'*

'Confirmed,' Kord's voice was low, steady. 'We are at the kill edge.'

*'Good fortune,* War Anvil.'

He did not reply to the sign-off. The rattle of his machine filled the silence which followed.

It was dark inside the hull. His breath had fogged the eyepieces of his enviro-suit. Six straight hours skinned inside the suit, breathing from tanks of air, unable to move more than a few inches; it was all so familiar that he had trouble thinking of how else war could be fought.

His machine was an old Malcador assault tank, its class named for one of the Emperor's closest courtiers. No doubt the man was a fine example of everything that was best about people who never had to see those who stood in the excrement beneath them. The tank was a brute though, with a name to match. She was called *War Anvil*, and was an ugly slab of tracks, armour and jutting gun barrels. A battle cannon stuck out from a turret high on her back, and a wide-mouthed demolisher cannon from a mount on her forward hull. Two lascannons nested in sponsons on the tank's flanks. A crew of six worked inside its hull. The primary gunner and crew squeezed into a space just in front of the commander's nest, so close that Kord could tap each of them on the shoulder without reaching. The machine's drive and ammunition took up most of its bulk, with the sponson gunners isolated behind crawl hatches on either side of a cramped central compartment. Both the forward gunner and driver were wedged down behind the front armour plates with just room enough for them not to be killed by the demolisher's recoil.

It was a reliable, but ill-designed creature. The battle cannon had a limited forward traverse arc, and the sponsons could not cover the machine's rear arc. Get behind it, and *War Anvil*'s armour counted for nothing. There had been a joke amongst the Jurnian officer corps that the Malcador hull was an 'assault tank' because no one could think of another use for a machine whose guns could only fire forwards. That did not matter to Kord. *War Anvil* had gotten him out of the fall of the Sapphire City, and made five kills in the process. Since then it had never failed, for all its age and flaws. If he had a home then *War Anvil*'s cramped and corroding insides was it.

*And now we are going back to what remains of the city we fled*, he thought. He blinked away a bead of sweat running into his eye, and rechecked the unit markers on the screen. All of his machines were there, rolling forward in a line half a kilometre wide. Executioners, Vanquishers, and all the other mismatched assortment that was now his regiment: the leavings, the dregs, the survivors. In truth it was barely company strength, but he was still a Colonel Commander, and rank meant that certain formalities followed, even out here, on the dead edge of existence.

'*This is not going to work*,' Sacha's voice lilted over the internal vox. He ignored it, just like he had ignored the goodwill sign-off from command. There was, quite frankly, no point in replying to either. He thumbed the unit vox, and winced as it shrieked in his ears.

'All units, this is *War Anvil*. We are in the attack path, estimate time to outer defence units two minutes.'

The acknowledgements came. Kord counted them off as he heard each call sign. Even if a machine was still moving, and showing an identification signal, that did not mean its crew were alive. Sometimes the seals went on a tank's hatches, and the virus-laden air would eat through the crew's air feeds without them noticing. Tanks had rolled on for kilometres with their crew dead inside them, their drivers' dead hands still pressing the drive levers.

'How much have we got out here?' It was Sacha again. She was resting her head on the breech of the battle cannon. He did not look at her. The screen in front of him was more important than her need to talk her nerves out. 'I mean,' she carried on, 'how many machines are in just this wave? Five hundred? A thousand? Throne, that's just us tank riders. I heard the Titans are walking for this. That's enough rolling iron to shake the ground all the way back to the stars.' She laughed nervously. 'They just expect the Iron Warriors not to have spotted it?'

Kord was watching the distance to their waypoint count down across the auspex screen. He keyed the external vox.

'All units–'

'I mean, is this plan just based on us being dumb, or them being dumber?'

'Light weapons and fire free. Anything in front of us is a target. Repeat, light weapons, fire free.'

Sacha sat up and rolled her shoulders and neck, the heavy folds of her enviro-suit squeaking as they rubbed together.

'And if they are not dumb–'

'Sacha,' he said, leaning in to press his eyes against the forward sight.

'Yeah?'

'Load the gun, and then be quiet.'

A second later he felt the thump as the cannon's breech closed on a shell. Explosive, and incendiary; he did not need to check that Sacha had remembered the mission briefing. Her inability to shut up had nothing to do with her memory, or how she handled the main cannon.

'Fog's not thinned.' It was Saul. Kord could almost hear the forward gunner trying to force down his fear and fatigue. Kord squinted into the swirling green light of his own gunsight, and keyed the regimental vox.

'*Razor*, this is *War Anvil*, what can you see?'

'*Nothing, looks clear,*' Origo's voice came back straight away, clipped and sharp, '*but they are there. I know.*'

Kord nodded. Origo's scout squadron was half a kilometre in front of them, spread out and watching for the enemy.

'Never a good start,' muttered Sacha.

'Passing waypoint one,' called Mori from the driver's nest. Kord took a slow breath, counted long seconds as he breathed it out again. Just in front of him Zade leaned into the battle cannon's sight, and flicked the guard off the firing trigger.

Kord keyed the regimental-wide vox.

'Okay, let's light this up. All units on my word.' He was sighting into the murk which boiled across the forward sight. 'The word is Vengeance.' He pulled the trigger, and the dark, shrouded world became a sheet of light.

*The air of Isstvan V was fire. Hrend could not see the horizon. A firestorm rolled above and around Hrend. The shrill of his armour's integrity and heat alarms had ceased several minutes before. He could feel coldness creeping across his flesh. He was breathing fumes and smoke but he could not smell them. He felt like shivering despite the flames all around. He knew what that meant. The air in his lungs, in his nose, in his throat, was burning him from the inside. The seals around his waist and knees had melted, and the fire was seeping in. He was cooking inside his armour. He was dying.*

*'Iron within…' he rasped, feeling blisters form on his lips and tongue. He kept wading forward, armour hissing and shrieking as it fought*

against damage. The ground sucked at his legs as he forced himself towards the cover of the wreck of a... He was not sure what it had been, a Rhino perhaps, but his helmet visor had dimmed to near blackness, and the wreck was a twisted shell. The vox scratched in his ear, but he knew better than to respond. It was just a ghost of distortion, the inferno laughing at him for his defiance. He was alone out here, in the swamp made by the burning blood of his brothers and their war machines.

'Iron without...'

He had failed. That much was clear. Surrounded, betrayed and outnumbered, the Raven Guard and Salamanders were doomed. But they still had teeth to bite back with. He should have anticipated how they would respond. He should have deployed differently. He should... He should have died when the first rocket salvoes hit. That was the reward he had earned by his weakness, and if he ended now it would only be because he had proved weak again.

He reached the wreck. The edges of its shattered hull were glowing like metal pulled from a forge.

'Iron...' he heaved a burning breath. His vision blurred as the moisture cooked in his eyeballs. 'Iron...' He slid to the floor, and the fire closed over him... burning...

'Master.' The word sent a buzz of pain through him, and the dream of Isstvan melted into waking. For a second he felt as if he were drowning, as if warm, black water were all around him. Then his nerves reconnected him to the Dreadnought, and he was ironclad again. The remains of his body flickered with a memory of pain. For a second the weak core of his being wanted to scream.

'Master,' the voice came again.

Waking was worse than dying.

Silence surrounded him. When he had been alive, before he had been reborn as a Dreadnought, he had never noticed the soft clamour that life made: the beat of hearts and blood, the rise and fall of breath, the almost imperceptible noises of muscle and bone moving together. When he woke now it was to blank nothingness.

Slowly he activated the Dreadnought's senses. Sound came first. The wind whistled around him. Then he became aware of his limbs, of the pistons and servos waiting for his will, of the weapons which were part of him. Last he activated the sensor pod set into the sarcophagus like a helm in a suit of armour. He looked out through his machine's eyes. Through *his* eyes.

Fog swirled in the green murk before him. Rangefinders, infra-sensors and auspex arrays began to overlay his sight. He could see the enemy now. Distant pinpricks of heat growing brighter as they came closer.

*'Master, do you hear?'* The voice broke through the moan of the wind.

'I hear,' he said, feeling the machine take the words from the flayed nerves of his throat and cast them across the vox.

*'The enemy are advancing,'* said the voice. *Jarvak,* he thought, watching the input from his machine senses scroll across his view in columns of data. All of the war machines of his command were in position, scattered through the ruins around him. They had been waiting for twenty hours, three minutes, and forty-five seconds precisely. Jarvak had woken him at the correct time.

Hrend watched the enemy advance. The pattern of their deployment was not ideal, and their formation lacked precision. They had also yet to detect Hrend or any of his force. Part of him wondered why they were attacking in this way. It was hopeless. The Sightless Warren would not fall. It was born of iron, and guarded by iron, and would never fail.

'Stand ready,' he said.

*'By your will,'* came the reply from Jarvak.

Hrend saw the data-stream change as the status of the three Predators, and two Venators changed to active. Their systems were still half dormant, their heat and electronic signatures small enough that they should be invisible to auspexes. At least that was the intention. That left his two ironclad brothers.

'Orun? Gortun?' he spoke their names. No reply came for a second.

*'I wake, master.'* Orun's voice was flat and metallic. It was the mirror of Hrend's own voice.

Gortun's answer was a growl of static.

Hrend watched and waited until the enemy units were on the edge of the kill zone created by his group's guns.

'Iron,' he said, and then paused. A squall of dull blackness pulled at him, and somewhere he felt the cartilage of his charred throat try and form the next word. 'Within.'

'*Iron without,*' came the reply from his brothers.

THE GUNSHIP LAUNCHED as its parent strike ship skimmed close to Tallarn. In the craft's cockpit Argonis watched as warning lights washed his view of Tallarn's orbit.

The planet looked like a ball of rancid yellow fat, shot through with smudges of smoke. Wreckage caged its orbits, glittering in long streams and banks of twisted metal. The fires of a void battle glittered above the planet's northern polar region. It looked like a big fight to Argonis's eyes. He corrected his course to ensure that they would come nowhere near the battle-sphere, locked onto his primary target, and pushed the engines to maximum thrust. Locked into the pilot rig, encased in power armour, he felt the hammer blow of full burn as a growing pressure.

'*Advise-warn you, current engine burn and trajectory will result in damage,*' Sota-Nul's voice scratched in his ears. He did not reply. He had not asked her to link into the gunship, but it was inevitable that she would. For a human supposedly divested of emotion in favour of pure logic she was remarkably predictable. '*Probability of engine output degradation currently at eighty-five point two-one,*' she added after a moment. '*Estimated.*'

He did not reply. There was no point.

His target was coming up fast. The outer picket ships of the *Iron Blood*'s first defence envelop were growing from distant dots to slabs of metal picked out in starlight. He threw the gunship into an irregular spiral, and watched two warning runes flick from amber to red in his helmet display.

'Combat display active,' he said, and space all around him became a network of blue, red and green arcs of potential targets. They disregarded warships of course; he doubted if even the smallest of them would notice if he fired at them.

'Auspexes and multiple targeting arrays have locked onto us.'

'Transmit the identification signal,' he said.

'Compliance,' droned the tech-witch. 'Suggest we cut speed, alter course to a steady trajectory, and disable weapons.'

'No,' he said, without pause. 'Transmit the signal, and then see if they still think the best course of action is to blow us out of the void.'

The outer picket ships were now vast cliffs blocking out the sight of Tallarn and the light of its star. Beyond them the inner shell of ships waited, and within their sphere the vast, notched chisel outline of the *Iron Blood*.

He yanked the gunship into a jagged skid and flicked into a spiral, as the tones of target locks grew in his ears.

He waited, feeling the familiar tug of G-force at his flesh inside his armour. He had missed this, had missed the feeling of mingled control and danger singing in his senses. It made him feel alive again, and let him forget how close he had come to death at the hands of his lord. There was another reason to dance through the Iron Warriors gun sensors. Skimming in, weapons live, targeters active, daring them to fire and then cutting them dead: it was a message, a statement of intent. Do not confuse might with power, it said.

Still, he would not like to have to do this in reality.

'The Fourth Legion vessels have dropped their target lock,' said Sota-Nul.

'Good.'

'They are hailing us.'

'Give me the vox.'

'Compliance.'

Static popped in his ears, rose in pitch and then faded.

*'The warships and warriors of the Fourth Legion welcome you, honoured emissary.'* The voice paused. Argonis thought he recognised it, the sour tone, the sharp edges used to command but not to courtesy.

Forrix, of course. Not the Lord of Iron, not yet, not until they were sure why Argonis was here.

'From whom do you come?' asked Forrix's voice carefully.

Behind the black faceplate of his helm, Argonis smiled without pleasure.

'I come from the Warmaster,' he replied.

IAEO OPENED ALL her eyes, and began to hunt. The info-verse surrounded her. Images, pict-feeds and abstract data extended off into a holo-hazed distance. Ninety-eight out of her ninety-nine data-taps were still in place, the lost one an unfortunate consequence of the Iron Warriors strike against the signal cable node south of the ruins of the Crescent City. That was not optimal, but not as bad as it might have been.

She looked through her scattered swarm of net-flies, and her vision spilt into facets. She had loosed the tiny creatures into the shelter complex sixteen hours before, when she began to think that *they* might have found her. The chromed insects sat in key positions throughout the shelter. They watched without ceasing, parsing every face they saw and hearing every voice.

The shelter complex was vast. Like all the shelters buried across Tallarn, it had been intended to host the mustering of armies for conquering the star systems. Now those same shelters housed the survivors of a viral bombardment which had killed all life on the surface. In the rockcrete-lined tunnels a lucky few had survived, and then struck back at the destroyers of their world. It was a battle fought in hell for revenge.

The shelter Iaeo watched was one of the largest in loyalist hands, and it lay below the ruins of a city. She had been here since the fall of the Sapphire City, and the arrival of the first loyalist reinforcements to come to Tallarn. Before that she had been on Tallarn for a year, moving through the world above, ghosting through data looms, watching with her swarm eyes, drawing a web to snare her target. Her target had been a cell of Alpha Legion operatives, who were working through worlds on the margins of the greater war.

The cell specialised in subverting, corrupting, sabotaging worlds of potential, but not current, strategic importance. They were not a target she had been given, but one she had identified and selected herself. That concept still made her uncomfortable.

Assassins of the Vanus Temple usually operated remotely, manipulating events through altering data to bring about the termination of a target. The noble killed by a jealous lover, after the discovery of rather explicit pict images; the cartel bosses eliminated by their business partners, when they discovered evidence of theft; the city wiped out by a plague because the shipment of vaccine, which would have saved it, never arrived – all these were the murder trade of the Vanus Temple, and, for most, the executioner did not have to see their target, or set foot on the killing ground. In fact most of Iaeo's clade siblings did not take to the field. Direct methods were the preserve of the other Temples, but occasionally one of the Vanus Temple was designated as an Unbound Infocyte, and became an exception to the rule. It was not a condition set lightly.

An Unbound Infocyte both designated and executed their targets. Once they had eliminated one target they selected another, and so on, extrapolating from termination to termination, until their Unbound Condition was withdrawn. Death at the hand of a Vanus was normally ordained and delivered with the remoteness of an angel enacting the will of a deity. To be Unbound was to be both the eyes that saw and the hand that cut.

Iaeo had been placed under an Unbound Condition two years before, and had been killing ever since. Sometimes she thought of her current state as akin to the virus which had killed Tallarn: multiplying and changing, creating death without end. She understood why it was necessary in a war like this, but she did not like it. It lacked definition.

As the shelter filled her senses, she let it linger for a second at the edge of consciousness. No, there was nothing unusual, and she saw no change in the macro patterns of data. She focused on the shelter's command room. It looked crowded. From her viewpoint she could see the strain on the faces, the lines of tension turned to gullies of shadow in the low light. No one was talking. She heard the rustle of fabric as someone shifted their weight. The comms officers, hunched over signal equipment, were glass-eyed with fatigue. She could almost taste the brittleness in the room. It would be five more minutes before reports from the attack on the Sightless Warren would come in, and another hour before the commanders could begin to gauge victory or defeat.

It would be defeat, though. Iaeo knew that already. The Iron Warriors knew the attack was coming. They had probably known before most of the loyalist forces now rumbling towards their attack positions. It still had to play out, but Iaeo did not doubt her projection.

She flicked between other viewpoints: the muster chambers, empty apart from a few machines too damaged to be on the surface, the billet chambers where a few slept under worn blankets, the lifts of the shelter's main axis shaft. Nothing. Not even the beginning of a hint that she had been right. But the feeling was still there, just like before, itching at the edge of awareness. Somewhere in this complex there was at least one high-grade Alpha Legion operative, and they knew that Iaeo was there too.

She was of the Vanus, an assassin of information. She dealt with possibility, with projected outcomes and webs of data. Uncertainty vexed her, but absences worried her more. And that was what looked back at her from the data: a blankness where there should be something, as though someone had edited it out from reality. The Alpha Legion was here, and they did not even cast a shadow.

That was not optimal. Not at all. That meant they were close, that they had a read on her actions. There was even the possibility that…

She pulled the visor from her eyes, folded and stowed it, then slid down the air duct towards an access grate in the duct's floor. The grate slid out of its housing and she dropped into the empty corridor below.

At least it had been empty two seconds before.

She saw the three figures as she dropped from the ceiling. All were utterly still, their shapes blurred outlines of grey, like graphite smeared on paper. Deductions spun through her mind in the stretched instant of the jump.

They must have been there for some time, long enough for their cloaked presences to dissolve into the data feed from her net-flies. Long enough that she had not seen them. That meant they had planned this. They had tracked her and predicted her actions.

*Clever*, she thought, as she heard the buzz of arming weapons.

She hit the floor.

*Their enemies had given the Iron Warriors fortress its name. They called it the Sightless Warren. It had grown from the broken shelter beneath the Sapphire City, spreading underground as the Iron Warriors captured more shelters and tunnel networks. Though they knew it was huge, none amongst the loyalist forces knew the Sightless Warren's true size.*

*Beneath the ground it was possible for Perturabo's forces to pass unseen, and emerge in the ruins of cities or in the empty, fog-shrouded wastelands. Artful concealment protected most of the peripheral entrances, their ramps and blast doors hidden in the shells of buildings, or in folds in the ground. The main gates to the Warren sat amongst the corpses of cities, ringed by slaved weapon emplacements, mazes of mines and the eyes of tank patrols. From its heart in the ruins of the Sapphire City to the outlying bunkers on the heights above the black sludge of the Crescent Ocean, the Sightless Warren ran for hundreds of kilometres.*

*Victory for the loyalists while the Sightless Warren existed seemed impossible. So it was determined that it must fall, and the strength of thousands were sent to see it done. In six months they had tried twice and failed. Victory in the third attempt, as had been said of the first and second attempts, was beyond question.*

# TWO

Machine war
Lord of Iron
Combat projection

KORD COULD BARELY see or hear. Metallic thunder rolled through *War Anvil*. Every surface was vibrating. The sounds of the engines hammered against the ring of shrapnel and the beat of explosions. He kept his eyes to the ground in front of *War Anvil*. He was using his own eyes. Infra-sight had become useless after the first seconds of engagement. Shapes, shadows and light crowded his eyes as he tried to keep his gaze steady. He could see a target, could see the chipped chevrons crossing its hull. Throne, it was close.

'Zade!' he shouted.

'Firing!' the gunner replied, and the battle cannon shouted its wrath into the chorus of battle. The shell hit the Iron Warriors tank square on the front of its left track and ripped down its side. The breech block snapped back in front of Kord. Sacha was already yanking it open, ramming the next shell into its mouth. The Iron Warriors tank was slewing around, its left track shredding.

'Saul, finish it!' he shouted. *War Anvil* bucked as the forward demolisher cannon fired. The Iron Warriors tank vanished in a plume of rolling fire. Kord was already pulling his eyes from the forward sight, glancing down at the cracked screen of the auspex. It was a mess.

Runes and tactical markers swarmed through distortion. His regiment still held together, but only just. They had taken some hits, but were still pressing forward; however, their eastern flank had been struck from the side and ripped in two. Its lead vehicles were wrecks and those behind them were bottling up as they tried to get around their dead comrades. From the moment they had fired the first shells the assault plan had started to fall apart. The ruins of what had been the Sapphire City, now an irregular plateau of debris, had welcomed them with mines, concealed tank snares, heavy weapon fire, and counter-assault groups ready and waiting. They had not even made the second waypoint yet. The second wave was coming up behind them hard, and they were running out of space. They should have been within a kilometre of the Sightless Warren's outer entrances by now. They were nowhere near that close. Ten minutes from the first shot and the attack looked like a disaster.

'Bastards knew we were coming,' Sacha shouted, as though she had read his thoughts. She yanked the handle of the breech block down, and it slammed shut. Zade was already traversing the cannon. Kord could hear the gunner swearing into the vox without pause.

All of *War Anvil*'s other weapons were firing, sponsons whipping energy out into the chaos. Saul would be dragging another shell into the demolisher's maw. Something hit the back of the hull. Kord's eyes flicked to the runes identifying his regiment's machines. *Claw* and *Razor* should have dropped back to cover *War Anvil*'s rear arc. He saw *Claw*'s rune fade out, the heat of its death blooming across the auspex screen.

'*Claw*'s out,' Origo's voice cracked across the vox from the remaining scout. '*Enemy machines to our rear.*'

'Understood,' replied Kord. For a second he closed his eyes. This attack was dead and done, and now it was just a matter of what the price was, and who paid it. 'Bring us around fast,' he yelled. 'Fire on all targets.'

✠ ✠ ✠

HREND STRUCK THE tank's side plating with his right fist. The armour plates twisted. Pistons in his arm and legs rammed his weight forward, and heaved the side of the tank up. Its tracks churned. Dry dust and rubble fragments spun through the air. Its turret tried to turn, pointlessly, desperately. Hrend slammed his other fist up into the track. His hand clamped shut, and the drill teeth on the end of each finger spun to life. The tracks shattered, metal links churning out as the drive wheels kept turning. The tank began to skid away, its other tracks digging into the ground. He triggered the melta-guns in the palms of his fists. The tank's armour glowed from red to white. Molten metal ran like spilled blood over Hrend's fists. Then the melta-jets hit a fuel line and the top and side of the tank blew out and up, in a glowing wet spray. Hrend cut the melta weapons and stepped back. The tank crashed back down to the ground, turret pivoting around like a head on a broken neck. He stepped back, fire washing over him. The tank was still, flames roaring out of its split hull, soot spreading across its corpse.

The sky above turned to white brilliance. His sensors fizzed, his view dimming. He paused, twisting to look upwards as the sheet of light faded into glowing streaks. Gods of metal stood above him, their shapes shrouded by fog and fire light. Plough-fronted heads swayed beneath backs bent by weapons. They stepped forward as one, and within the fluid of his sarcophagus Hrend thought his remaining flesh trembled. The Titans fired again, and again the sky became a blank sheet and the ground a frozen tableau. The stilled tongues of fires licked the mangled corpses of tanks. The shapes of battle automata and Dreadnoughts strode, or fell, or burned. Tanks tumbled, or ground forward, the spray and dust of their track clouds frozen in the moment of vanishing. Overlapping explosions blossomed and blurred together. Flare shells burst high above, scattering motes of blinding light. Smoke blended with the patches of remaining night. A shell or fuel cell detonated inside the wreck of the dead tank beside him. Shrapnel pinged against his body and limbs.

He felt nothing, not the ring of the sharp fragments against his iron skin, nor the gouges left as bright scars on his body, nor the heat of the burning tank. Iron without, iron within, cold, unyielding, unliving. His world was a gunsight view washed with data, his feeling the cold feedback from servos. He took a step and the pistons in his limbs responded.

Voices washed across the vox channels. He saw one of the Sicarans in his group slew around a wreck, turret turning, and its cannon thumping shells into the distance. Orun and Gortun were close to him though he could not see them. Threat runes began to bloom in his sight as the enemy's second wave hit the ruin of the first.

He began to run. Pistons shortened and rammed down. A Predator in streaked white broke from the bright fog. Two hunter missiles loosed from his shoulders even as the recognition formed in his mind, White Scars, 5th Brotherhood. The Predator's cannon twitched towards him. The missiles hit the turret collar, and ripped it from the hull in a blazing plume.

Hrend kept running into the embrace of destruction, and felt nothing.

'Why are you here?'

Argonis listened as his words drained into the silence of the throne room. Perturabo's black eyes glittered back at him from pits sunken into the primarch's skull. At the foot and sides of the throne the still shapes of Perturabo's Iron Circle automatons stood unmoving, shields held before them. Only Forrix stood at his lord's side, the only triarch or senior Iron Warrior present.

Behind Argonis Sota-Nul swayed, the black mesh of her robes rustling on the floor. He heard her tri-ocular lenses whir as they refocused. A step further back Prophesius was utterly still in his green silk shroud, his breath a low hiss from behind his eyeless iron mask.

Perturabo's silence extended. Argonis fought to maintain his gaze under the pressure of the Lord of Iron's presence. The primarch and his First Captain had changed from when Argonis had seen them last. Forrix seemed diminished, shrunken in presence, if not in size, the twinkle of malice in his eyes replaced by emptiness. Perturabo himself seemed both more, and less, than he had been. His flesh had thinned on his bones, and the light clung to recesses of his skull in a way that Argonis's eyes could not read. The Logos, the Lord of Iron's war armour, was lost beneath the pistons and struts of black iron and brushed plasteel. His head nested in a mass of cables and metal tubes. In places the primarch's skin seemed to have grown over the implants. Argonis noted the weapons bonded to the armour's arms in bulbous clumps.

'I do not answer to you, emissary,' said Perturabo at last, his voice a measured rasp of steel. Argonis did not flinch.

'You answer to the Warmaster, and I am his emissary.'

'And that is why my brother sent you here, to ask why I am here?'

Argonis heard the edge in the words. He inclined his head, half in deference, and half in acknowledgement.

'You sit above a dead world, pouring the strength of your Legion into its belly. You call our allies to you and spend them in battles without end, or purpose. Your Warmaster wishes to know why?'

'You speak so?' said Forrix. He raised an armoured finger and pointed it at Argonis as though it were the barrel of a gun. 'Our commitment to Horus is beyond question.'

'Our lord, the lord who holds your fealty and oaths, speaks, and asks, as he pleases.' Argonis looked up at the bronze and ruby eye which capped the black pole in his hand. 'And here and now I am his voice.'

Forrix's mouth opened, but Perturabo's eyes twitched, and the First Captain fell silent.

'I will be at my brother's side when the gates of our father's realm fall. I will break Terra's defences at his command, and stand beside him when the false Imperium is cast to the flames. Nothing, and no one, can prevent that.'

'That is not an answer.'

Perturabo turned his head slowly, his gaze settling on the dark at the edges of his throne room.

'This world was a vital base during the Crusade. The alignment of warp routes that spread from it, and the capacity and resilience of its shelters mean that if it is not ours then it will be used by our enemies. There are many routes to the Throne World, emissary, each one guarded by worlds such as this. The end of this war will not be won just by strength, or numbers, but by who controls those Gates to Terra.' The Lord of Iron paused and rotated his gaze back to Argonis. 'This is one such gate, and I will deliver it to the Warmaster.'

'The forces you have gathered–'

'Are what is required.'

Argonis held the primarch's stare, but felt the chill spread through him under that gaze. It was like being submerged in ice. It was like standing in the presence of Horus Lupercal. After a second he bowed his head low, taking care to ensure that the banner remained upright.

'I will remain, lord,' said Argonis, taking care that his tone held defence, respect, and strength. 'And watch the conclusion of this… endeavour.'

Perturabo inclined his head a fraction.

'As you wish.'

The doors to the throne chamber began to grind open at an invisible signal. Argonis straightened and walked from the room, the banner of the Warmaster held in his hand. Sota-Nul and Prophesius following in his wake. As soon as the doors began to grind shut behind him, he clamped his helm over his head. Sota-Nul's dry cog voice filled his ears as she spoke over the short-range vox. The signal was encrypted, and the tech-witch had sub-vocalised her words.

'You were not satisfied-convinced with the Fourth Primarch's answer-response.'

Argonis kept looking ahead, kept walking. Iron Warriors watched him pass, eyepieces coal-red in the low light. The sound of his footsteps seemed to echo as they walked down the wide passage.

'Send the signal,' he replied after a second. 'Let's see what Alpharius's asset knows.'

✠ ✠ ✠

IAEO'S WORLD NARROWED in the instant it took her to hit the floor. The feeling of her body had vanished, the sensations of her flesh flattened to data sorted by her subconscious. Her kind were created as weapons, as murderers and executioners, but they did those deeds from a distance. They were not Eversor, or Calidus, or even Culexus. Vanus killed like gods, without ever having to hold the blade or touch the blood. The problem space of combat was uncomfortably small, the variables too fine and too easily misjudged. It was messy. It was inelegant. Wasteful. But occasionally necessary.

The blur-suited shapes were moving too fast to track. That did not matter. Reaction was not the way of the Vanus Temple. Prediction was everything.

The stink of ionising air was thick in her nose.

*Data: Three weapons, energy-based, volkite 93 per cent likely. Cycle from charge to fire 0.03 seconds.*

She came up from her roll.

*Projection: Adversaries training and conditioning will mean that they anticipate target movement prior to firing.*

She twisted and dropped flat to the floor, limbs splayed like a spider. Two red pulses of energy cut the air where she would have been.

*Data: One adversary still to fire.*

Her muscles bunched.

*Projection: Shot held in case other two adversaries missed. Clever/ competent/dangerous.*

She leapt off the floor, with a single snap of muscle. The volkite beam struck the floor, and exploded a circle of rockcrete to dust. She twisted as she flew through the air. Her hands grabbed the edge of the still-open vent hatch.

*Projection: Other exits from ventilation shafts compromised.*

She yanked herself into the air duct.

*Data: Corridor door, 20 metres away, currently sealed, only viable exit.*

She could hear the soft, swift sounds of the figures in the corridor beneath her. Her hand had already slipped into a pouch and found the small, smooth sphere.

*Projection: There is no way of escape while they live.*

The grenade was of alien manufacture rather than human. Its surface was smooth, like ground bone, and it always seemed the same temperature as her skin when she touched it, never warmer, never cooler. Where it had come from was data that she had not been given. She knew only what it would do when it detonated. That knowledge was enough.

Iaeo dropped the grenade through the hatch, and she pulled her body into the vent space.

*Data: 1 second since grenade release.*

A beam vapourised the edge of the hatch. A blast of heat washed over her. The skin of her face charred and blistered.

*Data: 2 seconds since grenade release.*

The grenade detonated with a sound like countless needles scraping metal.

*Data: Silence. Projection: Adversaries eliminated.*

She snapped the visor back over her eyes, and blinked her way to the net-fly feeds from the corridors around her current position. Empty, or at least they seemed so. An increased error/subversion factor now had to be applied to all direct data inputs. The compressed awareness of combat was fading. The skin of her face was severely burned. Her hands were cut to the bone, and she was bleeding. She needed to move. A clock began to count in her consciousness.

*Count: 2 seconds since enemy asset elimination.*

She slid out of the damaged vent hatch, and hung beneath it for a heartbeat. The corridor space was red. A thick jelly of pulped flesh covered the walls and ceiling. Hard objects lay amongst the wetness. Her eyes found the grenade, its shape glossed with blood. The monofilament strands which had exploded from its surface had withdrawn beneath its eggshell casing. A flick of her eyes identified, dismissed, and then selected other objects from the flesh soup.

*Count: 5 seconds*

She swung down, and landed with a small splash. She picked up the grenade, then made two quick steps to pluck up a trio of what looked like implanted comms units. A calculated jump took her to the edge of the spreading pool of blood. She stripped to the overalls she had been wearing, and stepped from them without losing her stride. Beneath, she was a matt black statue from the neck down, the pouches bonded to the synskin breaking the outline of her muscles across her back.

*Count: 11 seconds. Projection: 9 to 15 seconds until enemy aware of asset loss.*

She began to run. This was going to be messy, but there was no other available path to take. She was under direct threat, and that meant that the possibility of total mission failure was very real.

*Count: 13 seconds.*

The sealed door from the corridor into the rest of the shelter was in front of her. The visor was projecting the scene from an expanding sphere of rooms and passages around her, as her net-flies repositioned to form a shell around her.

*Count: 14 seconds.*

The net-fly on the other side of the door caught movement as a figure stepped into the corridor beyond. She took in the field overalls of the Sectanal Regency Guard, the rank pins and status implants around the eyes: an officer, mid-grade, support echelon. She had no idea if he was what he seemed, and at that moment it was irrelevant. The corridor she stood in was filled with the liquidised remains of three Alpha Legion operatives, and there was only one way out. The projections indicated that survival was a low probability.

*Count: 16 seconds.*

She opened the door, rammed it wide, and burst through it at a run. The Regency Guard officer turned at the noise, his mouth opening. Her hand came up and the digi-needler on her third finger spat a sliver of crystallised toxin into the roof of his mouth. He began to fall. Released air sighed from between his teeth. If anyone but a very, very highly trained and suspicious specialist examined the dead officer, they would conclude that he had died from a sudden massive heart attack. She ran past his corpse.

*Count: 19 seconds.*

The other Alpha Legion operatives would likely clean up the remains of their dead comrades. They had no interest in alerting the loyalists that there was a silent war being fought in their midst. A corridor of blood would cause as many problems for them as it would for Iaeo. That at least was what the projections said. That was what should happen. That was the best outcome.

She needed to leave the Crescent Shelter complex. She needed to get out, link back into her sources of data, and find a weapon to take her enemies down.

*Count: 23 seconds. Projection: enemy aware of asset loss, 78 per cent probability.*

She ducked into a small room, and wrenched up a rusted grate set in its floor. A long dark space looked back at her.

She would see this execution completed. But now she needed to run.

*Count: 26 seconds. Projection: enemy aware of asset loss, 99 per cent probability.*

She let out a measured breath, and dropped into the waiting dark.

*The Sightless Warren held. In truth the loyalist attack failed to even penetrate its surface defences.*

*When dawn broke over the site of the loyalists' assault, its weak light touched fresh fields of dead war machines. Smoke stained the thinning fog soot-grey, and the flames of still-burning wrecks created pools of red light. When the fires had died the failed assault would be just another layer of devastation on a landscape of ruin. The Sapphire City had long ago ceased to exist in all but name. Its buildings had been broken by the Iron Warriors assault which had taken the shelter beneath. Attempts to crack open the Sightless Warren with orbital bombardment had reduced what remained to rubble, and before the failed attempts could reach the Sightless Warren only a few defiant ghosts of the city's past remained.*

*The corpse of a Warlord Titan stood slumped against a spire of girders and rubble from a building now a memory lost in crushed rock and shattered metal. The god-machine's head was a merged lump, its carapace cratered and rippled by heat. The fused crystal of its eyes looked out over the tidelines of battle marked by heaps of metal.*

*Along the one-time coastal plains the loyalist forces withdrew in a ragged herd. The Iron Warriors harried them, deploying fresh reserves to bleed their defeated enemies, and the loyalists fought to stop the withdrawal becoming a rout.*

*High above the plains the grand cruiser* Memloch *held in low orbit. Flanked by the* Veratas *and* Son of the Red Star *it had beaten off three attempts by the Iron Warriors to bombard the retreating forces. It was its last action in the Battle of Tallarn. An hour before the last retreating units reached safety, the* Memloch *fell from the sky. Its hull pierced in dozens of places, it plunged into the sludge of Tallarn's northern ocean. Debris fountained into the already clogged atmosphere. Its reactor exploded and sent a shudder through the earth that was felt thousands of kilometres away. On another planet this alone would have been a catastrophe. On Tallarn few even noticed.*

# THREE

**Dreams of Order
Cracked
Unscarred**

'There has to be another reason,' said Kord, taking the optics from his eyes, and massaging the bridge of his nose. 'Stands to reason.'

He looked up at the face of Colonel Augustus Fask, and wished the man was not there. The other officer looked like he had been soaked and then hung out to dry. A damp sheen clung to Fask's jowly face, and his Jurnian officer corps uniform looked like he had slept in it many times over and never washed it. But then there was little enough water in the shelter complex to drink, let alone ensure that uniforms were cleaned and pressed. Even if you were a command-level officer with strategic control, you wore the same uniform for months. After a while you just stopped noticing the smell.

Fask had turned up in Kord's cramped billet, with a smile and a bottle of liquor, an hour after Kord had got through decontamination. The bottle was already a third empty, and Fask's breath was rank with the smell of the spirit as he settled into the folding chair opposite Kord.

'Terra, Silas, this is how you relax now?' Fask's eyes were skating over the maps laid out over the folding table next to Kord's cot. Inked lines crossed the maps in different colours. Notes in neat, printed hand filled the spaces next to areas marked with circles. Kord wished he had been able to put them away before Fask had started reading them. 'Everything all right?' asked Fask, after a long pause. 'I mean, you holding together?'

Kord shrugged. He was very, very tired. He did not want to sleep, but he did not want to talk to Augustus Fask either. They had ridden war machines together back on Jurn, and then on Iconis. They were both squadron commanders then, younger, and full of the more comfortable sort of lies that went with a soldier's life. Kord supposed that history allowed Fask to think of him as a friend. Only problem was he did not like the man, never had. And Fask was not there to check he was all right, at least not in a friendly sense.

Kord stood and made to fold the maps up. Fask put his glass down on the maps as Kord reached for them. Some of the liquid slopped over the chipped rim of the glass, and began to pool on the parchment.

'I mean it, Silas. Is everything all right?'

Kord took a step back, and controlled the stab of anger needling at the back of his eyes. He reached into a pocket in his fatigues and found a lho-stick. He turned away as he lit the stick.

'I wound up sitting on my hands on a backwater world while the rest of creation tore itself apart.' He sat down on the folding chair, and breathed out a slow, smoke-heavy breath. 'That planet gets virus bombed. The Iron Warriors decide to turn the sludge that's left into a battleground. Then our side decide to get in the fight. I get my command all but wiped out, in what was, until last night, our biggest defeat. And we are still rolling around trying to break an enemy that has made its reputation out of being unbreakable.' He paused, nodded to himself as if satisfied. 'And we have no idea why they are here, or why it started. So yeah, everything is all right.'

Fask sat down on Kord's bunk, his glass back in his hand.

'Don't need to know answers to fight,' said Fask, and took a gulp.

'No,' Kord nodded, 'but it might help if we want to win.'

Fask shook his head, picked up the bottle, and began to pour himself a fresh measure. After a second he snorted and raised the bottle to Kord. The oily liquid splashed against the bottle sides.

Kord shook his head. Fask grunted.

'You really are as twisted around as they say.' Fask put the bottle down. He wrapped both hands around his refilled glass, but did not raise it to his mouth. All pretence of humour had gone from his face. 'Central command's worried about you.'

'Thought it might be something like that,' nodded Kord carefully.

'Look, it's just the way it is. This theory of yours worries them.'

'Worries them?' Kord raised an eyebrow. 'How?'

'All this stuff about why the enemy are here, about there having to be *another reason*. You keep it to yourself, sure, but people talk, and in this place...' Fask gestured at the cot, table and chair pressed between bare rockcrete walls and the metal slab of the door. 'People hear, people talk.'

'That why they sent you, to stop me thinking about it?' Kord looked at the floor so that Fask would not see the anger he could feel boring out of his eyes. 'You know where I have been? Eighteen hours in a machine, six going out, six in direct engagement, six coming back while the Iron Warriors try and turn our loss into a victory slaughter.' He stopped and nodded, his face set into a frown as though considering deeply. 'Good timing.'

Fask was shaking his head, impatience seeping from him as he sighed.

'You know, this was meant to just be a friendly talk.'

Kord nodded and tried to make his face reasonable, moderate. Calm.

'When did you last ride a machine, Fask?' he asked, softly. 'On the surface. You know, that place up there with the dead people, and the gunfire.'

'Throne, Silas.' Fask stood, stepped to the door and yanked it open. 'You know what, do what you like. I look forward to reading the discipline report.'

After a second Kord got up, closed the door and sat down at the table. Carefully he dabbed at the pool of spirit which had blurred the ink of the map. He stared at the lines, circles and notes again. It was incomplete, there was only so much information on engagements with the Iron Warriors and their allies that he could get hold of, but even so it meant something.

'Searching,' he said to himself.

Carefully he reached under his cot, and pulled a bottle out. The liquid inside was honey gold, and clung to the bottle sides as he unscrewed the top and took a swig. He inhaled sharply. Then took another gulp. He nodded again to himself.

'Searching.'

THEY TOOK HREND back to the silence of sleep. He had walked from the field of battle as the fog had begun to lighten with the coming of dawn. Far below the earth, in the caverns of the Sightless Warrens the adepts and Techmarines had begun to pull his machine body apart. He wondered if others of his kind thought of it as a relief. That had been how some of the tech-priests had talked of it when he had been amongst the living: a release from the pain of an existence snatched from death, a return to the peace of oblivion. Hrend did not think of it that way.

They took his power to move first, shutting down his neural connections to the Dreadnought frame so that the impulse which would have moved an arm, or lifted a leg, now did nothing. Ghosts of his old limbs returned to him: the feeling of his left arm twitching, the fingers itching even though they were no longer there. They took sight and sound after that. Silent blackness enclosed him with the suddenness of a disconnected plug. Those were the moments that were the worst. In the silence, he could imagine himself as nothing, just a tangle of stray thoughts and ghost sensations held in a box. What was worse was that in those moments he thought he should be angry, but instead he felt empty. And then, at last, they would drown his thoughts with sedatives, and give him to his dreams.

The dreams were his home now. Sometimes he went back to Isstvan and burned again. Sometimes he felt pain. Sometimes he forgot that it was a dream, and thought that he was dying again. When it ended he would try and remember the feeling of moving, of breathing, of being alive. He dreamed of the past. He dreamed of how he had become an Iron Warrior. He tasted the blood in his mouth again, and felt the razors filleting skin and muscle from his bones. The pain was a sea of ice and burning acid. There was no relief; to endure was to become stronger. He had looked up into the Apothecary's metal mask, and seen his own reflection in the circular lenses. His heart had beat in the open cavity of his chest.

'What do you wish?' the Apothecary had asked, the ritual words rising over the sounds of the bone saw.

'To be... Iron,' he had gasped through his own blood.

They had given him his wish.

He dreamed of the fields of a thousand battles, the ground chewed by shellfire, the flesh of the dead pulped into the mud. He saw faces he had never realised he would remember. He saw his life jumbled into chunks of colour and sound and smell, and they were more real than waking.

He had died on Isstvan V. His flesh had boiled in his armour. They had clamped his dying flesh at the heart of a body of pistons, plasteel and servos. They had woken him for the first time, and told him that he would serve the Legion still. They had given him a new name, one cut from his old name, like a word formed by mutilation. He had become Iron for a second time.

He remembered all this, and lived it again, screaming mutely as the unsettled tides of sleep came up to meet him. He struggled for an instant then fell...

And fell...

The true world snapped back into being, sharp and unforgiving. He felt his nerves mesh with the machine again, felt the silence form around him.

He was waking again, his fall into oblivion halted.

A voice came to him out of the dark, crackling with static.

*'You rise again, Ironclad. The primarch has called you to him.'*

✠ ✠ ✠

'The Fourth Primarch's words were false-incomplete in truth-value,'

Argonis did not bother to open his eyes to look at Sota-Nul. The servitors were peeling his armour from him, piece by piece, muttering in their machine voices as they moved around him. They did not like being near Sota-Nul, he could tell. They moved like curbed animals whenever she came close. He could not say he blamed them; he did not like being near her either.

The room was large, its floor polished rockcrete, its walls brushed metal, and the light came from globes floating in bronze cages. Red fabric softened the hard lines of the walls, and hung over the straight-backed chairs. Statuary – a rare thing to see in the presence of the Iron Warriors – stood in the room's recesses, the features of each sculpture bluntly stylised. The chamber was amongst the more luxurious living quarters he had seen aboard a IV Legion ship. The point was not lost on Argonis; he was honoured, but he was different, softer, not of the Iron.

Argonis felt the cool air of the chamber touch his skin as the servitors released the plating from his torso. The armour was sea-green and black. Cthonian kill glyphs spidered across the plates in beaten gold wire. A burnished crest of wings spread across the chestplate, and enamelled laurels ringed the brows of his helm. A bolt pistol and gladius hung at his waist, the grips of both decorated by mirror coins.

Black tattoos of wings and the geometric lines of Cthonian gang glyphs ran across the muscle beneath his armour shell. To anyone who had been born in the warrens of Cthonia, his skin would have shouted his past, from the kills he had made in his youth, to the honours he had won as a warrior of the XVI Legion. A killer, they would have read: nightwalker, oath taker, and one who has won loyalty through blood. Crescent wings spread across his neck and shoulders, a full moon set between their feathers. That last symbol told that he was Chieftain of the Isidis Flight, the pilot cadre oath bound to the First Company elite. Pale scars crossed the flesh of his arms, back and chest, the hair-fine lines hatching his skin. The Unscarred they called him, half in reference to the fact that his face was untouched by war, and partly in ironic reference to the years of knife bouts which had left their razor marks on his body. He flexed his shoulders and the inked feathers rippled.

'Do you not concur with my truth-analysis?' Sota-Nul asked, and a prickling of his skin told him that she was looking directly at him. 'Perturabo lied about his war.'

'A primarch's reasons and motivations are their own,' he said. 'They are beyond truth and falsity.'

'I have shut the ears of all who would listen to us. We can speak openly.'

'I was. Perturabo speaks the truth, in part at least. Tallarn is important, or could be, and he has never failed to answer the Warmaster's bidding before.'

'That view does not match your actions. You have summoned the operative. Why, if all is as it seems?'

The last plates of his armour came away and he felt the fabric of a tabard slip over his neck. Sota-Nul was looking at him. The cluster of nine lenses on the left side of her dead flesh face glowed green in the low light.

'Nothing is as it seems,' he said carefully.

A sudden scratching made both turn. Prophesius was moving, each step a sinuous transition between instances of complete stillness. A blank mask covered his head in its entirety, the metal scored with symbols which Argonis did not understand and did not like to look at. A lock-like mechanism held the mask shut at the back of the head. The key from that mechanism hung around Argonis's neck, its presence a promise he wondered if he would have to keep.

Hands had appeared from beneath Prophesius's green silk robes. The fingers on each were withered and twisted as though they had been broken and healed before they were set. His right hand clutched a tablet of wax set in a silver frame. A long metal spike capped the index finger of his left. After a pause he stabbed the spike down into the wax. His head was lolling back, his hands moving as though pulled by wires.

*he is marked*

The gouged letters showed clear on the pale wax. Prophesius paused, once again utterly still.

Argonis stared at the astropath, and then at the words on the tablet. He had no idea what they might mean. Blood was oozing from the edge of Prophesius's nails, running down onto the wax tablet.

'You refer to the primarch, to Perturabo?'

Prophesius's hand jerked to life again, slashing words into the wax.

*the eye has seen him he has passed through it has seen him he has seen*

Argonis opened his mouth, a question forming on his tongue.

Sota-Nul flinched, as though woken from sleep by a sudden noise. Argonis turned to her.

'Return signal from Alpharius's asset received...' she began.

'I thought this area was shrouded,' he growled.

'Signal confirms contact,' she continued, shaking her head as though struggling to hear. Then she looked up at Argonis, the light in her nine-fold eyes hard and bright. 'He will come to us.'

She passed the time by breaking the Alpha Legion communication ciphers.

It had been sixteen hours since Iaeo had folded herself into the crawl space, and she estimated that it would be another eight until she moved. Stillness was the key to invisibility. That truth was one of the first lessons taught in the Assassin Temples on Terra. Another strategy might have been to move continually, to make herself impossible to pin down. That strategy had merits, but most of them applied when you had somewhere to go. At present she had no location to reach, and getting out of the Crescent Shelter would be difficult, bordering on impossible. Not actually impossible, of course, but that was the way it might seem based on probabilities of detection/death. She was hunted, and she needed to stay alive if she was going to complete her mission.

So she had scrambled down into the deep reaches of the shelter, where the tunnels were choked with cables and pipes, and the dust and grime told its own story of how many had made the journey before her. The feeds from the cordon of net-flies were showing nothing concerning. Air temperature, sound levels and vibration were all steady at background levels. The multifaceted eye of the swarm showed her nothing other than empty shafts, ducts and tunnels. Everything was quiet. There, folded into a space small enough that even a child would struggle to reach her, she waited, and ran codes through her partitioned mind.

She needed to watch the swarm of net-flies – which currently watched every connection to her current location – but that only took half of her awareness. Cracking the Alpha Legion's comms had seemed a good use of the rest of her mind.

It had taken her a few awkward minutes to activate and expose the workings of the comms implants she had taken from the dead operatives. Two of her flies had bitten into the blood-slicked machine, and encrypted communications had begun to flood her awareness. The data was most likely low level, nothing big, nothing of critical importance, but she existed to make lethal situations from tiny fragments. Besides, cracking the ciphers gave her something to do.

The Mechanicum of Mars now claimed the realm of technology and its mysteries as theirs and theirs alone, but the traditions and mysteries which would become the Assassin Temples had been born in Old Night, and they had secrets of their own. The Red Priests might claim dominion over the machine, logic and calculation, but Vanus were not machines, they were the powers of human reason refined to a sharp point. And they lived for information. It was not just a skill, or training, or even the modifications made to their brains by razor, gene graft and alchemistry. It was a compulsion, a drive burned into her that she had to satisfy. There were sacred logic engines on Mars which could have cracked the ciphers, machines which would have creaked and wailed to the same solution, but they lacked the human component that the Vanus so treasured. They lacked obsession.

The cipher was complex, even for covert communications. She enjoyed knowing that, it made watching it fall apart more satisfying.

It took her five hours. When she cracked it at last she allowed herself a few moments for the data to wash around her senses. It felt like light, like fresh water, and warm air. The comms unit was not picking up transmissions any more, but fragments of what had passed through it still remained, scattered like shards of a shattered window. She dipped her mind into them, noting, collating and archiving. There was some valub–

Her mind stopped dead. Then her heart began to hammer. Blood flushed into her brain, as lines of deduction and possibility began to form, combine and expand. She had to move, she had to get out of the shelter no matter how.

She began to squeeze back out of her bolthole. Once able to crawl she began to move faster. Once she could run and climb, she was a blur of black synskin rising through the depths of the shelter. The lines of computation in her mind spun on, hungering for more data, promising conclusions. At the core of each accelerating thought the single fragment of Alpha Legion signal echoed and glowed, like a message written in fire.

*...THE EMISSARY HAS ARRIVED...*

War never ceased on Tallarn. In the face of victory and defeat, it ground on without pause.

In the six hours after the retreat of the Third Assault of the Sightless Warren, a force of four hundred war machines set off from the Cobalack Shelter. Supposedly they were to link up with loyalist elements which had fled north after the attack, though no one would later be able to recall who had given the order. No trace of them was ever found.

In the void, the ragged fleet carrying the Legio Kryos and the survivors of House Caesarean dropped from the warp, cutting its way through loyalist ships to drop its forces onto Tallarn's southern pole. From above, the ships of both sides watched as the clouds above the southern land-mass danced with flames as they, the traitor Titans and Knights, matched themselves against the maniples of the Legio Gryphonicus.

In the Cassildian Mountains the loyalist bunker complex fell when decontamination measures failed. The complex's last signal echoed across the planet's electro-sphere for hours after the last of its inhabitants had died.

In the command rooms of the loyalist shelters, and in the strategiums of the vessels circling in the void, the fractures in command split wide. Colonels, captains, praetors, generals, and others of countless vaunted ranks began to blame, insult, ignore and rebuke each other for a failure which all of them had had a hand in creating. It was Dellasarius, Governor Militant of Tallarn before its murder, and in name still commander of all forces on its surface, who silenced the squall of voices.

'We will attack again,' he said. 'We attack again, and again, until there are no more of us who can. And then we find a way to do it again until we break them.' Then, into the uneasy silence which followed, he added. 'Remember where this is, and the price we have paid to reach this day. This is not just war, this is vengeance.'

# FOUR

**Quiet
Father
Lies**

*'Did you see that,* War Anvil?*'*

*'*This is *War Anvil*. What are you seeing, *Razor?'*

*'Movement to the south. Visual only, nothing on the auspex. Might just be the wind.'*

Kord shifted the view on the cracked auspex screen. Nothing. They were ten hours out from the Crescent Shelter, running across the Tesilon Flats in a pair of staggered lines. There were twenty machines in his command, barely a company strength from the regiment as it had been. The battle tanks, a mix of Vanquishers and Executioners, rode in a box formation with *War Anvil* at their centre. The scouts were further out, running fast before going still to watch. Nothing usually came across the flats, not from either side, but caution was what kept you alive on Tallarn.

Kord keyed the vox again.

'You get a sense of what direction it was going?' The static swallowed his words. Origo's voice came back a second later.

*'South-east, but that's just a feeling.'*

'Strength?'

'Hard to say,' replied Origo. 'If it was real, more than one, less than a hundred.'

'Just a patrol sweep,' said Zade, across the local vox. The gunner had been listening in.

'Could be one of ours,' Sacha added.

'Could be...' Zade's voice shrugged for him, without Kord needing to see him.

'They don't normally come through this way,' said Kord softly. 'Too far out, no targets.' *This could be it,* he thought, *one of the strange Iron Warriors patrols he had been mapping for the last months.* His mind was ticking through the possibility of taking his machines to investigate the sighting. The least efficient machines in the group had air and fuel to last another sixteen hours of straight running, more if they stripped back the power taken by the tactical system. Command would not like it. No, command would hit the roof. He thought of Fask's blotched face and the stain from his drink leeching from the lines and notes he had made on the maps.

'Sir,' Origo's voice hissed in his ears again. *'If we leave it much longer we might not be able to acquire them again. What do you want to do?'*

Kord stared at the key of the vox for a second, and then nodded to himself.

'All units, this is *War Anvil*, hold formation on my position, heading south-east. Weapons cold, we have enemy in sight, so stay quiet.'

HIS FATHER CAME to him in the cavern beneath the earth. Hrend knelt as the Lord of Iron entered the chamber. The shield-bearing automatons of the Iron Circle formed a wall around them, facing outwards. The cavern had once been a muster area of a shelter which was now part of the Sightless Warren. The Mechanicum had filled the space with the devices of their art. The dark reaches of the cavern growled and sparked with the pulse of great machines. Here Hrend, and his Dreadnought brothers, slept and waited to be called to battle. All the tech-priests and adepts had left before Perturabo arrived, so that Hrend and his primarch were alone in a circle of cold light.

'Lord.' Hrend's voice rumbled from his speakers. Perturabo stood in silence for a long moment, his metal-wrapped body seeming to breathe with him.

'You were Sollos Hrendor,' said Perturabo. 'Master of the Seven Hundred and First Armoured Cohort.'

'That was who I was, my master.' Hrend felt his ghost limbs twitch.

'I have need of you,' said Perturabo, and his armour seemed to buzz in time with the words.

'I obey.'

The Lord of Iron paused again. In the silence Hrend heard his master's armour creak, like dry bones. When he spoke again, his voice rolled through the air, as deep and dangerous as an ocean.

'No, Sollos. No, this time I will not command you. Rise.'

Hrend stood, extending to his full height with a hiss of oiled metal. Perturabo stood shorter than Hrend, though somehow seemed to be greater. The primarch's exo-augmentation gleamed with oily reflections. Armour plates layered the frame, the machinery below visible through the gaps where the plates parted and overlapped. The primarch had changed since Hrend had last seen him. But then hadn't they all? They had gone beyond reality and returned. They had been betrayed and offered up to otherworldly powers. Who could not be changed by that?

'It is not enough for you to obey,' said Perturabo. 'You must know what I ask you to do, and why. You must believe.'

The servos in Hrend's head unit hissed as they tried to interpret the signal to bow his head.

'How may I serve?'

ARGONIS STEPPED INTO the light of the hangar bay. Sota-Nul and Prophesius followed a step behind him, one gliding as though on polished ice, the other shuffling. His Storm Eagle sat in a pool of stab-lights. Her name was *Sickle Blade*, and her black and sea-green fuselage made her seem an interloper amongst the brushed iron skins of the Iron Warriors craft. Servitors moved over her. Thick trunks of fuel lines snaked away from her belly into the deck.

Human serfs in tan overalls and blank faceplates moved amongst the servitors, performing rote maintenance too complicated for the half-machines. An enginseer in layered red robes stood to the side, utterly still apart from the light of scrolling data glowing in the darkness of its hood. A false wind blew through the hangar bay, stirred by the engines of the larger gunships. Parchment tapers fluttered from the catches on *Sickle Blade*'s open inspection plates.

'Master.' A serf, wearing a breath mask and with a senior rank code tattooed across his scalp, knelt at Argonis's approach. Argonis did not pause or reply. His eyes were roaming over the gunship, noting the care the Iron Warriors had taken over readying the machine.

Twelve days had passed since they had received the initial signal from the Alpha Legion operative, twelve days in which they had heard nothing more. Argonis had begun to wonder if the asset was real, or just another part of the Alpha Legion's endless misdirection. That, or perhaps the asset could not reach them. Having an asset embedded in Perturabo's forces was one thing, getting a clear, open channel signal onto his flagship without him noticing was another. Yet the assets had picked up Sota-Nul's contact signal, and acknowledged in turn, which meant that they had the means to bypass the Iron Warriors countermeasures.

'Master,' the serf spoke again. He was trailing just behind Argonis's head and shoulders bent, eyes pointing down. 'I am commanded to tell you that your craft is still being made ready for launch.'

Argonis did not reply. The serf bobbed his head and hurried to keep pace. The human's words were unnecessary; Argonis could see that both the *Sickle Blade* and its escort were still several minutes from launch readiness. Once they were ready, the descent to Tallarn would begin. For such a simple flight the tactical planning had been extensive. The *Iron Blood* would move closer to the planet, as a sub-fleet performed an attack run against the enemy forces in orbit. Argonis and his escort would drop to the surface above a deserted area to one of the Sightless Warren's landing fortresses.

There was a certain risk to the operation, but nothing substantial. On one level that disappointed Argonis.

The last minutes before a launch were amongst the few pleasures he allowed himself now. The smell of fuel and oil, the sound of engines test-firing, the itch of passive anti-grav flickering across his skin. He let it all wash over and through him, sharpening him. It reminded him of the knife fights he had fought before he had become a legionary, the moments just before everything became the flicker of razors, the moment when he felt a knot of doubt in his heart: would he live or was he about to walk down a tunnel that had no end?

He came around the rear of the *Sickle Blade* and ducked into the open assault hatch. The space within was dark, lit only by the light from the hangar and the glow of instrument panels set into the walls. He stepped inside, eyes checking the position and readiness of every detail. Prophesius and Sota-Nul followed. The sound of a third set of feet on the assault ramp made his head turn. The serf was still following them, head still bowed in respect. Argonis opened his mouth, but the serf was already moving, all semblance of respect gone.

The bolt pistol was free from his thigh and rising as Sota-Nul began to turn. The serf was already at the door controls and the hatch was closing. Argonis's finger closed on the bolt pistol's trigger. It froze. Frost was spreading from his trigger finger up his arm. Beside him Prophesius was twitching, masked head shaking.

'That would be a mistake,' said the serf as he turned to face Argonis. Beads of sweat formed on the man's forehead, catching the light as they ran down to the rim of his breath mask. 'Please relax your trigger finger. I can stop you shooting for a few more moments, but with your masked associate so close it is taking a lot of effort.'

Sota-Nul hissed. Argonis noticed that an array of exotic weapons on metal tentacles had sprouted from beneath her robes, each one poised like a dozen scorpion stings. Prophesius was still twitching and shaking. The air had become heavy and thick.

'You are?' he asked, though he felt he knew the answer.

'A gift from Lord Alpharius,' said the man. Argonis nodded, relaxed the tension in his trigger finger, but did not lower the pistol. 'My thanks,' said the man, reaching up to unfasten the breath mask covering his lean and hairless face. Green eyes looked up at Argonis without fear. 'Greetings, Argonis. I offer apologies for the manner of my arrival. This is one of the few places in which it is at least moderately safe for us to meet. I would have organised our meeting sooner, but care had to be taken. You understand.'

'The proof of who you are,' said Argonis, the barrel of his weapon still level with the man's forehead.

A smile twitched on the man's lips, but the eyes stayed cold and steady.

*Reptile eyes*, thought Argonis.

'Of course.' Patterns began to spiral across the man's face. The rank code on his forehead vanished, swallowed by green scales and blue feathers. The patterns grew thicker, until the man's exposed skin was a tangle of crawling serpents and spread birds' wings. He blinked, and the patterns slid down onto his eyelids. Carefully, he pulled a heavy glove from his left hand. A simple symbol glowed on the centre of the palm: two lines joined to make an open-bottomed triangle. The alpha, the mark of the XX Legion.

'My name is Jalen,' said the tattooed man. He let his hand drop. Two heartbeats later Argonis lowered his gun. He glanced at Sota-Nul, but the tech-witch's weapons had already vanished beneath her robes. 'How may I serve the Warmaster's emissary?'

'Why are the Iron Warriors here?'

Jalen blinked slowly, nodded.

'We do not know.'

'You–'

'There is a reason they are here, of that we are certain, and it is not the reason that they have given you. Most of their own warriors do not know the truth, because they have been told a lie. The same lie told to you. It is a good lie, and like all lies it has been grown from a seed of truth. But it is not truth.'

'Your breed would know.'

Jalen smiled, white teeth bright in a tangle of colour.

'Yes, we would.'

'Why are you present-here?' asked Sota-Nul. Jalen glanced at her, raised an eyebrow, and the pattern of scales around his eyes rippled. The tech-witch's eye lenses pulsed as if in imitation. 'Your Legion-warriors are fighting on Tallarn,' she continued. 'If you do not know why the Fourth Legion are present-engaged, then your Legion must have its own reason.'

'We were here before they came.' Jalen shook his head. 'You think that all the worlds that declare for the Warmaster without a fight do so willingly? Tallarn's use to the Great Crusade had passed, but in this war it could have been useful again. We were... realigning its loyalties.'

'And now?' asked Argonis. 'What are you doing now?'

'Making the best of the situation.'

Argonis watched Jalen carefully. Every instinct bred and trained into him was screaming that he should turn the operative's skull into blood mist, or drag a bloody smile across his throat. Jalen's eyes twitched, as though in response to the thought. Argonis remembered the force holding his trigger finger still, and answered Jalen's smile with one of his own.

'You know that they lie,' Sota-Nul's voice buzzed into the silence, 'but you have not found what it masks-hides.'

'Not for lack of trying, I can assure you,' replied Jalen. He glanced at Argonis. 'Since the Iron Warriors have arrived we have done nothing but try and discover why they are fighting this battle.'

'And tried to bring about a swift victory for our forces, no doubt,' said Argonis.

'We have made a contribution, but there are wider concerns at play.' Jalen cocked his head, his eyes fixed on Argonis. 'Otherwise you wouldn't be here, emissary. Otherwise you would not have summoned me. Otherwise the Warmaster would not be considering ordering Perturabo to abandon this fight. Is that not right?'

A sudden shudder rolled through the gunship's hull. Argonis

recognised the metallic thump of fuel lines disengaging. They were almost ready to launch. A low rumble filled the gloom as distant machines began to hoist other craft into launch rigs.

Jalen turned away and made for the hatch controls, his hands fastening the breath mask back in place.

'I cannot give you the answer you want, emissary,' he said. 'But I can tell you that you travel in the right direction.' He keyed the hatch and it folded down. The light of the hangar bay beyond pulsed with amber alert lights. Jalen stepped onto the ramp and looked back, his tattooed face a painted mask. 'Whatever keeps the Iron Warriors here, it is down there, on Tallarn.' Argonis held his gaze for a second, and then Jalen stepped down the ramp, and the tattooed patterns drained from his pale skin.

'How do you wish us to proceed-continue?' asked Sota-Nul. Argonis did not look at her. He realised that he still had his bolt pistol drawn, his finger still on the trigger.

'We go down to the dead world,' he replied.

THE GIRL DIED quietly, her neck broken and her dead weight caught before it hit the floor. Iaeo was already pulling the corpse into the maintenance niche before the last air had sighed from the girl's lungs.

Pict images from her net-flies winked at the corner of her sight. A group of three tank crew in overalls turned into the passage, talking in low voices and exhausted glances. She watched them pass the shadowed niche. Once they were past, she began to work fast.

The dead girl's uniform fitted Iaeo to a reasonable approximation. She pulled it on, feeling the rubberised seal squeeze over her head, noting with a detached interest that it was still warm from body heat. She had studied the girl's face for hours through the eyes of her net-flies, but she glanced at it again, trying to make sure that her facial features were a rough estimation of the leaden exhaustion written over the dead face. She hoped the uniform would be enough. If someone looked closely they might notice that it did not fit her properly. A guess of size and body shape was all she had been able to manage in the time she had. Even then finding the correct moment to remove the girl had been uncomfortably open to error. She was no Calidus.

*Data: 605 seconds to patrol muster. 907 seconds to terminal projection deadline.*

She stood and moved into the passage. Behind her the corpse lay hidden in shadow. It would be found, but by that time she would be beyond reach.

She began to walk faster, hurrying towards the blast doors to the muster cavern. The enviro-suit hood swung from her hand.

*Messy. Imprecise.* She did not like this, not at all.

Behind her the four net-flies watching the passage buzzed after her. They landed on her shoulders and crawled into her hair. The rest were already dormant, their silver bodies gripping her synskin inside the enviro-suit, like hatchlings clinging to a mother queen.

Getting out of the shelter had not been a difficult problem, but it had not been easy either. Getting into a vehicle was a low-grade sub-problem. Getting into a vehicle that she could take control of quickly was another factor, but not a significant one. The number of other machines accompanying a potential machine was more important too many others and she would not be able to break away from them. That shrank the field of selection to a few. Then there was the matter of time. It was a strong assumption that the Alpha Legion might be drawing their snare tighter. The more time she spent in the Crescent Shelter the smaller that snare became. On the other side of the calculation was the fact that she was working quickly, and errors clung to haste like maggots to a corpse. Go too fast, take too many shortcuts and her plan would fail.

The time at which all the risk factors became overwhelming was her terminal projection deadline, and it had drawn closer with every second after she had killed the girl.

*Data: 581 seconds to patrol muster. 883 seconds to terminal projection deadline.*

She walked into the muster cavern. Rows of vehicles stretched away under the stark light of lumen-strips and stab-lights. The corrosive toxins saturating Tallarn's air had pulled the colour from their war paint. Exhaust fumes stained the ceiling, and the smell of oil was thick. The air chimed with the sound of metal: metal cases rattling as belts of ammunition snaked into hoppers, tracks clanking over rockcrete, hatches hinging open and closed.

She took it all in with a glance, and extrapolated to a 99 per cent accurate estimation of machines and personnel in the chamber.

*675 war machines, 356 operational, 100 in need of fuel/service/rearming, 170 in need of repair, 49 likely to be scrapped and broken for parts, 980 humans, 680 servitors, 64 tech-priests. 23 per cent were tank crew either coming off mission or preparing to go out. Level of activity consistent with standard levels of operation post arrival of...*

'What machine are you on?' She looked around, blinking fast. A man in a green and grey uniform was looking down at her.

*Data: Rank pins – Lieutenant, Fenellion Free Guard, Logistics Rated.*

She realised that she had not replied and began to open her mouth.

'You going out?' he asked. 'What machine?'

'Vanquisher 681, Saraga Armoured Continuity Force Lionus, Fifth Subdivision, Gamma Squadron.' She took a breath, then thought, and added, 'Sir.'

The lieutenant let out a sigh, bloodshot eyes focusing under a frown.

*Data: Eyes and breath odour indicate spur addiction.*

*Projection: 78 per cent probability of chronic insomnia, 56 per cent probability reduced fine motor function and sensitivity in extremities, 34 per cent probability of ni–*

'You floating on something?' he said.

Iaeo froze for a second. She had a deep compulsion to look around her. She felt blind, her awareness confined to the data coming from her base five senses. There could be eyes watching her, feet moving closer, hands reaching for weapons. She ran her tongue over her lips, eyes darting over the lieutenant's face.

'You know...' she began, 'gotta... stay on top of it somehow.'

She had once heard a soldier say those words, and then watched him consume a large volume of alcohol. It had seemed to be a form of explanation.

The lieutenant stared at her. She hoped that the correct/expected facial expression was on her face. After a second he nodded.

'Down that way, second row over.'

'Thanks,' she said, but he was already moving away. She had to hold back the instinct to run. Instead she moved as she thought people would move in a hurry. She saw the machines she wanted within a second. She had looked them over remotely, and reviewed each detail of their specifications. They were as familiar to her as her own hand. Except, of course, she had never been inside a tank.

Heads turned to look at her as she hurried closer. She scanned the faces, found one whose cardinal facial points corresponded to the squadron commander she was looking for, and saluted.

The woman's face was flat, and seemed to be sheened in a mix of sweat and bearing grease. The black hair framing her face was clumped and matted.

*Data: Lieutenant Casandra Menard, two years' service in Saraga Armoured Continuity Force Lionus. Fought in the battle of–*

Iaeo cut the data recall from her awareness. This was a crucial moment, and she needed to get the interaction right. Useful though the data she had sucked from the shelter's regimental records might be, right here and now it was utterly irrelevant.

'What do you want?' the lieutenant asked, barely looking up at Iaeo.

'Gunner Vorina reporting for duty.'

'I don't need a gunner.'

Iaeo spoke the next words carefully. She had constructed them from a patchwork of observed and recorded interactions between officers and tank crews. She had practised the cadence, intonation and studied weariness in the words one thousand seven hundred and eleven times. She was still wondering if that was enough.

'Regiment sent me over.'

'All right.' The lieutenant nodded as though Iaeo had a point. 'But I still don't need a gunner.'

'They said that I was for tank 681. Something about the gunner for that one being out, and you needing someone in the slot for a surface run.'

'Huh. Cali's out? What happened?' Iaeo was about to answer when the lieutenant waved her hand. 'Never mind, probably fell over her own boots.' She jerked a thumb back over her shoulder at a Vanquisher with a long gouge across its front armour. 'That's 681. Commander's called Fule. Get comfortable quick. We are rolling out in three minutes.'

*Data: 243 seconds to terminal projection deadline.*

Iaeo stood for a second, her mouth ready to give a reply that now did not fit the pattern of conversation.

She had selected the squadron, tank and crew member she would replace with all the care she could afford. She had falsified a medical record that would confirm that the gunner of Vanquisher 681, Saraga Armoured Continuity Force Lionus, Fifth Subdivision, Gamma Squadron, had fallen and broken three bones in her arm. She had constructed a functional – if imperfect – ghost identity for herself, and implanted orders into the command chain which replaced the now absent gunner from Vanquisher 681 with her ghost identity. All of it balanced so that no one would spot the inconsistencies and contradictions, unless they were looking very closely. It was not the most delicate web she had ever created, but under the constraints it was still functional.

'Need something else?' asked the lieutenant as Iaeo continued to blink.

'Err... No.'

'Good. Then get moving.'

Iaeo nodded, and jogged over to the Vanquisher. Crew were already dropping the hatches on nearby tanks. Engines gunned and breathed hot exhaust into the air. She reached the Vanquisher, swung up, and dropped through the turret hatch. The metal hull was already vibrating to a rising pitch.

*Data: 61 seconds to terminal projection deadline.*

She pulled the hood of the dead gunner's enviro-suit over her head, plugged her breathe-line into the Vanquisher's air supply, and pulled the hatch closed above her.

*Projection: Probability of exodus from Crescent Shelter 88 per cent.*

*The battle for Tallarn was a matter of numbers: numbers of ships, numbers of war machines, numbers of war machines damaged, numbers of war machines lost, numbers of crews, numbers of officers to lead crews, numbers of reserves to make more crews, numbers of stores, numbers of shells, numbers of bullets. The simple truth, believed by both sides, was that they were involved in a battle that would be decided by who had most, and who would run out soonest.*

*In the strategiums of the Sightless Warren the Iron Warriors calculated their active and potential strength ceaselessly. This was war as they had mastered it, the application of force and logistics until the enemy broke. Since they had come to Tallarn the numbers had changed drastically. They had begun with the overwhelming strength, and then seen that eroded by the flea bites of the resistance. They had pulled in more strength. Then the first forces loyal to the Emperor had arrived, and the advantage had shifted from overwhelming to simply significant. More had come to both sides, and losses for all had risen and risen. Which side possessed the numerical advantage had become far from clear.*

*A new set of numbers became significant: the number of units each* side had active on the surface. One side might have more war machines, or greater capacity to sustain, or recover from damage, but if the other side could outnumber and overwhelm them for a short time the reserves and stores would not matter. Governor Militant Dellasarius called it 'the depth of cutting edge', and by the time of the Third Assault on the Sightless Warren, it was the guiding principle of the loyalist strategy. The raiding tactics of old had become the past.

'Just one vast push at the right time and the battle will be done,' went the oft-repeated wisdom amongst the loyalists. Some commanders disagreed, some even took contradictory action, but their defiance meant little. It was a matter not of the small numbers, or of individuals. The groundswell of force, of strength and weakness, as measured in hundreds of thousands, in millions; that was what mattered, and individuals held no significance.

# FIVE

**Iron Warriors
Dagger point
Questions**

'All units, cut engines!' Kord shouted the command as another sonic boom rang through *War Anvil*'s interior. Sacha was swearing, hands pressed over her ears. Kord was watching the auspex. It must have been a direct orbital drop, straight down from the edge of the void, fast, the kind of thing you only did if you were going straight into a war zone. He could see the aircraft now, small pips of light streaking across his screen as they banked east. Another sonic boom split the air above them, then another and another.

'It's a full flight!' shouted Zade. Kord was adjusting the screen, throwing its viewpoint as wide as it would go. Blurred markers streaked the screen. They were out on the edge of the vast plateau which the Tallarn-born called the Khedive. The enemy formation they were tracking was forty kilometres in front of them, just at the edge of sensor range.

Another thunder crack. Zade was not wrong, a full flight of warplanes had just dropped directly above their position. That might mean they were seconds away from being wreckage. The only thing holding him back from that conclusion was that they were still alive.

'How did they find us?' shouted Sacha.

Kord ignored her. He took a quick breath, felt his pulse steady, and flicked over to the regiment-wide vox.

'Squadron leads, this is *War Anvil*, what are you seeing?'

'Six aircraft, so far. They are coming back around, banking towards the east,' the voice was loud but level. Zekenilla, Kord knew without looking that she had shut down her squadron on a coin as soon as he gave the order.

'They ours?' Abbas from the First Squadron lead tank, his breath ragged. Shock? Possibly, more likely anger. That was normally the way with him.

'No signals,' said Origo. 'They are spitting out a hell of a lot of auspex distortion. If they hadn't come down on top of us we wouldn't have known they were here. Probably not ours, but probably not looking for us either.'

'Doesn't mean that they might not take the chance to come back around and pick us off,' snarled Abbas.

'This far away from anything else, maybe they are just wondering what we are doing,' said Zekenilla.

'If we stay still maybe they will think we are already dead in the dust,' added Origo.

Kord took another breath.

'Hold position,' he said. 'If we find we are still alive in a few minutes we can worry about other things.'

He listened, straining to hear the aircraft over the vox hiss. Was that rumble them, or just the wind on the silent hull? The screen showed him a series of distorted marks that might mean that the aircraft were still banking, or had already cut a course to the east. The seconds stretched on.

The roar of rockets and the crack of lascannons did not come.

*That does not mean they won't*, thought Kord. *This is a battle of hunters and prey. Assume you have escaped and you make your death certain.*

'Sir.' Origo's voice cut into his thoughts. 'I have a read on the quarry. They are still moving. Much longer sitting here and we lose them.'

He switched the view on the auspex. The estimated position of the patrol they were tracking was drifting into blurred uncertainty.

'Sir,' Abbas said. Kord could almost hear the Tallarn-born lieutenant purse his lips as he chose his words. '*Colonel, with all respect, what are we doing out here?*'

'Searching for answers,' said Kord.

'*Sir,*' still Abbas, still holding his emotion on a lengthening leash, '*it's just a sweep patrol. Might not even be Legion machines.*'

'*I saw a silhouette as the mist thinned five kilometres back,*' said Origo. '*It looked like a Predator.*'

'Even if it is,' pressed Abbas, '*they are just looking for targets to take out. Targets like us. If we go much further the smaller machines aren't going to have enough fuel to get back to the shelter.*'

'They aren't on this planet to fight!' snapped Kord, and regretted it as soon as he said it. Silence.

'*Sir?*' It was Zekenilla, her oh-so-steady voice touched with concern.

Kord shook his head. All of his officers, and most of those that rode under his command, knew what he believed. They never asked him, and he never talked about it. It was an unspoken understanding that had never been tested. Except now they were on the edge of their fuel radius, watching a quarry, which only he believed was important, disappear into the distance.

He shook his head, closed his eyes, and began to speak, suddenly unable to hide his weariness.

'They thought they had won as soon as they let the first bomb fall. So why come down here after that? Why not just move on?' He opened his eyes, wishing that he could take the suit off and rub them. 'You have seen it as well. Legion patrols far from their bases, in areas that have no strategic value. They are not looking for targets. They are covering the ground, or keeping it clear for others that follow them. This is one of those patrols, way out, heading towards nothing important. If we want to know what they are here for, we follow them.'

'*That's full of it!*' Abbas spat. An uneasy silence fell, like the pause between seeing the flash of a bomb and being hit by the blast wave. But when Abbas spoke again his voice was filled with exhaustion rather than anger. '*There needs to be no reason for this war. We are* here because we are. We lost at the Sapphire City because we were out-gunned and out-fought. There is no other reason. No hidden truth that makes sense of it. It just is.'

'I will let you have that, lieutenant,' said Kord, and his voice was stone. 'This one time.'

'Command authorise this, sir?' asked Abbas.

Kord said nothing, there was no point. They all knew the answer.

'Origo, you got anything to say to this?' asked Kord.

They all respected the scout. He had volunteered, one of the first. He had been there with the rest of them at the fall of the Sapphire City. Cold as a knife blade, that was what most of those who met him said.

'There is always another side to things' said Origo at last. 'Always.'

'Aircraft have passed, sir,' said Zekenilla.

Kord shook his head slowly, glanced at Zade and Sacha. They were looking away, leaning on the gun. They looked as though they were trying to catch a few moments of sleep. They were not of course. His crew would have heard the exchange, but he knew that they would not say anything. He had got each one of them out of the ruin of the Sapphire City, and they would follow him without a word. But Abbas had a point. This was the last moment they could turn back, and if they were going to step into what waited beyond they had to do it willingly. All of them.

'All units, this is *War Anvil*. You know why we are out here. We are chasing ghosts that no one else believes in. Some of you might not believe in them either, but you know me. Whether you believe me or not, you all have a choice to make now – turn around and head back to the shelter, or follow me. We move in twenty seconds. *War Anvil* out.'

He shut the vox off.

'Mori, warm the engines up. Everyone else, you heard that, I'm afraid you don't get the choice.'

'Don't really need one, sir,' said Sacha.

*War Anvil* woke to life. Kord waited, counting the seconds off in his head. When he reached twenty, he keyed the vox again.

'All units, start up the engines. Let's get moving.'

Gradually, one after another the machines of the Tallarn 71st began to roll across the earth and into the mist. One machine, an Executioner, peeled away from the others as they fell into formation around *War Anvil*. The lone machine turned south. After a few minutes it was lost from the screens and sights of its comrades.

'So,' Kord heard Abbas's voice over the vox, and could not help smile. *'Igra decided this was not for him. Shame. Where are we going, colonel?'*

'Into the unknown,' replied Kord.

HREND PAUSED ON the edge of the tunnel threshold. The wind wound yellow vapour over the land before him. He had not slept again since the primarch had come to him, and he would not sleep again until he returned.

*If you return*, itched a thought at the back of his awareness.

His Dreadnought brothers stood to either side of him. Blunt slabs covered Orun's Mortis frame, the barrels of his doubled lascannons catching the passing streams of fog like fingers held in running water. On his other side, Gortun was turning his head unit slowly from side to side, spinning the drill claws of his fists up, and then letting them spin to stillness, over and over again. The tanks of the Cyllaros assault group were formed up behind them, tracks still on crusted earth. At their centre sat a Spartan carrier and a bloated mobile drill machine. Of all the machines in the group these two had to survive if the mission was to succeed. Everything and everyone else was expendable.

*'Master.'* Jarvak's voice spoke the word to him. He did not reply. He knew what his lieutenant was going to ask. *'What do we wait for?'*

'Nothing.'

The tunnel mouth they stood in opened in the side of a mountain range. A shallow slope slid down to meet low hills in front of him. Beyond that the land undulated away into the fog like the waves of a frozen sea. Above the tunnel mouth the bare rock of the mountain reached up to the hidden sky. The tunnel itself had been the entrance to an abandoned mine network. The Iron Warriors sappers and stone-wrights had connected it to their growing network of the Sightless Warren within a few days of the first shelter falling to them. Now it had provided Hrend and his force a door into a silent corner of the surface.

*What are we that we have made this?* The thought pulled at Hrend.

He adjusted his view, zooming in on where a line of pylons marched across the crest of a hill, and into the murk.

'Do you think of the past, Jarvak?'

'No, master.' Jarvak's voice cut into comms static. *'I think of the task I must perform. I think of my duty.'*

'Duty?'

*'The duty we have to the primarch.'*

'What is that duty?'

*'To never fail. To never prove weak. To never break.'* Jarvak's answer came without hesitation, but Hrend caught the note of puzzlement at the edge of the words.

'Why?'

'Master?'

'Answer.'

*'We are Iron Warriors.'*

*We are Iron Warriors.* That found an echo in his own thoughts. *We are the Olympian-born, the Legion that did what others would not deign to do, the breakers and makers of war. We are the wronged, the slighted, the forgotten strength of an Imperium that turned its face from us even as we gave it the iron of our blood.*

'What does it mean to be an Iron Warrior?'

'To be iron withi–'

'Now. What does it mean now?'

A pause, filled with the sound of the wind blowing the death shroud of a planet.

*'What it always meant,'* said Jarvak at last.

Hrend said nothing, and then spoke across the vox to his entire group.

'Forward.' He stepped out of the tunnel mouth, and into the waiting desolation.

THE SICKLE BLADE hit the edge of Tallarn's atmosphere, and threw a cloak of fire across its wings. It trembled and sang as it plunged down through the air. Black ceramite shutters blinked closed over the gunship's canopy, and suddenly the view of the rancid planet was gone from Argonis's view. A projection of the world beyond filled his eyes instead, the complexity of reality stripped down to lines of light and sensor data. He was flying by hand, feeling the craft twist against bands of thickening air.

Behind the gunship, the Iron Warriors void-fighters peeled away to circle the re-entry point. The remaining six craft swung in closer to form a box, four Lightning Crows and two Fire Raptors. Argonis heard the terse words of each pilot flick across the vox. They were good, each movement and formation change crisp and precise, but Argonis could not shake the idea that the Iron Warriors flew with the same blunt efficiency as a resentful serf who wanted a duty done as quickly as possible. That was not fair, of course. The Iron Warriors were formidable in every sense. They just lacked something under their skin of iron.

'You trust-believe the operative Jalen?' Sota-Nul spoke across the vox. They had not spoken in the hour since the *Sickle Blade* had launched, but she spoke as though continuing a conversation that had continued without pause. Perhaps in the tech-witch's mind she had simply cut back into the discussion of Jalen's lack of information, as though resuming a recording from a mark.

'Them, not *he*,' said Argonis. 'When you talk of the Twentieth Legion you should never think that you see them all. If you see ten then there are a hundred you do not see. If you see a hundred assume that there are a thousand. If you see one alone assume there are ten thousand.'

'Is that your own wisdom?'

'The Warmaster's.'

'He does not trust them…' said Sota-Nul, and he thought he heard something rattling and serpentine in her voice. 'Despite their alliance to his cause?'

'His remarks,' he said carefully, 'were, I believe, intended as a compliment of their mode of war.'

Argonis watched as the altimeter counted down. They were within the lower bands of atmosphere. He blinked a rune, and the shutters flicked back from the canopy. A swirled soup of fog pressed against the armourglass. They were above a huge plateau that bore the name Khedive, diving directly downwards, accelerating into the grasp of the planet's gravity. Just above the ground they would flick up from their descent, then slam into a ground-hugging curve. The XVI Legion called this manoeuvre Ahagress, 'the dagger point', in Cthonian. The Iron Warriors had simply referred to it as Assault Manoeuvre 23-b. The ground was coming up fast. He triggered the gunship's ground-sweeping auspex. The shapes of war machines blinked in his sight, bright with heat and hard metal edges.

'You have not answered,' said Sota-Nul.

'No,' he replied. 'I neither trust nor believe the Alpha Legion, and what the Warmaster believes is not for me to know.'

'But you are his emissary.'

'Yes. I am.'

'*War machines active in insertion zone.*' The heavy voice of the Iron Warriors escort commander cut into the vox. '*Threat status unclear.*'

'*Leave them,*' snapped Argonis. '*Even if they are hostile they won't be able to touch us. Maintain pattern and course.*'

'*Confirmed,*' said the Iron Warrior. Argonis watched as the altitude count drained down into smaller and smaller values.

'Yet...' Sota-Nul's voice lingered on the word. There was something unsettling about it, something more flesh than machine, but still not human. 'Yet even though you neither believe nor trust the operative Jalen, we still follow where he guides us.'

'You do not need to trust a weapon to wield it.'

'And that is what you do? You are sure?'

The altitude value at the edge of his sight pulsed amber then red. Beyond the canopy the fog parted for a brief instant, and a bare plain expanded beneath him. For an eye-blink he saw the scattered shapes of tanks. Then he triggered the anti-grav and the gunship snapped up. G-forces hit him like a blow. For a wonderful, terrible second it felt as though he were both floating and falling without control. Then he slammed power into the thrusters and *Sickle Blade* punched forward, and the thunder of its passing vanished behind it.

SHE WAITED IN the dark and talked to herself.

It was cold. Her enhanced physiology let her discard the discomfort of the dropping temperature, but she still registered it. She had left the enviro-suit on. One of the suit's very limited advantages was that it kept the chill out. She had cut all power in Vanquisher 681 before she had killed its crew. That part of the plan had been simple.

The machine's controls were not complex. She had waited until the rest of the squadron had spread out, and then let one of her net-flies crawl out of her suit and bite into the tank's vox and comms systems. From there it had been easy to slowly guide the squadron to where she needed it. Over the course of an hour she had teased Vanquisher 681 further and further away from its comrades without anyone realising. By the time she cut the power in the tank there was a very small probability that the rest of the squadron would find it. The crew had not panicked at first, and when they had it had played to her advantage. Then the waiting had begun.

She had begun the self-dialogue after four hours.

'Question: What is the chance of error in the termination projection?'

'Answer: High. The factors are unknown and all outcomes are approximations.'

It was a basic technique of the Vanus Temple, one of the first that initiates mastered. As much as mental skill and data were the foundations of the Vanus arts, doubt and questioning were trained into their psyches from childhood. The first stage of this training came from responding to the questions of a master, and then by mimicking that technique through assuming the viewpoint/ intellectual framework of another person. Eventually the question/

aggressive-doubt technique became part of their basic awareness. In time the back and forth of self-interrogation sank down into the architecture of their subconscious. Most Vanus rarely revisited the technique consciously, but Iaeo had taken to doing so during her deployment. At first she had thought of it as a form of mental cleaning, keeping her functions grounded. After a while she wondered if it had become a consequence of operating without direction, a compulsion.

In the quiet of the Vanquisher's hull she flipped between questioner and answer, vocalising both. In her mind the questioner was always Master Senus, her mentor for her first decade in the Temple. His sour shrunken face grinned out each challenge from a pict-perfect memory.

'Question: What is the basis of the current termination projection?'

'Answer: That the presence of *an emissary* is seen as significant by the Alpha Legion. That the presence of the emissary represents a change in the problem field. Where there is change there is opportunity.'

'Question: State your current target.'

'Answer: Apex Alpha Legion operatives within the Tallarn war locale.'

'Question: Name and identify individual targets.'

'Answer: Alpha Legion Apex Operative, cognomen Jalen.'

'Question: Outline target's current location, nature, capabilities, connections and resources.'

'Answer: Demanded information unknown.'

She paused. In her mind the memory image of her mentor's face grinned. It was not a pleasant expression.

'Question: Outline base-level information related to target.'

'Answer: Multi-level infiltration of loyalist forces on Tallarn by human, or human approximate operatives. Sub-level of bribed, coerced, or converted assets likely to exist within survivors of Iron Warriors viral attack, because of prior infiltration of Tallarn by the Alpha Legion.'

'Question: Project the likely meaning of "emissary" in the context of the problem field.'

'Answer: An actor sent by an external power as formal representation of that power. As the Alpha Legion is not dominant within the enemy forces, the emissary is not to them. The Iron Warriors are the dominant authority within the enemy forces at present. The emissary is, therefore, an individual sent to the Iron Warriors from another power base. This analysis has a 76 per cent accuracy value.'

'Demand: Expand beyond primary analysis.'

'Answer: Given a blank reading of power values within the enemy forces, *an emissary* implies at least a peer relationship of authority, and suggests a dominant relationship. The emissary is from a higher authority than the Iron Warriors. The emissary is from Horus Lupercal. This expanded analysis has a 38 per cent accuracy value.'

In her mind's eye her mentor's desiccated mouth spread into a dagger-slash smile.

'Question: How does this offer a termination solution on the designated target?'

She paused again.

'Answer: The presence of an emissary from Horus represents a change in power structures, an overall alteration in the problem field.'

The memory of her mentor just stared at her, eyes glittering in mocking triumph.

'Answer clarification,' she began, paused, felt her own hesitation, and shivered. *To doubt brings truth,* said another voice in her head, *to be unclear is to fail before you begin.* 'Answer clarification: The emissary allows for an expansion of the problem space, and possible elimination of targets by manipulating ignorance and knowledge within the enemy forces.'

She stopped. She could hear her own heart beating through her blood in the silence of the Vanquisher's interior. She saw the memory of her mentor lean forward, looking down at her, the light catching the implanted membrane over his eyes, turning them to blank silver.

'Assertion,' he whispered with her voice. 'You are clutching at uncertainties.'

'Response: There are possi–' The words caught in her throat.

'Assertion: You don't see a clear outcome path. Assertion: You don't know what you are doing. Assertion: You are going to make an error.'

She blinked. Suddenly aware of the cold inside the Vanquisher again.

'You are going to make an error, Iaeo,' she said quietly to herself.

She stayed still and quiet for a long while after that, eyes staring into space while she counted seconds.

At last the probability that the squadron were still searching for Vanquisher 681 shrank to nothing.

It was time.

She uncurled herself, and reached across the slumped body of the tank's commander. The tank's communication and vox systems came online. She triggered the signal she had prepared. It was a broad-spectrum distress broadcast. Dozens of these signals washed the comms network of Tallarn, the dying gasps of war machines who could not reach home. Both sides tracked down the sources of such signals near to their shelters. Functioning war machines were valuable in this war, even if the dead were pulled out of their hulls.

The signal began to ping out into dead air, and Iaeo listened and waited for the Iron Warriors to hear. She had positioned Vanquisher 681 close to the patrol screens which ran around the Sightless Warren's southernmost entrances. Somewhere in the Iron Warriors base the signal would be heard, and recovery vehicles would come to pull the dead hull beneath the earth. Once she was inside the Sightless Warren she could begin the next stage.

She curled back into a ball, and watched the signal transmission light pulse. She considered beginning the self-dialogue again, but decided not to. The sound of a rising wind rattled down the outside of the hull. After a moment she thought it became a voice scratching at her from memory.

*You are going to make an error, Iaeo,* it said.

# PART TWO
# PILGRIMS

*Tallarn was changing. Dawn broke across the planet in a ragged line. On the surface the light grew brighter, dissolving into the fog so that the air seemed soaked in a dirty brilliance. From orbit, if one looked down at the correct angle, the new day was a luminous cord pulled across the planet's surface. Each day had begun like this since the virus bombing, and it seemed that it always would. Except that, here and there, the new light found holes in Tallarn's shroud.*

*In places the fog had thinned, and the ground had begun to dry, black sludge caking to a dry layer under the sun. Shrinking pools of slime dotted this landscape. In places the hard crust covered deep sink holes of black liquid beneath. War machines had been lost to these hidden wells, their weight shattering the crust and plunging them into the void beneath. The turrets and barrels of some stuck up from the ground like dead hands reaching for air.*

*Dust began to replace the fog in these dry places. Winds shivered across the flats, picking up the powdered layer from the top of the ground and tumbling it up into the air. The human crews of tanks began to recognise the dust storms by the dry rattling sounds they made on the outside of their hulls. 'The voice of the dead' they called it.*

Six days after the failed third attack on the Sightless Warren, the first squadron of war machines was lost to a storm on the plains of Khedive. Their wrecks were found by chance three weeks later. Lightning from a massive storm had crawled over their hulls, fried their systems and detonated their munitions. The wind had then stripped the corroded paint and soot from their hulls.

The fog swirled on the edge of the drying areas. It still covered much of Tallarn, but it too was changing. Churned by fire from battles, and the pillars of energy hurled from warships, it boiled with its own currents, spinning across the seas and slime-sheened mountains. Heavy with soot and the residue of great and terrible weapons, it spawned storms that dragged sheets of black rain through the dissolving rubble of cities.

The survivors of Tallarn felt the changes too.

The Hell Above was dying, they said. In place of the death mire of the old, a new land was emerging, fathered by war and mothered by poison. It was a hungry child too, filled with spite and hunger for their lives. As with so much of the battle, the survivors reached into the language of their past to name the changing surface of Tallarn. 'Yathan' they called it – the 'land of lost pilgrims'.

# SIX

**Comrades**
**Black Oculus**
**Observer**

'Origo?' Kord spoke the name carefully. His head was swimming, hovering somewhere on the boundary between exhaustion and hallucination. 'Origo?' he said again, checking as he did so that the vox was set to the scout machine's frequency.

*'Yes, sir,'* came Origo's voice, dry and wrung out. Kord licked his lips. His tongue was dry.

They had lost the quarry three days before. The Iron Warriors had simply vanished; one second the scouts were saying that they could see them, and the next the vox was filled with confusion. Finally a numb resignation settled into Kord like ice water. The auspex screens were showing merely static, as though the air itself had become nothing but a blizzard of distortion.

They had carried on for another twelve hours on the same heading after they had lost their quarry. No one spoke except to check headings and status. Kord remained quiet, even as the instinct to ask for fresh reports itched at him. They had settled into the silence for four hours, and at the end of it Kord had given the order to move out on the same bearing as before. No one had said anything other than the briefest of acknowledgements. That had been two weeks before, two weeks of pushing onwards sipping recycled water and nutri-paste from tubes inside the suit. They had not seen anything in that time, not a silhouette of a vehicle, not a scratch of code on the wind. At first he had been able to hear the tension in the voices of the others over the vox. Then that had faded to a dull monotone, which blended with the fog beyond. Even Sacha and the rest of his own crew had faded into soundlessness. He could not say he blamed them. He was not sure if he felt alive himself.

'Was there something, colonel?' asked Origo.

Kord breathed. He was not sure why he had begun this.

'What should I do, Origo?' the words came before he could help them. They hung in the pause that followed. *I sound so weak*, he thought. *Weak, broken,* cracked.

'With all due respect, sir, that is not how the chain of command works.'

Kord almost laughed. He felt giddy.

'We won't find them again, will we, Origo? The ghost I was following is gone, isn't it?'

*'If this is the old flats south of Kussank, then we could travel the two hundred kilometres we have already covered again before we saw its edge. They might be anywhere within that space, or somewhere else entirely.'* Origo did not add the implication of those facts. He did not need to.

Kord clicked the vox to reply, but said nothing. After several seconds of fizzing silence he released the transmission key. He closed his eyes, but kept the vox open. He began to notice the heat and noise of the machine, the warm clamminess of sweat on the seals of his suit, the stuttered clatter of the tracks turning, the way that Sacha twisted to get comfortable every few minutes. It was as though his mind and senses were reaching for something to take the place of the thought that kept rattling through him.

*I was wrong.*

Three hours after the last sighting he called a full halt. The regiment had scattered into a ring, guns and sensors facing outwards, power, heat and air turned down to a minimum. He had ordered all crews to sleep. He wondered, however, how many of them would sleep. He could not, he knew that without trying.

After several minutes he opened the vox to Origo again.

'Is there supposed to be anything else out here?'

'*There was a settlement on the northern edge of the flats, a shelter too. We could perhaps make it in thirty-six hours if we went straight and fast.*'

'Are you saying that we should run for safety?'

'*Isn't that why you're asking?*'

'They are out here. We lost them but there are others.' He paused, realising that the words had come without him thinking about them.

'*You believe that, sir? I mean really?*'

'Yes…' he began, and he heard the truth come wearily out of his mouth. 'Because there has to be a reason doesn't there? A reason for why this all happened, a reason why Horus is fighting the Emperor, a reason why the Iron Warriors came here, a reason why we are here, a reason for where we are going.'

'*Where are we going?*'

He looked down at where the glass of the auspex screen blinked with runes.

'I don't know.'

'*Sometimes… sometimes, knowing the answers does not help.*'

'No… perhaps… but we have to believe they exist.'

'*Who are you trying to convince, sir? Me, or yourself?*'

'Both.'

'*Well I–*'

'*Colonel,*' Abbas's voice cut through Origo's. Kord felt the tiredness slide back behind a layer of adrenaline. '*I am getting a signal. Very faint, but it's there. Seventy-five degrees from north.*'

Kord began to work the vox set. He could hear the signal now, a shift in the tone of the static. There was something there all right. It sounded like a voice.

'All units, this is *War Anvil*. Engines and weapons live. Heading seventy-five degrees from north. Crescent formation. Slow and careful.'

They moved out, tracks clattering through slow revolutions. Muttered signals snapped between the machines.

'*I see something!*' Abbas's voice came across after they had gone five kilometres.

'Steady,' said Kord.

'*Visual contact,*' called Abbas. '*It's a tank. Can't identify class.*'

They moved closer. Kord could almost feel the eyes of every member of the regiment scanning their sights and screens.

The faint sound in the static suddenly became a voice.

'*…please help, can anyone hear…*'

'*I don't like it,*' Zekenilla's voice cut in. '*Why did we not hear their call until now?*'

'*Powered down perhaps, until they saw us,*' said Origo.

'Keep on heading,' said Kord.

'*…Please, oh golden gates of Terra,*' came the distorted voice. '*Please, I can see you, please…*'

And then Kord saw it. Sitting beneath a low rise was a Vanquisher, its turret rotated to the side, the tip of its long barrel touching the ground. Dust and corrosion had rubbed the red-and-black of its heraldic colours into a series of pocked patches.

'Acassian Line Breakers,' said Sacha. 'Been out here for a while. Can't see any damage.'

She was right. The machine looked intact, but it was slumped to one side, its right track submerged beneath the grey crust.

'*Please,*' said the voice again. '*Please. I know you're there. We don't have much power left…*'

'Sir, what are we going to do?' asked Sacha.

Kord was staring at the Vanquisher's hull.

'Sir?'

'All units full stop. Origo move the scouts close. Get your eyeball pressed against its hull. All other units hold position. Stay sharp.'

Kord switch his vox to the frequency the pleading voice was speaking on.

'Unknown unit, this is Colonel Kord of the Tallarn Seventy-First, please identify.'

'*Thank goodness,*' the voice sobbed back. *Male,* thought Kord. '*Thank goodness…*' The words crumbled wetly, so that Kord could almost hear the tears.

'Identify,' he said again, turning his head to nod at Sacha. She returned the nod and pressed her eyes to her gunsight. The main gun was already loaded.

'*Gunner Tolson…*' the voice gasped, '*Acassian Eight Hundred and Seventh.*'

'What is your situation?'

'*My situation… can't you see?*'

'Listen to me, Tolson. What happened?' asked Kord. A sob sucked over the vox, but then he heard the man take a series of breaths. When the voice came back it was steadier.

'*We ran into an enemy unit running to the east,*' said the voice. Kord felt the words shiver over his skin; he was aware that he was holding his breath. '*We lost two. We ran. Then the track sunk, and we could not get out.*'

'Where is your commander, Tolson?'

'*We…*' the man's words caught. '*We started to run low on air…*'

Kord blinked, suddenly aware of the air as it passed over his tongue.

'You are alone?'

'*Yes, but I can drive it, the machine, I mean. I think it could move if it was shunted out.*'

Kord nodded. The machine looked like it could be pushed out of the soft ground that had caught its track. He keyed the vox onto another channel.

'Origo, tell me what you see.'

'*It's jammed, but could come free.*'

'Anything else out there?'

Kord flicked his view to a straight magnified display down *War Anvil*'s gunsight. Just beyond the stranded tank and the three scattered scout machines, the fog swirled in uneven cliffs and curtains.

'*Not that I can see, sir,*' came Origo's reply.

Kord nodded to himself.

'Abbas,' he said, 'Get *Grave Call* and her dozer blade up here. Shunt the machine out.'

'*Sir*,' came the curt reply.

'Tolson, we are going to shunt you out of there and get you moving. Then you are coming with us.'

He cut the man's tears and thanks off as they started.

A second later Abbas's squadron swept into sight. The dozer-equipped Executioner *Grave Call* was in the lead, its three siblings spread around and behind it in a V. Kord zoomed his view closer, tracking the machines. Getting the stranded tank free, that was one thing, but he was not thinking about that. All that he could think of was the enemy force that the surviving crew member had mentioned. If they could get the man calm enough to work the tank's auspex he might be able to backtrack to the enemy's last position. There could not be many Iron Warriors patrols out in this isolated reach of Tallarn, and that might mean that they had just stumbled on a lead.

Something caught his eye in the fog as he pulled his view back to the stranded tank. He did not know what he had seen, it had been so brief, an image caught as it vanished behind a curtain.

He swept the gunsight back. The fog beyond the low dirt ridge had thickened again. His mouth opened.

What had it been?

Cold on his skin.

Had it been... a figure...

*Grave Call* was within ten metres of the stranded tank now.

No, that could not be. Except...

His hand found the vox.

'Tolson,' he said, trying to keep his voice steady. The vox crackled. 'How long did it take the air to fail?'

'*Sir*...?' Tolson's voice was ragged with relief.

The *Grave Call*, had rotated its turret so that its gun pointed to its rear. The pistons holding its dozer blade extended, dropping it to the ground.

'How long?'

The fog parted along the ridge behind the stranded tank.

A figure was standing there; still, graphite black, the dust of the drying earth falling from its joints and armour plates. It was not human, it was not even trans-human. It was a cyborg. A Thallaxi. And it was looking directly down at Kord.

'All units!' the shout roared from his throat.

The stranded tank exploded. Jets of molten metal blasted from each face of its hull. The *Grave Call* blew apart as the jet cut through its hull. A sphere of plasma flew out from the dead machine, struck another tank, and flipped it onto its side like a toy slammed by a child.

The cyborg brought its thick-barrelled meltagun up and fired. A red neon line split the fog, touched Abbas's tank, and a second, brilliant white sphere blinked into being.

Kord jerked his head back from the sight as white-bright light bored into his retina. *War Anvil* shook as overlapping blast waves broke over it. There were voices shouting all around him, shouting across the vox, through the pressed tight space of the tank. He tried to blink away the bright smudges burned into his sight. Beyond them he could see shapes moving on the auspex screen, red threat marks rising from the dead dust of the ground to close on him.

*The memory of Perturabo's voice came to Hrend as he dreamed.*

*'What are we?' Perturabo asked.*

*The question surprised Hrend, but the answer came without him thinking.*

*'We are iron.'*

*'And what is the purpose of iron?'*

*'To endure. To cut.'*

*'To be weapons of war.' Perturabo nodded, and turned half away, the plates of his augmented frame flowing over each other. He raised an arm, and turned it over seeming to examine the weapon bonded to its back. Hrend did not know the exact design, but recognised volkite charge discs and energy feeds. 'But we are fighting a war that is not like the wars*

*of old. The edge has been taken from our blades, the strength from our shield. The universe we thought existed was a lie.'*

The dream ended, the lingering image of Perturabo crumbling into the static swirl of fog in his sensors.

For a second the feeling of fading dreams and memory lingered, more real than unreal, even as they vanished. He shivered and his Dreadnought frame creaked in sympathy. He turned his head and looked around him, trying to remember where he was and what he was doing.

A line of black jagged rocks rose through the thinning fog to his left, biting up into the air, and marching down a slope to a valley floor which waited somewhere out of sight. The assault group were lined up beside him, stationary on the crusted earth slope. The brick slab shape of Spartan 4171 loomed to his left. Orun and Gortun stood a short distance behind him, and the rest of the group's war machines formed a diamond around them. All of them had their engines and systems wound down to minimum power. He remembered where they were now.

A voice was talking, the last word it had spoken sliced off at his wakening.

'*–h out a specific target. We could meet resistance in either direction.*'

He still did not feel fully part of what was going on around him. Reflexively he checked the time lag since he had last been conscious. Less than a second had passed. He looked at the seconds click past, and felt his recent memories return.

He and his group were halted in the lower foothills close to an area the humans of Tallarn had called Nedden. They had stopped to make the decision on the direction in which they should proceed.

'*East...*' A new voice trembled across the vox, draining down into a panting breath. The voice trailed off, and Hrend could feel the silence on the vox thicken uneasily.

'You tell us to go east, Navigator?' he asked.

'*Yes...*' said the rustling voice. The fingers of both Hrend's fists clamped shut at the sound. Even from the vox it was like sand grating over glass. '*The rift opens. Its scent calls. The taste of night is like sugar. East runs the water though there is no stream, only the eyes... eyes like the dark-bright moon...'*

'Silence,' he growled, and the Navigator went quiet.

Hrend had only seen the creature once as it was being loaded onto Spartan 4171. It was not an experience he wished to repeat. It had moved with an irregular grace, gliding, twitching and veering without discernible pattern. The exposed flesh of its head and hands was grey, and crazed with black veins which stood proud of the skin. A metal plate covered its forehead, keeping its third eye locked behind closed, plasteel leaves. The eyes beneath were blood-red from edge to edge, the irises a broken swirl at the heart of each. Hrend knew its name: Hes-Thal. He, for it had been a male, was one of the Navigators who had been at the tillers of Perturabo's fleet as it had plunged into the black star at the heart of the Eye of Terror. They had still had their third eyes open when the ships fell into that other space. It had killed many of them, and altered the ones who remained. 'Black Oculus Navigators' was what the primarch had called them. Hrend had become one of the few that knew of their existence when he had accepted this quest. It was an honour he did not relish.

Whenever he had to interact with the altered Navigator, he felt a hunger to be ignorant of their existence again. But without Hes-Thal their task was impossible; the Navigator could see, or sense what they sought, though that sense seemed as erratic as the creature himself.

'We turn east,' said Hrend, into the waiting vox. He began to walk. The tracks of the tanks began to turn.

'*Ironclad...*' the Navigator's voice slid into his ear.

'Yes.'

'*I see you, Ironclad...*' Hrend heard the words, and suddenly was sure he could feel something inside his sarcophagus, something delicate tracing lines across the chewed remains of his skin, something with long, thin fingers. The Navigator's voice returned. '*I... see... you... a morsel of flesh pulled from the death father's mouth... I see you curled in your tomb... I see you dream...*'

Hrend saw the land around him, but suddenly everything was different. The fog stripped back as if burned away by sunlight. Everything was brilliant and clear and bright. Everything was burning. His feet were moving, and beside him the block shapes of Sicarans, Predators and Venator hulls shimmered in pools of shadow. Sounds came to him as he looked at them, sounds like the snicker of blade edges and the rattle song of bullets feeding into a gun.

'What?' he began, but the word hung on its own because the Navigator's voice came again.

'I... see... you... I see the whole... I see the seed... and I...' The voice trailed away. Hrend's sight suddenly cleared, and the sensation of fingers stirring the fluid around his body vanished. He was striding over the ground, his sensors peeling back the fog not with light but with the stark stream of scrolling data. He knew without knowing why the Navigator within the Spartan had turned its gaze from him.

'What?' he said again, as though clearing it from a jammed thought.

'I see you, and I...' whispered Hes-Thal as though falling asleep. '...and I am sorry.'

Hrend marched on, following a line into the east, trying not to hear the Navigator's words scratch at the back of his thoughts.

THE MASTER OF Core Reach I came to Argonis in his chamber complex.

The rooms were three levels down, in a region of the Sightless Warren that had been the first to be assimilated into the buried fortress. The Sapphire City Shelter had been its name before, but the Iron Warriors had stripped it of that name when they had remade it. Core Reach I was its new title, and the blunt efficiency of the IV Legion now pervaded its every corner. Work details moved through its corridors in tight groups, hauling loads of shells, armour plates and provisions to the areas that would need them. Harsh light and fresh air billowed through the passages and chambers from repaired and carefully maintained lighting and ventilation systems. Every door and lift shaft had a guard. Most were from the human regiments bound to the Legion. The iron skull and bonded unit numbers marked their armour and skin. Legionaries watched over more vital areas, flanking doors or looking out into chambers, like worn steel statues.

Argonis and his entourage had been given a cluster of sparse chambers close to the central command areas. They had been permitted to go wherever they pleased, and no one had questioned their presence anywhere. The Eye of Horus opened all doors. Even so they had learned nothing besides the manifest truth that Tallarn was a battlefield, which gave up victories sparingly and drank the blood of all who trod her surface. Argonis had walked the miles of the Sightless Warren, had reviewed battle plans, and seen caverns filled with troops and machines. None of it had told him anything besides the fact that the IV Legion were trying to win Tallarn the way they always won wars, by battering their enemies to ruin. He had found nothing: no suspicious facts, no concealment, nothing.

Had his instinct been wrong? Was the truth they were hunting a ghost?

It had been the tech-witch who had suggested that they change their approach. Argonis had resisted, but as the days became weeks, and the weeks clustered into months he had agreed that there was no alternative. If there was something hidden then looking at the surface of things was going to tell them nothing. They had to peel the skin off and look beneath, and that meant that they were about to do something that brought a taste of bile to his tongue when he thought about it.

He turned when the chamber doors opened. The Iron Warrior who entered was a little shorter than most Space Marines, and the face was a flattened lump of scars and stitch marks. A blank silver ball stared out from where his left eye should have been, while the right met Argonis's with pale green coldness. A crimson-and-yellow centurion plume rose from the plough-fronted helm held under the newcomer's left arm, and his right rested on the pommel of a sheathed short sword. Bronze lightning bolts split the dirty iron of his breastplate and shoulder guard. Behind him stood two warriors in the chevroned bronze of the Legion elite. The Iron Warrior's name was Volk, and he held command over much of the Sightless Warren, and he was there because Argonis had summoned him.

Argonis waited.

After a long second Volk spoke.

'The Commander of Core Reach One gives honour and greetings to the emissary of the Warmaster of Mankind.' Volk bowed his head, just enough to show respect, but not enough to imply deference.

'The honour is ours, and we give you thanks for the efforts you have made to aid our mission.' Argonis bowed his helmeted head, careful to make sure the gesture was not as deep as Volk's. The relative depth of his bow told everyone present where the higher authority lay. Most importantly it told Volk. Behind him he heard a rustle as Sota-Nul bowed in turn. 'It is pleasing to see that you have come in person to ensure that our latest request is met.'

Volk's expression flickered, his scarred features rippling.

'We deny you nothing, emissary, but I do not understand how this request is relevant?'

'He is not unintelligent, this one,' said Sota-Nul, her voice a private whisper from his helm's vox. 'That could be problematic.'

He ignored it.

'Relevant?' he let the word hang in the air. 'Everything is relevant.' He watched a muscle twitch under Volk's metal eye.

'If he will not comply there are other ways-methods that can be used,' Sota-Nul said in his ear.

'The primary armouries are yours to see. All seventy-two of them.'

Argonis nodded, still not breaking eye contact.

'The Lord of Iron has laid his preparations for war well.'

'As always.'

'A long war...'

'For whatever might be needed.'

'Need is decided by who is judging that need.'

Volk laughed, the deep sound growling through the bare chamber. His armoured frame shook with the sound. Argonis saw broken stubs of teeth flash in the crooked line of Volk's mouth.

'Do you ever let an opportunity to sound like an arrogant cur pass?'

'Sometimes,' Argonis reached up and unfastened his helm. He smiled himself then, stepped forward and clasped Volk's extended fist in his own. 'But you provide so many opportunities it would seem impolite.'

'Does Cthonia only breed weaklings with sharp tongues, or is it just you?'

'Does Olympia still just breed halfwits and siege dross?'

'Only the best of both.' Volk's scars twisted into a smile again. 'It is good to see you. Even in all of this, brother, it is good to see you.'

'All this?'

'This war. It is a long way from Carmeline, and the Reddus Cluster.' Volk let a breath hiss from his nose, and shook his head. 'A long way along a strange path.'

'It is,' said Argonis, holding his expression and head still. 'And things change.'

'Yes. They do.' Volk said the words carefully, frowning. 'You come from the Warmaster. In person. As the bearer of his presence. Somehow I never thought that kind of honour would be yours.'

'Neither did I.'

Volk raised an eyebrow, but did not press the point.

'And as you can see I have had my wings clipped. A hawk on an iron perch.' He grinned, and tapped the metal sphere of his left eye, and then pointed at Argonis. 'But even with just one eye I could still tear you out of the sky.'

'I doubt it. Unless half blindness has somehow improved your skill as a pilot.'

'Oh-ho. So the high orbits of command have not taken your claws. Good. Do they still call you – what was that ridiculous title? The Unscarred – that was it wasn't it?'

Argonis smiled briefly, and then allowed his face to harden into seriousness

'What happened?' he asked. 'Since Isstvan, what happened to the Fourth?'

'I went to the Cathian Gulf after the Massacre.' Volk closed the fingers of his hand with a clack of ceramite on ceramite. 'Broke the holdings around Selgar. But the primarch summoned us here, and so here I am. I am sure that all of our activities are fully known by the Warmaster.' He shrugged, and did not look back at Argonis.

'Things have changed, old friend,' said Argonis.

'Civil war will do that.' Volk nodded, his mouth a hard line. Argonis thought of the squadron master he had known and fought with for almost a decade. The warrior in front of him was the same, still the combination of wit and brutality that seemed at odds with his Olympian birth. But there was a weight there now, as though thoughts he could not speak were churning within.

'Why are you here? Why is your Legion fighting this battle?'

'You have asked the primarch that?'

Argonis nodded. 'Then you have your answer.' The Iron Warrior turned and made for the door. From far off a distant rumble shook the still air. A thin thread of dust fell from the ceiling. Everyone in the room looked upwards.

'Surface bombardment,' said Sota-Nul. 'They are attacking again, as predicted.'

Volk's eyes flicked to her then back to Argonis.

'You have unusually poor timing on this occasion, brother. My attention will be needed soon, but the armouries are open to your inspection... Emissary.' A hard note of formality had returned to his voice, and he gave an abrupt gesture to one of his two guards. 'Taldak will be your guide.'

'My thanks,' said Argonis. Volk bowed in reply, and then he turned and was gone out of the door.

Argonis looked at Taldak's blank, masked face, and clamped his own helm over his head. Sota-Nul's transmitted voice spoke to him as soon as the helmet's connections closed.

'That one is dangerous and clever.'

'He always was,' he replied, making for the door. Taldak fell in before him, his bolter held low in his hands.

'His presence and the presence of this guide may cause us complications.'

'I am not sure I will tolerate what you are implying.'

They crossed the door out of the chamber and began to walk down the curving passage beyond. An alert alarm began to sound. Yellow lights began to strobe in the ceiling. Another tremor ran through the floor. Despite himself he felt adrenaline spiking his blood.

'You should overcome your reluctance,' purred Sota-Nul. 'We might need to kill more than him.'

'There will be no need.'

'There may be every need,' she said.

IAEO FELT ELATION as she watched the emissary and heard the tech-witch's words. The emotion washed through her, raw and burning. She had to slice it out of her awareness before it corrupted the calculations.

Her primary phase manipulation had worked. It had worked. Even if she denied her emotions she could not deny that truth.

*True danger lives in the moment when you feel invulnerable.* The aphorism floated through her thoughts even as she refocused her mind. There were many, many reasons why she should not feel victorious.

Her own security was tenuous at best. The Iron Warriors controlled the tunnels of the Sightless Warren with ruthless precision. While the loyalists were scattered and broken into different commands, the Iron Warriors infused every aspect of their operations with control. Security was not simply tight; it was a coordinated pattern of overlapping countermeasures and contingencies. Guard patterns changed. Movements of personnel and material were continually catalogued and crosschecked. Sweep and search patrols probed deserted areas at random. She had only seen comparable compliancy once before, and that had been during a short-lived incursion onto the Phalanx several decades before. She could not help but admire the craft in the IV Legion's paranoia.

Despite how aesthetically pleasing the Sightless Warren's countermeasures were, they had slowed her progress. She had overcome the problem in the end by making a series of boltholes in places where safety only came from the ludicrousness of trying to use them as hideouts. The skull-space of a Reaver Titan of Legio Fureans undergoing repair was her bolthole for the first two cycles. A set of faulty decontamination airlocks proved most useful, as did the piles of damaged and blood-marked hulls awaiting repair. She moved between these locations according to purely random patterns. It was not ideal, but it was the best solution she could achieve.

She had needed to establish a workable pattern of evasion before she had been able to turn her energies to the emissary. At first she had thought that she would need to find a way to reach one of the Iron Warriors ships, but that had proved unnecessary. The emissary was there in the Sightless Warren. The tech-witch had been a problem at first; her presence had killed a dozen net-flies before Iaeo had compensated. Once she had done that she had been able to throw her awareness over the trio and begin to squeeze for data. Every movement they made she saw, every word they said, every signal they thought private, all of it went to Iaeo.

She began to build prediction profiles and individual data-models of Argonis and his entourage. They lived in her skull, shadows projected by the living creatures she watched.

The model of the astropath called Prophesius was a sketch of ephemeral possibilities. She was almost certain that the creature was not fully human, or that its nature had altered substantially, probably by psychic means. In its actions she had seen total obedience. There were also signs that it had almost no self-determination, beyond the ability to obey commands. The mask locked to its skull was clearly not a simple device. She had also decided not to remember the shape details of the runes cut into the mask's metal. Looking at them had distorted her thoughts. But even though the data-model was thin it gave her enough to deduce Prophesius's role and importance; the astropath was a link between the emissary and Horus himself, but a link that had yet to be used.

Sota-Nul was another matter. She was like no other tech-priest Iaeo had encountered. Her physiology was at variance to her kind. There was as much of the biological about Sota-Nul as there was mechanical. The line between the flesh and metal was also narrow. That was also unusual, almost unprecedented. Almost. Then there were her speech patterns. She had a human voice, produced not by machine, or vox, but by air, throat and mouth. Iaeo was certain of this; she could hear it in the texture of Sota-Nul's words. But she had never heard her breathe. Worst of all were Sota-Nul's decision/reaction patterns. Where the rest of her kind often eschewed emotion in favour of logic, the tech-witch seemed to follow both instinct and logic in ways that Iaeo found hard to predict. She did things because of calculation, and because of emotions such as anger, hunger and spite. That was not good. It was not good at all. All the little factors meant that Sota-Nul could only be one thing; she was one of the reborn of Mars, one of the so-called new priesthood, the Dark Mechanicum.

Then there was Argonis, beautiful Argonis, so filled with the echoing martial pride of a lost age. He was a warrior, noble, loyal, focused, ruthless, but he was also a betrayer, with blood on his hands. He was so loyal yet so bound to his own principles, a person cut in two and then bound back together. She was not certain, but there were indicators that he had not been sent to Tallarn as an honour, but as a penance, or as a form of exile. She wanted to know why, she wanted to know why very badly indeed. There was possibility in that silent space, the possibility of death and mayhem. Sometimes, when she played recordings of his voice over and over, she thought she could almost see the truth, a hidden shape betrayed by its shadow.

Between these three she could feel her projections spiral and whirl. She knew almost all that they knew. She knew they had contact with the Alpha Legion Operative Jalen, and that they did not trust him, that they almost believed that everything they saw on Tallarn was a lie.

And of course it was.

*Ships upon ships had come to Tallarn since the battle had begun. Many had died, some had fled back to the warp, but most came in small groups, ragged clusters and lone battlegroups. Not since the Iron Warriors main force arrived had a substantial fleet arrived together. The fleets which vied with Perturabo's forces were an amalgam of all the disparate forces drawn to make Tallarn their battleground.*

*The coming of the Golden Fleet broke that pattern.*

*It came from the warp without warning. Clusters of war barques, bombardment barges and battle cruisers, spread into a wide sphere from the wounds of their re-entry. The* Eagle Claw *drifted at their centre, its ancient hull glimmering in the thin light of the stars.*

*In the time of the Great Crusade the* Eagle Claw *had changed from a lone ship reeving far ahead of the Emperor's crusade forces to the flagship of a fleet. Each ship of that fleet had been a prize of conquest, as had the wealth which filled their holds with mercenary companies from across the galaxy. The fees paid to the Sacristan Geneo-het warriors alone were said to have been enough that they would have beggared kings. Yet* the mistress of the Golden Fleet had paid them for a hundred years of service in advance, and they were not alone.

Beside the forces bought by coin there were those bought by oaths and loyalty. The orphaned Knights of House Klaze walked at the Fleet Mistress's command beside automata painted in auric and ebony to show their perpetual service. Three hundred warriors of the XIII Legion rode in the *Eagle Claw,* and the bodyguard who stood at the ship mistress's shoulder had stood in the battle lines of the first battles of unity. During the Great Crusade, some had objected to the half-mocking title given to the Emperor's privateer pathfinders, but it fitted the Golden Fleet and its mistress to perfection. Rogue Trader, they had called her, and now she had brought her war fleet back from beyond the edge of conquest, and found a war.

From her throne Rogue Trader Sangrea, Mistress of the Golden Fleet, looked on the light of Tallarn, and listened. She had left the Imperium from Tallarn a decade before and struck out into the dust cloud reaches of the Morai Veil. She had served and built the Imperium since a time when its name and nature were still fresh with newborn strength. Yet for all her power, she knew that she would never be a part of the Imperium she was building. People of her kind had faced a choice with the coming of the Emperor: serve out in the dark, or be destroyed. She had chosen to serve, but a part of her had always hoped that she could return and die in the lands she had helped create. The truth that formed piece by piece as she listened and read the data from her auspexes said that the Imperium she had left had died, that everything she had helped to build was burning from within.

When she spoke her words were quiet.

'Take us in,' she said.

# SEVEN

**Machines
Will of the father
The trust of allies**

THE WORLD OUTSIDE was spiralling smoke and blood-red sheets of flame. Kord could not look through his sight for more than a few seconds. When he did, he saw death rising from the ground and walking to claim him.

The spindly black silhouettes of Thallaxi advanced beside the hunched shapes of battle automata. They began to fire. Spirals of lightning flicked out, struck a scout machine, and crawled through its armour. The scout detonated in a spray of igniting fuel and tearing metal. Kord's sight danced with nausea-bright pixels. The auspex was sparking, its screen a swirl of spiralling images. The external vox was screeching like a chorus of dying crows.

Kord sucked in a breath; it tasted of electricity and metal.

'Fire!' he shouted. Sacha was still shaking her head, eyes blinking widely behind the lenses of her suit mask.

'I can't see,' she said.

'Fire! Now!' She reached for the gun's control and pulled the trigger. The battle cannon slammed back. Kord felt *War Anvil*'s demolisher fire a second later. The shell landed blind, burrowed into the ground and exploded. Dirt fountained up into the smoke. He saw walking machines.

Zade was already feeding shells into the cannon's smoking breech.

'Forward, full speed,' he roared. He was not looking at the auspex. There was no point. This was a disaster, a complete wild disaster. He had lost. That was certain. He could not see where or what of his units remained. The enemy had complete surprise, and there was no way out. No way at all.

He looked through the sight again in time to see an automaton turning ponderously, towards him, guns tracking for a target.

No way out.

The automaton had them. Sensor blisters on its torso scattered laser targeting lines towards *War Anvil*, like reaching hands.

No way at all.

'Forward! Full speed!'

Kord saw the laser lines converge on him and *War Anvil* as the tank hit the automaton with full force. The impact shook the hull. The automaton was scrabbling at the front of the tank, its legs dragging beneath as it rammed onwards. Kord could see the cog marks and glyphs scored into its armour. *War Anvil* lurched forward, tracks turning faster and faster. The automaton vanished. A sound of breaking and tearing metal reverberated from beneath the tank as it lurched on.

Kord was breathing hard, eyes flicking between any battle information he could see, vision blocks, gunsight, the memory of where all his machines had been before. They must be on the bottom of the ridge, the enemy spread in front and to either side of them. Skins of smoke and flame sliced the view in all directions in narrow corridors. He just hoped that somehow, someone was covering *War Anvil*'s rear arc. Lascannon light was whipping through the air, and he could feel the skin-itch of exotic weapon discharge. The main gun fired again. He had no idea what they were shooting at. High notes of shrapnel and the thump of explosive rounds overlaid the engine roar. Something hit one of his sight blocks and crazed the armourglass as he looked through it. He snapped his head back. His head spun for an instant.

Behind them a disc of rust-red metal and chrome rose from the loose earth like the back of a turtle breaking the surface of the sea. The figure standing on the disc might have started as human, but that was long ago. Its body was a frame of brass and blackened plasteel. The poison winds blew through the latticework of its ribs. Cables snaked from its back. Sparks flashed in the air around it as disc and rider rose. The fog-heavy air shimmered around it as it slid forward. Red beams ringed with concentric circles flicked from the disc. A teeth-aching screech followed each beam, audible even over the roar of explosions and churning metal.

'What is that?' screeched Zade. Kord was staring, he knew what it was, what it must be: a war magos, a master of machines and death, and it was there for them.

'Got you!' shouted Sacha. The main gun fired. The shell struck the disc and its rider true, and shattered into fire. Sacha punched the air, her growl of victory lost in the ringing echo of the explosion.

Kord had half turned away from the sight when the disc broke from the fire cloud. The robes of the rider fell from it in charred scraps. The body beneath was like a model of a human made by a watchmaker. A bubble of actinic energy flickered as it grated against the fire and smoke. The disc tilted. The air beneath it shimmered. A black sphere sat at the centre of the disc's belly, like the pupil of a great machine eye. Kord felt a void open within him. In front of him Zade was still sliding a fresh shell into the breech, Sacha was screaming at him. Tendrils of sickly light were pouring across the disc as though draining into a hole. The black sphere ached in Kord's sight. He felt something tug at his sweat-sheathed skin. He could taste electricity on his teeth.

A beam of purple-wreathed blackness shot from the black sphere beneath the disc. For a second the world seemed to freeze, colours to flip to white, light to dark, shadow to bright brilliance. And then there was a sound like a thunderclap in reverse. Kord felt warm liquid running from his nose. He felt like he was spinning through the air, waiting to hit the ground.

'*Noon Star*'s gone!' Sacha's voice was a shriek of hysteria. 'Gone, just–'

'Fire,' he croaked.

But all he could see was the disc rotating towards him, and the power begining to build around the black sphere

'Fire... Someone, fire.'

A flash of las-light cut across his vision, shattering the disc's shield into a cloud of oily sparks. *War Anvil*'s demolisher cannon fired an instant later.

The shell hit the disc's centre and broke the black sphere. Darkness rushed out from the broken disc, as though trying to swallow the light of the explosion. Kord felt tears gush from his eyes. The pain of a thousand needle punctures stabbed his face.

'Finish it,' he managed to call. The main cannon fired. The blackness shattered, then sucked into a pinprick of night before vanishing. Kord felt himself swaying in his seat. Through watering eyes he saw battle automata stutter to a halt, then stagger and begin to slump to the ground. Everything was very far away though, and swirling, swirling like water. He was... the last thought that interrupted his fall into oblivion was to wonder who had fired the lascannon bolt that had broken the disc's shield.

*'Where do we begin?' he had asked. His father and master had lowered his head, the black gloss of his eyes spreading to pool in the sockets of his eyes.*

*'Within,' Perturabo had said.*

*'The powers that exist beyond the walls of reality mock our strength, and try to turn this war to their own. There is no one left to trust besides the Warmaster, and serpents coil around him. There are two wars now, the war to topple the Emperor and the war against those who would betray us in turn. And in that war we need to be sharpness and obliteration, we need weapons, we need to be iron once more.'*

*'Your will is mine.'*

*'You do not know what I ask yet.'*

The memory, which was half a dream, fell away from Hrend's sight. He was standing on the side of a valley, the machines of his assault group spread out beside and behind him. Before him the valley side fell away in spills of grey schist. Above him the fog held to the hidden mountain caps as a rippled yellow ceiling. The air in the valley was clear, but the jagged shapes of the rocks made the returns from the sensors dance with ghost shapes. To his left the mountain pass itself opened beyond a wide canyon mouth which split the bare rock of the valley's end like an axe wound. The canyon beyond formed a pass between two mountain peaks, and must have borne a road in Tallarn's past. Cracked slabs of stone formed the remains of a crude road surface within the canyon's walls, and signs of its course could be seen tracing a line across the valley floor. It had begun to snow while they waited, the wind spreading black and yellow flakes across the grey ground.

Above him, further up the slope, Spartan 4171 waited, hull-down behind a ridge. Even at this distance he thought he could feel Hes-Thal looking out at the world, and seeing... He had no idea what the Navigator saw, only that it had led them to have to cross the mountains.

'Target is two kilometres distant,' said Jarvak, his voice juddering as the signal was shredded by the walls of the pass. 'Speed and signatures consistent. Unit count is sixteen. Force strength is heavy. I count two heavy-grade signatures, Baneblade or equivalent yield. Twelve battle tank hulls. Two smaller units, scouts or armoured cars.'

Hrend listened to the words as he cycled through the raw sensor data. It was not clean, but he had told Jarvak to make sure that he was not seen or detected. That put limitations on reconnaissance information. They had picked up the enemy force moving into the canyon as they were moving into it themselves. Hrend had considered simply meeting the enemy force head on and battering their way through, but had decided to withdraw to the valley and wait. Jarvak's machine had carried on alone, its systems flooding the space before it with distorting sensor ghosts. Now he had seen the strength of the enemy force, Hrend judged his decision to withdraw correct.

'We hit them as they exit the pass,' he said.

'They are wary,' said Jarvak. 'There is wreckage in the valley floor beneath the pass. This is not the first time this place has been a battleground.'

Hrend made to reply, but suddenly the world was gone.

*The sound of breaking steel rolled over him. There was fire, the strobing blink of white starburst, and he was burning, his skin melting into his armour...*

His sensor sight jumped back into cold awareness.

'*Master, what is your will?*' asked Jarvak. Hrend looked at the time count at the corner of his sight. He had been silent for almost two full minutes.

'Estimate time until they exit,' he demanded.

'*Thirty minutes,*' said Jarvak. Hrend added the timing to his battle plan. Nothing needed to change, he had crafted every point correctly. Every unit in the Cyllaros had absorbed the plan and was placed to execute it. It was a future moment of destruction ordained in every detail. Now it simply needed to become.

'Withdraw to the designated position,' he said. 'Wait.'

He engaged the fingers of his fists. They moved. He did not feel it. He would...

*...the fire was his skin, and his screaming was the roar of muzzle flare, and the hungering crash of rending metal. He was breathing ash, and every breath was a blaze of white fire...*

'*Enemy will exit canyon in ten minutes,*' called Jarvak. Hrend tried to blink as sensor data spilled into his vision. His Dreadnought frame clanked as servos tried to answer the dead nerve signal. He saw Jarvak's Sicaran emerge from the canyon mouth, its position painted by cold blue markers. It settled into place behind a low rise on the opposite slope of the valley.

'Waken weapons,' he said. The Cyllaros obeyed. He tried to blink again, and again his body twitched in confusion. His hands were burning. The fire held in their palms were blisters of bright pain in the cold dark. He had to let go, had to allow the fire free. He had to...

Coldness, and the dead silence of a lightless amniotic tank.

'Two minutes.'

The first tanks emerged from the pass, two smaller machines, running fast on narrow tracks. They split and moved to either side of the valley. Hrend could hear their auspexes as faint, metallic whispers. Two blocks of battle tanks came next, spreading into two lines behind the scouts, bracketing the valley floor as they came forward. The air was thick with sensor waves now. They were not as powerful, nor could they see as far as the sensor eyes of Legion machines. That limitation and the Cyllaros's cloud of countermeasures would hold for a little longer.

The first of the true giants rolled onto the valley floor. It was a Baneblade, the father of a dynasty of destructive children. Its hull was twice the size of the three battle tanks which rolled in front of it. The turret atop its gun-studded hull turned with slow purpose, the gaze of its vast gun tracking across the snow-shrouded land. Behind it came its cousin. Twin clusters of multi-barrelled mega-bolters jutted from the block of armour atop the second super-heavy tank. It was a Stormlord, and the sight of it made Hrend pause as fresh combat estimations scrolled across his sight.

There was no choice, though; they had to act now. He waited as the twin super-heavy machines broke into a staggered pattern, and the last squadron of battle tanks took up line formation behind them. It was a significant force, and well arrayed. He could read experience, discipline and training in the way that the machines moved. The Cyllaros were outmatched in numbers and fire power. Normally the most direct method of addressing that disparity would have been to trap the enemy in the pass between the canyon walls. That was not an option here. Hrend and his machines had to pass through the valley and through the mountains. The pass needed to remain unblocked.

The enemy cleared the gates to the pass, moving forward at the lumbering speed of the two behemoths at their heart. Their overlapping auspex signals were clawing at the Cyllaros's sensor baffles. That concealment would not last much longer. Snow swirled down from the clouds above. The dirty flakes settled and began to melt on the metal skin of the war machines.

'Now,' he said.

The Cyllaros fired as one. Streams of energy converged on the valley floor. The Baneblade's turret blew into the air. An instant later the conversion beamers turned its flank plating into a molten cloud. Fire rolled out in every direction. Snowflakes became steam. Two of the three battle tanks riding in front of the Baneblade skidded and tumbled over. Lines of accelerator shells hit their belly armour, punched inside, and their death flames screamed to the already burning air. A third tank jumped across the ground like a kicked stone. Above the valley a glowing pillar of smoke spread into a thunderhead. The rest of the tanks were still moving forward, carried by shock and momentum.

Hrend watch three target runes blink out.

'Go,' he said.

THE TUNNEL SHOOK as they walked through the strobing alarm light. Spills of dust shook from the ceiling and dusted Argonis's armour. Sota-Nul was a too-close presence at his shoulder. Prophesius was a little further back, matching speed with him as though tugged by an invisible chain. Figures moved around them, hurrying, running, never coming too close, never looking at the trio directly. The tunnel shook again, then twice more in quick succession. None of them looked up at the quartet of strangers passing in the opposite direction.

Taldak walked ahead of them. Argonis had been watching the warrior since they had left their chambers. There was a stiff set to Taldak's shoulders, his movements powerful but rigid. He reminded Argonis of a bull grox he had once seen forcing its way against the current of a river, blunt head low, strength battering each step forward as though to do anything else was to admit defeat. It was a quality he both admired and found stifling. It also made the prospect of what they would need to do much more dangerous.

A series of deep tremors ran through the walls. The lighting flickered. Argonis looked up at the dust spilling past the strobing gloom.

*Orbital bombardment,* thought Argonis, as the bare slabs of rockcrete quivered. *Concentrated fire, at least two ships in firing pattern, possibly more.* They were hitting the area directly above the complex core. Seismic charges most likely. That and enough plasma fire to melt half the surface rubble to glass. He could not fault the usefulness of the timing.

'You are certain that what we seek will be there?' he said into his helm vox without looking around. To anyone observing them he would appear to be walking in silence, the short-range vox signal passing between them alone.

'No,' replied Sota-Nul. 'Nothing is certain, but it is likely that we will be able to gain access from the location we are bound for.'

'No killing,' he repeated, after a long pause of silence.

'It is not in the necessary parameters of our plan,' she said. 'As you know.'

'No matter what, if one of the Iron Warriors dies here we lose everything and gain nothing.'

'Not necessarily.'

Argonis's jaw tensed. Inside his helm his lips had peeled back from his teeth. Sota-Nul's voice scratched through his nerves even over the vox. Especially over the vox.

'I am surprised that such a prospect causes you concern,' she continued. 'You were present at the kill-cleanse of Isstvan, were you not?'

'They are our allies?'

Sota-Nul began to speak again. He was unpleasantly aware that her voice had added a mocking edge to its monotone.

'There are recordings I have heard-reviewed, the last transmissions between different Legions on Isstvan Five. They believed the same falsity-fact until we began to kill them. Perhaps some of them died still believing it.'

Argonis felt his hand twitch towards his weapons, then restrained the instinct. The tech-witch would have registered the gesture, he was sure. He would have felt satisfaction if he had thought she cared. He was certain that she did not. Nothing seemed to intimidate Sota-Nul. She was not without fear, but was as though she found the concept amusingly redundant.

'The Iron Warriors have denied us nothing,' he said carefully.

'Except the truth,' she said. 'That is why we are here.'

A unit of human troopers in heavy enviro-suits ran by, pausing to give a stylised salute that Argonis did not recognise. Taldak made no gesture of acknowledgement. They had not seen another warrior of the IV for some time. Even here at the heart of their fortress the Iron Warriors were spread thinly, tens of thousands dissolved into millions of human soldiers.

They walked on without speaking, the blare of alert alarms and the beat of the bombardment shaking the ground filling the pause. He glanced at Sota-Nul as she glided on, her robe rustling as it dragged along the floor. Her shoulders were moving, flexing as though she were breathing hard. But she was not breathing. In the time he had spent in her proximity he had never heard her breathe once.

'What is your concern in this?'

'One of my kind was requested by the Maloghurst, and sent by the most knowing and high Kelbor-Hal. I am an emissary to an emissary. I am here to lend aid. You know this. You are simply struggling with emotions.'

'Emotions?' he said.

'Yes,' her voice now the dead-toned texture of a static. 'Revulsion, possibly disgust, probably loathing. The current actions we are engaged on have elicited a heightened response that your mental conditioning is displacing into other existing areas of emotion that you can understand.' She paused and her voice slid into a tone which sounded all too human. 'You cannot feel fear so you are feeling hate.'

He did not reply. He was not sure which was worse: the accuracy of what she said, or that he could hear the relish in her voice.

They turned a corner, and a set of blast doors closed the tunnel before them. Gun servitors flanked the oiled steel. Targeting lasers flickered over Argonis and his entourage, found the authorisation they needed and dropped the aim of their weapons. Taldak took a step closer, and pressed an armoured hand against the doors. A clang rolled through the air, louder even than the alert sirens. The doors ground open. A bare platform waited beyond. Taldak turned his helm to face Argonis.

'Emissary,' he said. Argonis stepped onto the platform. The rest followed, and the doors closed on them. A heartbeat later the platform jerked and then began to descend. Argonis looked up. The shaft above them was a black hole boring into the lost dark.

'We are approaching the correct level,' said Sota-Nul.

'Yes,' said Argonis turning his face back to Taldak. Prophesius took a single, silent step forward.

'I am truly sorry,' he said. Prophesius reached out and up, his hand like a pale spider descending on a thread as it touched Taldak's head.

THE IMAGES FROM the net-flies watching the lift platform fuzzed with static. Iaeo switched view as black blobs formed and flowed over the image. Prophesius's hand closed on the Space Marine's head.

*Active psychic capability*, she added the datum to the cloud of observed facts on Prophesius, and switched her awareness to another portion of the net-fly swarm. She blinked as a different set of perceptions washed over her. She had only dared deploy the swarm into the datastacks in the hour before Argonis had begun his own mission to reach them. Part of her hungered to tap into the information held in the vast cogitator and data looms. There was so much there, so much possibility, so many additional factors which could...

No, she had her focus now.

She let out a breath and, as though answering a tremor, ran through the ground. A grumble of distant explosions rumbled in her ears. This time it was strong enough to make her senses flick back to the reality of her physical location. She was briefly aware of the confines of the Mars-pattern tank hull enclosing her. It was one of 156 burned or damaged hulls stacked in a row in armoury cavern 102-B. It had no turret, or sponsons, and most of its insides were gone. The through-and-through shot that had killed it let the light of distant welding torches flicker across her face. She had sat cross-legged on the floor of the machine for two hours. She had 7506 seconds before the probability of detection became unacceptable.

She flicked back to the feeds of data and watched Argonis. Part of her – a very, very small remnant of empathy – hoped that he would not get himself killed. If he did, that would be exceptionally awkward.

*There was always a ship burning in the orbit of Tallarn's star. Above the war world battles never ceased, as both sides fought to control the key approaches. Battlegroups came together in spirals of silent light, and broke apart again, leaving the cooling debris of their meeting. Even in the orbits close to the system's star ships clashed, as they tried to skim the gravity and radiation-thick zones to reach Tallarn itself. Further out on the system edge, battlegroups ran the outer reaches of the Oort cloud, hunting for ships fresh from the warp. Battle light never left the skies above Tallarn. But the coming of the Golden Fleet brought a fire to the void like no other.*

*The first ships to meet the Golden Fleet were a battlegroup bound to Perturabo's command. Their challenges were answered with reassurances, and respect.*

*They were on the same side, said the ships of the Golden Fleet. They had come to answer the Lord of Iron's call. Of course they would accept forces onto their bridges and move in system under escort. Of course…*

*The mistress of the Golden Fleet waited until they crossed the distance from black system edge to dead world. Then every ship in the Golden*

Fleet ran its guns out and turned the ships escorting them into wreckage and burning dust. The forces sent onto her ships were contained, ambushed, and slaughtered. The rest of Perturabo's forces scrambled to intercept the Golden Fleet, but it was already accelerating, bearing down on the dead planet like a sheath of fire arrows falling from a night sky. It fired at every ship that came against them, killing many, and leaving others as bleeding wrecks to tumble in their wake.

From her throne the fleet's mistress watched as the planet grew fat in the bridge's viewport. Signals from the forces opposing Perturabo called out from ships and from Tallarn itself. They went unanswered. She had made her judgement.

Ships from both sides filled the close orbits of Tallarn. Support fleets held station at different hemispheres, trading turbolaser fire at landers. Both sides had sensed a lull and rushed to drop supplies and troops on to the surface. Bulk promethium carriers, munitions barges and macro landers moved beneath shells of escorts. They were vulnerable, but both sides had deployed so that they were screened from enemy fire. They had not prepared for a battlefleet striking them from another quarter.

The Golden Fleet hit a school of bulk carriers which had just begun to sink into the planet's atmosphere. Above them ten battle cruisers held station to protect them. They fired at the Golden Fleet.

Flame swallowed shields and gouged the gilded ships' hulls, but they kept coming. They had selected their targets hours before, while Tallarn was still just a bright dot to the naked eye. They did not know, or care, what allegiance their targets were.

The lead ships of the Golden Fleet peeled back, scraps of shredded shields trailing them. The ships behind them were true battle cruisers, their hulls studded with weaponry, their armour thick under skins of gold. The nova cannons in their prows had been loaded, and the time triggers in each warhead were already running. If they did not fire they would die, but their command crews had come from the nightless moons of Creda and they had fought this way for their mistress many times before. They began to burn, their hulls shedding stone and molten metal as they rode down into the teeth of their enemy's guns. Ripples of shells and beams of energy struck their shields, and slammed into their prows.

The sphere of Tallarn filled the views of their bridges, its gravity tugging them down. The fuel transports and their escorts realised the attacker's intent and began to scatter. Heavy with fuel they began to break formation, but by then it was too late.

The Golden Fleet fired. A deluge of nova shells hit the fuel transports.

A flattened sun spread above Tallarn. The energy wave skimmed outwards, catching ships and orbital platforms in a freeze-frame instant. Hulls the size of great cities split, and spilled the blood of their reactors into the burning storm. And the tide surged on, growing in seconds and feeding off ships too slow to slip its embrace. The Golden Fleet fired their engines and flipped over. Kilometres of metal and stone screamed under the forces twisting through their hulls. They rose into the empty void as behind them a skin of fire spilled across Tallarn's skies, fizzing with the death of ships.

Down on the surface, a false dawn ran across the night side of the planet. Showers of burning debris fell like golden coins scattered from a hand. At the poles, auroras of fire and starlight hung in curtains against the sky.

The Golden Fleet left, running for the system edge and the cold black beyond, the light of its inexplicable act of judgement chasing the ships until they dived back into the warp.

Shock rippled through all the remaining forces in the system. Tallarn's disputed orbits had been stripped, the ever-shifting battle for their control reset to neutral. It took even the Iron Warriors a long moment to realise they were facing both the greatest opportunity and most dire threat since the Battle of Tallarn had begun.

In a time that would come later, scholars and poets would give that night a name to mark its place in time: they named it 'The Inferno Tide'.

# EIGHT

**Breath**
**Stormlord**
**Warning**

KORD WOKE TO the feeling of heat washing over his skin. He sat up slowly. Red and orange light flickered in from the view slits. He looked out. Fire washed over *War Anvil*. The burning wrecks outside nested close, the flames sheeting from their bones lapping against *War Anvil*'s hull.

Kord felt as though his body had been worked over with an iron bar. The roar of the guns still rang in his ears. He could not hear anything on the vox. He wanted to sleep. The urge was so deep and overwhelming that he felt his eyes begin to close. Sacha was slumped sideways next to him. He could see the crumpled form of Zade down in the space beneath the turret. It was all very quiet, the flickering wash of flames like the water of a molten sea pressing silently against a sinking ship's porthole. He shook his head to clear it, but that just sent grey blotches dancing on his eyeballs. What had happened? He could remember the disc and the explosion as it had detonated. After that…

How long had he been unconscious?

He looked at the auspex screen. It was a blank black, filled with swirling coloured blocks as he woke it. He muttered to the machine, pleading with it to work. It did. Slowly at first, then, with a blink, it showed him the world beyond the hull. Heat blooms swelled and pulsed across it. He could see the shapes of wreckage, lots of wreckage, each chunk outlined in heat. There was nothing else. He shifted the view wider, but the heat-drowned desolation just grew.

He keyed the vox. Static first, then a silence which seemed to wait for him to speak. He licked his lips, suddenly aware that his mouth was dry.

'All units...' he began. 'This is *War Anvil*...' he trailed away. Was the rest of his crew even alive? He looked at the air supply levels.

Throne, they were low. He switched to a total band broadcast.

'This is *War Anvil*, if you can hear, respond.'

From somewhere deeper in *War Anvil*'s hull he heard a clank as something metal unlocked. A second later a masked face look up at him.

'Sir,' said a female voice over the vox. It was barely a croak.

'Shornal?' he asked, and the sponson gunner nodded. 'Is no one else...?' he began.

She gave the sketch of a shrug.

'I don't know, sir. It's been quiet for a while. Since the shooting stopped.'

'Did we take any damage?'

'No. I don't...' She just sat down then, slumping to the floor.

'Shornal,' he said, putting every scrap of strength and calm into her name. Her head jerked up towards him. Her eyes were veined blotches behind the suit lenses. 'Damage?' he asked speaking the word clearly.

'I don't think so.' She swayed where she sat. 'But... but the engine went quite a while ago. Don't know why.' Her head nodded then came up sharply as though jerked by a string. 'Sir,' she added in a smudged voice.

Kord blinked as what she had said soaked into him. If the engines were down then... then... the air supply was running on reserve power. His thoughts were running like thick oil. He blinked, and brought his hand up to his face. The gloved fingers filled his eyes. He tapped the front of his mask, breathed in, felt the smallest trickle of cool air on his face, and realised that they were all very close to dying.

He reached over, trying not to move too quickly, trying to keep the grey fog to the edge of his sight. He pushed Sacha. Her slumped form shifted, but did not stir. He tried to move his legs, to slide down into the space beneath the turret. They would not move. They simply would not move. He looked at his hand, wondering for a dreamlike second if it too would refuse to move.

'Shornal,' he said carefully. 'Can you reach Mori in the drive cradle?'

'I... think so.' She began to crawl across the floor. Empty shell casings rolled under her. Inch by inch, she moved out of sight. Kord kept the vox open all the while, trying to take, very, very shallow breaths. The minutes bled slowly past.

'I'm here.' Shornal was breathing hard.

'Mori?' he asked.

'Not moving, sir.'

'Try and wake him.'

'He's... he is gone, sir.'

'Gone?'

'There is blood all over his eyepieces. Throne!' she swore, and Kord tensed. The grey clouds grew. He fought his heartbeat down. 'There's blood on the controls, sir. His face... he must have slammed into the rig when we took a hit.'

'Can you see the controls?' asked Kord measuring out the words.

'Yes.'

'There is a lever, a red lever just beside the controls. You see it?'

'Yes.'

'Pull it.'

The noise of a faint clank reached him. Then another. Then nothing.

'Sir–'

'Try it again,' he said. A pause, another clank, another silence. He heard her try and take a breath. How many more times can she try before she passes out, he wondered? Grey drifted across his narrowing world.

*These machines are supposed to have hearts that beat forever*, he thought.

Clank.

But all hearts could fail.

Clank.

He closed his eyes.

Clank.

*War Anvil* woke with a shudder of power. Air spluttered across his face and he gasped.

He coughed. The fresh air burned as it filled his lungs. He breathed, and breathed, and breathed as *War Anvil*'s engine plant shook its hull. Relief flooded through him. He looked at his hands, flexed the fingers, and found that he could move his legs. He glanced at the fire light still spilling through the armourglass vision slits. They had to get moving.

He slid out of his seat. He would have to unplug his air until he was in the drive cradle. He took a deep breath and snapped the hose free. A stab of panic gripped him as the air cut out. He dropped into the crawl space under the turret, his feet sliding briefly on the brass cases of shells. Shornal sat next to the driver position, her chest heaving as she swallowed down air. Mori's corpse hung half in and half out of the drive cradle. Blood had dribbled from his suit's broken eyepieces and dried in sticky brown runnels on his suit.

The breath he was holding in his chest had started to ache, and he could feel the grey fog pushing at the edge of his sight again. He slotted his air hose into place, heard the valve clink open, and breathed again. He looked around. He could see the unmoving shape of Saul, the forward gunner, hanging from the demolisher niche. He looked down to Shornal. She was breathing more steadily now.

'You ever driven a machine?' he asked.

'No.' She shook her head. He nodded, and pulled Mori's corpse out of the drive cradle. It lolled, the dead weight almost pulling him down as he lowered it gently.

'Go check all of the others. Wake them if you can.' She nodded, and began to crawl towards Saul in the forward gun niche.

Kord lowered himself into the drive cradle and looked at the controls. It had been over two decades since he had steered a tank. There was blood on the sight block and control levers. It stuck to his hands as he took hold of them. 'Saul's alive,' said Shornal. 'So is Kog, and Zade, though they are still out.'

'Sacha?'

'Can't tell.' He could hear the hesitation in her voice.

'Get into the turret,' he said. 'Watch the auspex and vox.'

He turned back to the controls. The assault tank was larger, heavier and more powerful than anything he had driven before. He glanced through the forward viewfinder. The augmented display had dimmed the light of the fires to near black, but he could see the wreck of a machine directly in front of them. Flames gushed from its hatches, and its front armour ended in a twisted ruin. A white blaze, somehow still visible through the soot and flame, ran down the dead machine's flank. *Mourner*, he recognised without having to think. Abbas's battered old face floated in his mind as he watched the flames.

Slowly he engaged *War Anvil*'s power, and the tank moved forward, gradually at first, and then with heavy purpose.

'Colonel!' Shornal's voice cut through his concentration. 'There is something moving out there.' Ice pulsed from his heart. One of the enemy had survived, or another ambush group had come to see what had happened to the first.

'War Anvil,' the tired voice, came over the vox. 'War Anvil, *this is* Razor. *Respond,* War Anvil.'

Kord felt his hands shaking on the controls.

'Origo?'

'Sir.'

'*Razor* is still going?'

'*Still alive, sir. Yes.*'

'Anyone else?'

The pause spoke the truth before Origo put it into words.

*'No other signs of life.'* Another pause. *'We were going to head north. I didn't think anyone else was alive... until* War Anvil's *plant started up.'*

Kord nodded, then realised no one could see. The fatigue that had been hidden beneath adrenaline began to nudge back into his limbs and thoughts. With it came another thought, one that he did not want to look at now, the thought that he had done exactly what Abbas had feared; he had killed almost everyone who had trusted him.

'North?' he said.

*'There's supposed to be a shelter up on the edge of these flats. At least if we are where I think we are.'*

'All right,' Kord said. 'North. Lead us out.'

'Sir,' replied Origo.

Kord began to feed power into the tracks again.

'And, Origo...' The words came without him deciding to say them.

'Yes, colonel.'

'Thank you.'

HREND RAN INTO the flames, his strides powdering stone to dust. His meltaguns were singing. The blast wave from the Baneblade's death hit him. The world vanished in fire and the hail ring of shrapnel. His shields fizzed as they reduced the debris to fire and dust. He could taste his weapons' need to burn. He could feel the death of metal, and the ring of shrapnel. He was burning, drowning in iron. He was...

...running down the slope towards the spreading shockwave of the Baneblade's death.

Gortun was running beside him, a wet roar bubbling from his speaker units. The rest of the Cyllaros accelerated across and down the valley floor. Each of them had a pattern of attack, and a set of secondary patterns and target priorities. The trio of Predators were already firing, conversion beamers and lascannons reducing the surviving battle tank from the Baneblade's guard to a scream of light and shattering metal. Orun and the two Venators were shifting position on the high ground. They would be ready to fire again in six seconds.

Directly in front of Hrend one of the enemy squadrons was pulling around. A pulse of las energy hit the stone beneath his stride. Rock splinters hit his shields, flashing to powder. The dust rattled against his skin. He saw the long barrel of a Vanquisher turn towards him. It promised an end, a chance to rest from war, to let go of iron. But it would never fire.

Hrend jinked to the side, raised his arms, fingers splayed. The Vanquisher was twenty strides away. The barrel of the cannon was a black circle in his eyes. Two spears of white heat leapt from his hands. The cannon barrel melted as it fired. The blast blew out of the top and back of the Vanquisher's turret.

He ran directly at the wreck. Behind it two more battle tanks were turning, hunting for targets. The air was hissing with gunfire, screaming as the fire rose to stain the clouds above.

A scout tank came around the wreck of the dead Vanquisher. It was fast and the human piloting it had reacted faster than Hrend had estimated. That was a mistake. Hrend levelled his hand. The energy built in his palm. Inside his cocoon of iron, he felt the heat spill up his nerves. It felt impossible. It felt like being alive again.

Gortun hit the scout an instant before Hrend was going to fire. Drill claws screamed into armour plate, as the other Dreadnought shunted the tank across the ground. Its tracks shredded free from its wheels as it gouged through snow and stone. It struck a boulder, and for a second Gortun reared up above it. The teeth of his drill claws glittered in the red, rolling light. Gortun slammed his claws down. Tatters of metal fountained up. Hull plates tore. Hrend could see a figure in a bulky suit scrabbling inside the split hull. Then the poisoned air found a weakness in the suit, and the figure juddered as his flesh became jelly.

Gortun reached into the wreck's guts, and his claws pinched shut. A ball of flame enveloped the other Dreadnought, but Gortun was standing, wrenching the burning wreck into the air. Hrend heard his brother's roar spill through the vox and air. Then he realised that he was screaming too, running on, his machine form flowing as if it were his own muscle, as if it were following a hunger he had not realised he had, a hunger to live again, a hunger to live and burn.

He killed the next tank with his hands. It was trying to turn, its tracks churning rock fragments in its wake. He struck it in the side. One hand clamped around its turning tracks and ripped backwards. A shattered length of track arced into the air above him. The tank slewed as its other track spun it into a circle. Hrend shook as the machine's bulk slammed into him. He punched downwards, just behind the block of a side sponson. The welded join shattered. Hrend gripped and fired his melta. Molten armour bored into the machine's heart and out of the other side. In his sarcophagus Hrend thought he could taste cooking flesh. Hrend stepped back. The wreck slewed to stillness. Flames were spewing from its back in a bright crest.

He stood for a second looking at the dead machine. The battlefield seemed almost silent, the sounds of explosions a dull rumble, like the crash of distant waves. He knew where each of his machines was, but everything seemed remote, as though something had just been unplugged from his awareness. To his left the Predator trio were moving in deliberately erratic patterns on the lower slopes. Lascannon light flicked from their sponsons. The Venators were shifting firing position again. Jarvak's machine was still on the opposite side of the valley, hidden from sight behind the wall of fire and smoke. They had torn the enemy force in half for no loss, the battle plan had unfolded exactly as it should have. Except something was wrong, something that had nothing to do with whether they would survive this fight.

Something was calling him, something within him, something that perhaps had always been there.

*Iron within.*

He could feel it gripping, pulling him in with a relentless strength. With his own strength. It felt like the promise of air when drowning. It felt like life.

*Iron without.*

And he wanted to let go. He wanted to let it become. He wanted to feel alive again. He wanted to be more than a corpse clad in iron.

He felt his limbs start to move.

The Stormlord broke from the curtain of flame.

Hrend twisted aside as the machine rammed through the wreck of the machine he had just killed. The hull hit Hrend with armour-cracking force. He fell, his senses filling with blinking warning runes. He hit the ground, gouging a track across the earth. He stopped and began to rise.

The barrels of the Stormlord's megabolter were turning faster and faster. One of Hrend's Predators on the valley side was dead ahead of the spinning barrels.

Hrend pulled a leg beneath him. There was oil on the ground, dribbling from his iron frame, black flecks pattering on dirty snow.

The muzzles of the Stormlord's guns were a blur. The Predators were breaking, scattering across the slope, their guns turning to point at the Stormlord.

Hrend stood. Amber warning runes painted his sight. His shields were gone. He felt pistons twist and gears snap. They felt like broken bones, and shredding muscle. He charged.

The megabolter fired. Shells breathed from the spinning barrels. The side of the valley vanished. Rock, dust and shrapnel spread in a roaring cloud. Shell casings sprayed from the Stormlord, raining on its hull as they fell. The Predators struggled on for a second, their armour distorting as round after round chewed into their hulls. Hrend saw the status runes of the three Predators pulse to amber and then blink to red. He began to run towards the Stormlord. Hrend had shut off his audio sensors when the first shot was fired, but he could still hear the megabolter. It shook the fluid-filled dark of his coffin and into his skull, like the roar of an iron dragon.

He raised his hands to fire. At the edge of his sight he saw two of his Venators moving, trying to outrun the storm of gunfire which churned the slope. They would fail. The megabolter was simply cutting Hrend's force to pieces.

The Stormlord twisted back, tracks screaming and shattering stone. A sponson gun swivelled to point at Hrend. He fire–

The shells slammed into his torso. Fire swallowed his sight. He staggered, his charge faltering. Shell impacts slammed through him. Blood seeped into the amnion around his body. More rounds struck, ringing his world to shrill silence. Part of him – the part which had been forged and trained to war – felt everything and catalogued it dispassionately.

The Stormlord's main gun was not firing at him; if it was he would already be dead. It was a heavy bolter. Its shells were substantial but not potent enough to crack his armour. Yet they could batter him down, hammer him to kneeling, shatter his sensors and leave him blind. They were not firing to kill him, they were firing to hold him until the main gun could turn and reduce him to shards and blood slime. That moment was coming, winding down into certainty with each second he was not moving.

He began to stand, fists raised, forearm plates reverberating as the bolter shells exploded against them. His sensors were blurring with threat markers and damage readings. The fire ceased. He took a step forward. His sight cleared. The Stormlord was pivoting its spinning barrels, glowing cherry red as they dragged fire down the slope, down towards him.

He took another step, damaged servos wailing as he began to level his guns. He willed the missile free from his carapace. Nothing, just a sparking blank feeling of blown connections.

A wedge-shaped hull broke from the screen of fire behind the Stormlord. Scorches marked the brushed metal of its plating. Hrend saw a trio of targeting lasers glimmer in the ash-thickened air.

'*Master*,' called Jarvak's voice, across the vox, and – as though the word were a command – the Sicaran fired all of its weapons.

The back of the Stormlord exploded in a gout of black smoke. The vast machine lurched, its tracks still turning for an instant before becoming still. Promethium flames spread up its back, as it rocked to stillness. It was not dead though, not yet. It fired all of its guns, panning them across the ground around it, like a half-blind warrior trying to fend off attackers. Hrend ran, feeling the damage to his frame dig deeper. This was foolishness, it was not optimal, and it was nowhere near rational. But he was no longer seeing the world through those eyes. He was the iron within, and he could feel more than he ever had, more than he had in life. He was a weapon, and a weapon could only live by killing.

He hit the front of the Stormlord, and bounded up the sloped front, fist rising. A spear of heat struck the cannon. A sphere of molten metal sprayed outwards. It hurt him. The plates of his armour cratered and blistered. He punched into the wounded Stormlord's hull, gripped onto sagging metal and fired his meltagun.

And the world became silent whiteness.

FROST FLASHED OVER Taldak. Argonis felt his own teeth clamp shut as the air became like tar. The Iron Warrior juddered where he stood. Pale mist rose from him. Argonis thought he could see faces and open mouths in the vapour. Taldak's helm was shaking in its socket. A smell of burning hair and honey flooded Argonis's mouth and nose. He gagged. Taldak's arms began to rise, straining as though against a great weight. Prophesius's fingers were glowing where they touched the Iron Warrior's helm. Argonis saw the shadows of bones and blood vessels within the astropath's hand. Taldak began to turn, slow heavy fingers reaching for Prophesius's arm, boltgun rising. Argonis stepped forward and clamped his own hands around Taldak's arms.

It was like touching lightning.

He blanked out. When he came to he was kneeling on the lift platform. The motionless shape of Taldak lay before him, fuming oily smoke.

He pulled his helm off and sucked a deep breath of air. It tasted of bitter iron.

'That was foolish,' said Sota-Nul to him. She was bent over an open panel on the platform. Prehensile cables snaked from her robes and buried themselves inside the opening. The platform jolted to a halt.

Prophesius was standing three paces away, utterly still, as though he had not moved. The iron-masked astropath raised his wax tablet as Argonis looked at him. A silver-spiked finger flickered across the tablet.

*he lives,* wrote Prophesius, scraping the words clean as he finished. *he dreams in the cradle of sharpness and delight. he will wake, and he will remember nothing.*

*i will stay.*

*i will watch him in his dreams.*

Argonis nodded. Relief and revulsion washed through him. He reflexively reached for the key to Prophesius's mask, and found it still there, hanging within the gorget of his armour.

Sota-Nul gave a low hiss, which sounded strangely like pleasure, and doors set into the wall of the shaft opened. Argonis stood. The space beyond was dark, but he could taste charge on the air. The hum of power conduits and machines pressed upon the exposed skin of his face. He slid his gladius free, thumb hovering over the activation stud.

'You predicted guards,' he said.

'Most certainly,' said Sota-Nul, disconnecting herself from the platform and gliding over to his side. 'They will be here.'

'If you are wrong and there are legionaries–'

'There will not be. This is not their domain. Even Perturabo respects that.'

'So they will be tech-priests, your kind?'

'Not my kind. Weaklings, creatures of a lower dominion, fools that happen to follow at the side of our allies. I am of the future, they still are of the past.'

Argonis did not know what she was talking about, and he was certain that he did not want to have that ignorance corrected.

He stepped through the door. The darkness beyond spread out in every direction. He paused as his eyes gathered the scraps of light from the gloom. A narrow walkway extended from where he stood. Beneath it empty space dropped down to a distant floor. Vast shapes rose to either side of the walkway. Sparks flashed occasionally across their surfaces, illuminating patches of metal and tangles of cable. These were the datastacks of the Sightless Warren. In the previous life of the shelter they would have held the data records of troops, supplies and shipping movements of crusade forces that had mustered and shipped out from the planet. The Priests of Mars had laid the core of these great machines in the early decades of the planet's compliance. They had grown since that time, so that now they spread through the charged gloom like mountains.

Sota-Nul slid past him, hissing with anticipation.

'Where do–'

'So new, so untouched,' said Sota-Nul. 'Ah, you have dreamed so long, but not known how to dream, my children.'

She shivered, her robes rustling in the charged air.

Argonis followed, feeling the weight of his blade in the cradle of his fingers. Worms of charge squirmed and vanished across his armour. He could hear a deep, throbbing buzz vibrating through the air and walkway. They kept moving.

The tech-priest appeared without warning.

Stepping from the shadow of one of the machine stacks, he must have been standing utterly still. Umbilical cables still linked him to the great machine. He blurted a stream of machine code. Weapons, or fingers, or fingers that were weapons, glinted at the end of his arms. Argonis began to move. Sota-Nul moved faster. She flew forwards. The air shimmered around her, oily slicks of light spiralled in her wake. A halo of silver arms spread from beneath her robes. Argonis saw turning blades and injector spikes beneath her robe. Wet flesh glistened with the rainbow sheen of oil. Eyelids blinked over clusters of crystal eyes inside nests of sinew and clockwork. She had no legs, just a column of tangled cables.

The tech-priest tried to twist aside, lightning building on his fingers. Sota-Nul hissed. The electricity arced from the tech-priest's hand. Sota-Nul rattled a stream of scratching machine code as she struck. She folded around the tech-priest. Her halo of tentacles punched down, and the tech-priest stopped moving.

Sota-Nul hung in the air, the twitching body of the tech-priest hugged closed, cables and articulated arms pulsing and squirming. Dark liquid siphoned down lengths of transparent tubes. Argonis thought he saw arcs of electricity running through the liquid. The tech-priest's body began to crumble, its shape seeming to lose structure and substance. Sota-Nul gathered the shrinking ball of its mass into her chest. A wet pulsing sound washed through the air for a long moment. Then she withdrew her array of machine limbs, and the black robes fell back into place. She turned on the spot, the shadowed hole beneath her hood pointing at Argonis.

'I said–' he began, but the tech-witch spoke over him.

'The eightfold wheel must be given its due. It is *their* work that we do.' She turned away, and drifted further down the platform. Argonis felt anger flair inside his thoughts, and then quickly crushed the instinct. Events were rolling now, blinking from instant to instant as time became a pressure wave of momentum. He began to run in Sota-Nul's wake. The tech-witch was singing, a low brittle noise, which ground against the throb of the datastacks. She turned as she moved, head tilted as though listening. Argonis kept his eyes moving across the shadows. Amber threat markers danced and dissolved into nothing.

Sota-Nul stopped at last. She floated in place, her sharp-edged song growing, and then she too rose into the air. A pair of silvered tentacles slipped out of her. They squirmed through the air, reaching blindly into space. At last she stopped and drifted to a panel set high in the cliff-face of a machine. Argonis had no idea how she had selected the location or how she had known it was there. The twin tentacles slid out, slithering over the machine's surface, and then into sockets.

Sota-Nul jerked, and became rigid. She began to shake. The datastack began to rumble. Argonis felt his hair rise inside the shell of his helm. He sheathed his blade. His bolter was in his hand. His helmet system was pinging warnings into his ears.

'It... is...' called Sota-Nul, her voice rolling higher and higher within each word. 'So innocent.'

Amber threat runes were moving across his sight as he turned his head. Out there in the gloom between the stacks things were moving.

'Come on!' he called, the need for silence banished by the need for haste. Sota-Nul's whole body was pulsing, swelling and contracting, as though she were breathing in, as though she were swallowing something larger than herself. Argonis could see the shapes of the things moving amongst the stacks, the glitter of machine eyes staring at him. Lines of targeting light began to flicker out through the dark. He raised his bolter. Target runes began to flash between red and amber.

'We go now!' he called.

Sota-Nul shivered, and then pulled away, silver tentacles yanking from the stack. She trembled in the air for a second and then began to spiral downwards towards him. Machine voices were rising from the dark. Sota-Nul landed and began to glide back towards the lift platform. He followed at a run.

'What did you see?' he called as the metal grating shook beneath his feet. 'What did you find?'

'A nothing,' she hissed, her voice dreamlike.

'Nothing?'

The lift shaft opened to greet them. Prophesius stood above the still supine form of Taldak. The doors began to close behind them.

'Not nothing,' said Sota-Nul. 'A nothing.'

Prophesius was scratching words onto his wax tablet.

*do you wish the iron one to wake?*

'A nothing?' Argonis called.

Sota-Nul nodded slowly.

'An absence,' she said, 'a void, a thing that is not there.'

*do you wish to wake?*

'What do you mean?'

'They have lied to you.'

*to wake?*

He stood and stared at her for a second. He had known it, had been all but certain ever since he looked in Perturabo's eyes, but he had hoped that he would not find a reason to bring fresh news of treachery to his father. He had hoped that in this war of broken vows some bonds stayed true.

Lights set into the shaft walls were flashing past as they descended. He turned to Prophesius, and thought of the key to the iron mask, cold against his neck. Then he looked back to Sota-Nul.

'Tell me,' he said.

'No,' she replied, her metal snakes working inside the platform's control panels. The platform began to move even faster, sinking into the shaft beneath. 'We must see it.'

The platform came to a halt two full minutes later. Quietness settled into the air. Argonis found it almost unsettling. His hearts were beating adrenaline-spiced blood through his limbs. Tactical markers were spinning in his sight, telling him that the air was cool here, but tinged with exotic chemicals. Ambient sound was almost nothing, just the distant noise of machinery stirring air. Sota-Nul extended a set of metal snakes into the controls beside the door. Sparks and smoke puffed into the air, and the doors opened. The corridor beyond was smooth rockcrete. Bare lumen-strips ran down its centre. Another small door of reinforced plasteel lay in the distance. Chipped hazard stripes marked its edges.

'You are sure?' he asked, keeping his eyes on the corridor.

Sota-Nul glided up beside him, metal tentacles slithering back beneath her robe.

'Yes, this is it. Not the main means of entrance-exit, but it should take us to it. The likelihood of detection is high.' She rotated her head towards him. He found himself imagining a grin hidden beneath the hood. 'You might even have to get your weapons dirty.'

'The records gave no indication of what they are keeping here?'

'None, just the name-signifier buried under three cipher layers. They called it Black Oculus.'

'Black Oculus...' he let the phrase hang in the air.

He glanced back at the still unconscious form of Taldak, and then at Prophesius. He nodded and stepped into the passage. The tech-witch and the astropath followed. They moved fast. The next door opened to Sota-Nul's touch, as she fed it the codes she had culled from the datastacks.

More corridors followed, all bare, all quiet. He did not like that, not at all. The air and light changed the further they went. A haze hung on the edge of sight, blurring the edges of walls and the details of distant objects. Shadows clung to recesses like folds of black cloth, while the lumen-strips shone brighter, but gave less light. The rhythm and regularity of deserted chambers and silent corridors began to press into his mind. He caught his concentration wandering several times. He would blink and realise he had walked several steps, and was not even aware of taking them. Every time he would pull himself back to focused awareness, only for it to drain away. It was difficult to tell if the tech-witch was affected, but Prophesius's hands clasped and twitched the further they went. The silence deepened, and the fog in their awareness thickened.

It almost killed them.

Another hatch door had swung open, and Argonis had been stepping through, gun pointing by habit as much as intent. The Iron Warrior standing on the other side of the hatch turned, bolter rising. A slowed sensation of shock ran up Argonis's spine. His senses cleared in a cold rush. He kicked the Iron Warrior's gun. The casing slammed back into the warrior's chestplate. Two rounds roared from the muzzle and hit the wall. Gunshot echoes, dust and smoke flooded the passage.

Argonis came forward fast, slamming his fist into the Iron Warrior three times before he was halfway to the floor. His mind was a sudden focused line, all hot fury and bared teeth. The lenses in the Iron Warrior's helm shattered. Blood misted from the broken sockets with his first and second blow. The Iron Warrior was falling, most likely blinded, but he was far from dead and brought his gun up as he fell.

The decision occurred so fast in Argonis's mind that he was barely aware of its passing. He fired his bolter. The round hit the Iron Warrior in the chest, exploded and punched the warrior back into the wall. Argonis fired three times more: once into the throat joint, once into each eyepiece, each shot a sliver of time apart. The Iron Warrior's head and neck exploded.

Argonis moved forward, gun ready, tracking the space beyond the headless corpse. Nothing, just a section of corridor with another small door in the wall opposite, and a large, circular hatch to his left. His helmet display fizzed as he stepped closer to the circular hatch, and then dissolved into a blur. Squawks of distortion rose from his vox. He pulled the helm off, and looked back at his two companions.

Sota-Nul was already gliding close.

'Very clean,' she said, the slight twitch of her hood indicating the dead Iron Warrior. 'Apart from the first instant when he nearly killed you. But the three kill shots, one to ensure the throat and mouth could not call an alarm, the other two to ensure fatality. Impressive.'

Argonis did not respond. Part of his mind had simply shut off all of his thoughts about what he had just done. He had not wanted to kill the Iron Warrior, but the only other option would have been to die and to fail in his mission.

'He may still have sent an alert,' he said without looking at Sota-Nul. 'He had time to speak before I fired.'

'No,' said the tech-witch. 'He sent nothing. His vox was disabled, as were most of his auto-senses.'

'Why?'

'Because of this.' She touched the circular hatch as she spoke. 'You will have to open it,' she said, and he could hear a tremor in her voice. 'I...' she began to say, but the word did not finish and she drifted to the floor.

He noticed Prophesius then. The astropath was still by the door they had entered through. He was trembling. His hand was jumping across his wax tablet, writing the same thing again and again.

...*black star, black star, black star, black star, black star*...

Argonis turned back to the hatch. A wheel sat at its centre. He could see no other lock, just the blank space and loose cables where an access system had been. He reached out and gripped the wheel. His armour was moving with slow creaks and groans of resistance, as though its system were failing. He began to turn the wheel. It spun until he heard a heavy clank from within. Then he pulled the hatch, his protesting armour grinding as he heaved it wide.

The space beyond was dark, and the light coming from behind Argonis halted at the door as though a barrier prevented its passing. He stepped across the threshold. The dark closed over him. For a heartbeat he could see nothing, then his eyes adjusted, and a scene in stark monochrome formed in front of him.

Thin human figures hung from frames of metal. Chains hooked into loops bonded to their arms and scalps. Some bore mutations: additional limbs of shrivelled muscle and stark bone, translucent scales, back-jointed legs, fingers grown to crescents of pale bone. A thick metal band circled each of their heads. Needle-tipped tubes connected their bare skin to bottles of liquid. A turn of his head told Argonis that there were dozens of them in the chamber. His eyes ached as he looked at them, and a dull crackle hummed in his ears.

He knew what they were, or at least what they had been. They were Navigators, dozens of Navigators chained in the dark and sedated. He stepped closer. His armour was a dead weight pulling against his muscles. The first figure he reached was a starvation-thin woman. Slowly he pulled the needles from her flesh. He waited, feeling the instincts in his spine and limbs telling him to get back into the light.

He waited, and time waited with time.

The Navigator's head came up. She gasped air to scream.

Then she went still, then tilted her head, first one way and then another. Argonis did not move or speak.

'I see you,' she said, and her voice was a cold shiver of sound. 'I see you, son of the moon-wolf.'

'What are you?' he asked.

'What are we? We are those who have looked into the light of eternity. We are the ones who have seen the black star.'

*...black star... black star... black star...* The words repeated in his thoughts, trailing down to silence.

'The black star?' he asked, and found that his lips were dry.

'The dark heart of all things. It was there, and we passed into it and through it, our eyes wide. And we saw...' The Navigator's voice caught, and for a second terror trembled her words. 'We saw all things. The black star... the circle beneath... the Gateway to the Gods... the Eye of Terror sees all.' She turned her head and looked at Argonis. He felt the look. It felt like ice, like falling, and falling without ever finding the release of the ground. 'It is here. It is within. And...' she was trembling again, limbs shaking the frame that bound her. 'And it is looking back at us.'

He left the chamber, and closed the hatch on the darkness and the sleeping Navigators within.

Sota-Nul had withdrawn to the hatch they had entered by. Her shape was swelling and deflating as he watched her, and there was no sign of either the corpse or the blood which had spattered the floor and walls. Argonis walked towards them, his armour moving more freely with each step he took from the door.

'We have to reach the *Iron Blood*,' he said, as he ducked into the passage that led back the way they had come. 'We have to reach Perturabo.'

IAEO WAS LISTENING to Argonis when her awareness snapped away from the emissary. The part of her mind watching the rest of her feeds had noticed something. This was not supposed to happen. She was in a deep focus meditation. Only something that could be an immediate personal threat could trigger a switch.

The image of a corridor filled her eyes. It was deserted except for a lone man, standing still, looking up into the eyes of her net-fly. Looking into her eyes. The man wore grey overalls marked with the numbers of the Iron Warriors labour cadres. His scalp was clean-shaven, his stare blank and unblinking. He smiled, lips moving as though pulled at the corners by wires. A swirl of colour tattoos bloomed on his face, and then faded as the smile slid down his face again.

'Be careful, assassin,' he said. 'There are only so many places to hide, and what might appear safe, might be otherwise.' He smiled again, reached up, and the image became static. She felt the net-fly die. Shock flooded her. It took several seconds for the conditioned routines to kick in.

*Data: Net-fly presence compromised.*

She performed a blink-fast inventory of her swarm and found all the rest in place and functioning.

*Projection: Subject who made approach wished to invoke psychological intimidation.*

She began to flick through the net-flies that watched over her boltholes within the Sightless Warren. After three she began to find the messages. Scratched, daubed or chalked within sight of her net-flies was a symbol: the first letter of the alphabet in a dialect of Old Terra, an Alpha.

She had to pause before she began to process these facts. She had kept subconscious watch on each of the bolthole locations that had been marked, and she had not seen anything.

*Projection: The enemy is not trying to intimidate. The enemy is trying to communicate sophistication and superiority.*

She was aware of her own breathing; aware of the narrowness of the vent she had folded into, aware of everything, and aware that she was shivering.

'You are making an error.' Iaeo started at the sound, and then realised she had spoken aloud.

*No, no, not now,* she thought, and suddenly her mind was tumbling out of her control. She had been warned about it, they all had. Even a Vanus mind could only take in so much data for so long before it began to clog, and misfire. Extended mission conditions, and overly complex problem spaces, could induce a chaotic state in which the mind walked down its own compulsive paths. Iaeo had been living within a supremely complex problem space for months.

'Demand: List known psychological qualities of the Twentieth Legiones Astartes, designation Alpha.'

She was speaking out loud. She could not help it. The old face of her mentor was grinning at her from her memory, and she catapulted through a loop of question and response that she had not begun and could not stop.

'Response: Known psychological qualities include superiority/inferiority complexes, sublimated into complex psychopathic behaviour requiring the acknowledgement of superiority by an enemy and/or ally.'

'Demand: Project data of recent confrontation in line with this data, and previous mission data.'

'Projection: The Alpha Legion know I am here. They want me to know who they are. They want me to know how good they are. They want me to know before they kill me.'

The memory of her mentor's cruel smile was there again, just inside her eyelids.

She was shaking, her contorted muscles aching. But her mind was clearing.

She was out of the fugue. Crucial time had passed, but she was still whole, still alive, still functioning.

She began to touch the strings of her computations again, tentatively at first, then hauling them back into her awareness. She had lost time, and time was a deadly factor in a problem space.

She looked again through her eyes, and blinked back to the net-flies following Argonis and Sota-Nul. They were moving to the lift. She was still uncertain exactly what Argonis's discovery meant. The implications were vast in their potential, and the projected possibilities were equally vast. She needed time, and for that she needed to cut away the agency of some of the actors. She performed a quick mental check, assured herself that her action would not have fatal consequences, and decided to change what she was seeing.

Carefully she fed a message into the Iron Warriors security systems. It was a tiny thing, just a seed that would grow into something greater.

The first security alarms began to ring out three minutes later.

*The greatest defence is being beyond the reach of your enemy. The loyalists had understood this ancient wisdom since the first reinforcements had come to Tallarn's aid. While hundreds of thousands of war machines rested in the vaults of buried shelters, as many remained in the void, kept in the bellies of warships and transports. The reasoning behind this was simple: strongholds could fall. The loss of the Sapphire City Shelter had proved that point beyond doubt, and when it had fallen the loyalists had lost tens of thousands of machines. Ground-based fortresses were also static. The dominance they exerted over the surrounding areas was a weakness. Forces bound to one location on one side of Tallarn could not easily be deployed to an engagement on the opposite side of the planet.*

*Forces held in ships were not so vulnerable. They could run beyond the reach of an attack, and could be deployed across the planet's surface. The ships might have to fight through enemy forces to reach Tallarn, but while they were there, the loyalists could never be defeated. It also meant that the full strength of the forces arrayed against Perturabo could never be brought to bear at once.*

*It was a trade: survival at the cost of strength on the ground. It had remained a central pillar of the loyalists strategy for months and it showed no sign of being overturned. For that to happen something fundamental would need to change.*

# NINE

**Rachab**
**Unbroken**
**Ambush**

WAR ANVIL TRAVELLED north, leaving the fires of the dead as a smear of red light in the thickening fog. They travelled through days and nights without noticing the boundaries between each. The surviving crew of *War Anvil* woke. Sacha did not regain consciousness, and her body remained slumped over the gun breech.

The flats seemed to go on forever. Kord had a suspicion that Origo had made more than one navigation error. He did not say anything, nor did he blame the scout. How could he blame any of them any more? They saw no other living thing. From his position back in *War Anvil*'s turret, Kord watched the two green runes of his remaining command glide over a featureless plate of drying earth.

Sometimes the fog outside the hull thickened, sometimes it thinned to almost nothing and the light of sun, stars, or moon fell down on them. The wind brought dust as well, great rolling banks which enveloped them in seconds. The first time the dust had come, Kord had ordered a complete stop, and they had waited while the hull had whispered with the swishing voice of the dust. When the dust had cleared it left them half buried beneath a black glass sky. As Kord had looked towards the promise of distant mountains, a great light had risen into the dark, strobing between blue and white, before vanishing, and leaving glowing skeins of light that had scudded across the sky. Shornal had sworn that she had felt the earth shake through the hull. Kord had felt nothing.

They had pressed on after that, the two tanks heaving themselves free of their shrouds of dust, and the desolation of days that were nights, and nights that were days, took them again.

In the dark hours Kord would sit and think of the reason why he had begun this journey into folly. His thoughts circled the images of the burning tanks, and he heard again all the warnings that he had not listened to.

But even then the old thought surfaced. There had to be a reason: a reason why this had all happened, a reason why the present was as it was, a reason that explained it all. To admit anything else felt like a surrender.

Time became difficult to measure, even with the numbers clicking over on *War Anvil*'s auspex. It was not that they could not measure the passing of days, or weeks, but the information lacked meaning. Fuel, water, air and nutrient fluid, and the status of the recycling systems became the true measure of everything, the slow countdown to nothing the only clock which mattered.

Then, with an abruptness of a gunshot, the journey ended.

The rocket exploded ten metres in front of *War Anvil*. Earth fountained up. *War Anvil* rolled on, the debris falling on its hull. The order to arm weapons began to form in his mouth, but he already knew they were dead. Saul and Kogetsu were in the side sponsons, but the main guns were cold and empty.

'*Multiple heat signatures,*' called Origo over the vox.

'Where the hell did they come from?' shouted Saul.

'I can't see them!' Kogetsu yelled.

'*I count six,*' said Origo. '*But their signal identifiers say they are–*'

'Unknown units, halt now and power down,' the voice cut across the vox. '*We have clear shots, and I will not warn you again before I fire.*'

Kord recognised something in its low tones, something that rolled cold down his spine. He cut the drive power, and *War Anvil* came to a juddering halt.

'Comply,' he said into the command vox. 'Stop and power down.'

*'We are still,'* said Origo a second later.

'This is Colonel Kord of the Tallarn Seventy-First, we have complied.' He took a breath and tried to make his voice reflect the title he had just invoked rather than the reality he felt. 'Now identify yourselves.'

*'Your weapons are still charged and ready, colonel. You have ten seconds to undo that.'*

'All weapons cold, now!' Kord roared.

'Colonel…' began Saul.

'Now!' Kord waited. He had not counted, but after what seemed like a long time, the cold voice growled across the vox again.

*'You will give reasons for your presence.'*

'Who are you?'

Kord closed his eyes and let out a breath.

'Colonel,' it was Shornal. 'Their identifier signals are green. They are with us.'

'Allies who open a conversation by shooting,' said Saul.

'Silence,' said Kord. They all caught the sharpness in his voice. A leaden silence waited for him as he opened his eyes.

'We are seeking sanctuary,' he said into the external vox. 'We have taken casualties, are undercrewed, underarmed and running low on water, food and air.'

*'You do not know where you are?'* asked the voice.

'Not precisely.' Kord let out a slow breath, considered not asking the question which had been rolling over in his mind ever since he had first heard the challenge come across the vox. 'What Legion are you from?'

A pause. A long ringing pause.

*'The Tenth.'*

*Tenth Legion*, he thought, *one of the sons of the dead primarch, one of the Iron Hands.*

'My name is Menoetius,' said the Iron Hand, *'and I give you greetings.'*

As if to accompany the words a low dark metal shape slid into Kord's field of view. It was a Predator, its oil-black lines rubbed with dust. Lascannons hung from its flanks. Kord recognised the focusing plates of a conversion beamer running down the barrel of its main gun. *'You will follow,'* said Menoetius.

'Where to?'

'You have found what you seek, at least in part. You are come to the Rachab, colonel. You will have safety there. Though, if you will leave again is another question.'

HE WOKE FIRST to the memory of his father's voice.

'Do you know our creed?' Perturabo had turned to look into the distance of the machine-filled cavern. Hrend had hesitated, the words coming in halting bites from his speaker grilles.

'From iron cometh strength. From strength cometh will. From will cometh faith. From faith cometh honour. From honour cometh iron.'

'Those are the words, but what do they mean?' asked Perturabo, his chin dipping into the collar of his armour, the skin of his face contracting around his stare.

'That we never break.'

'That we never break...' The primarch nodded, and then looked back to Hrend. 'But what if we have already broken?'

For a second he could not believe that he had heard those words. Then they began to seep in. They felt like poison. Perturabo watched Hrend, black eyes unblinking.

'Master,' Hrend began. 'We–'

'What if we were broken long ago? What if the choices we made, and the trust we gave made our iron rust, our strength weakness, our honour false? What do those words mean then?'

'They become a lie,' he said.

Perturabo nodded slowly.

'They become a lie,' echoed the primarch.

'But we have never broken.'

'Our word, our trust, our chains, our dreams...' A flicker passed through the depths of his eyes. 'Which of these remains unbroken?'

And Hrend woke a second time to the voices of his brothers.

*'He endures yet.'* The voice was Jarvak, hard-edged, neither pleased nor disappointed, a blunt statement stamping the truth on reality.

He lay beneath a ceiling of red and orange clouds. It was not a kind waking. There was pain, true pain crawling up his nerves from damaged systems, the sharp feeling of broken bones and seeping wounds. Both his machine frames and his true flesh were hurt. The sensations overlapped, contradicted, chimed against one another, pulling his existence between two realities.

Bit by bit his senses cleared. He became aware of the others, their presence blotches of signals and heat encircling him: four war machines and a single Dreadnought, all arranged in a circle with him at the centre. They had taken four casualties then: the three Predators, and one of his Dreadnought brothers. More important than this tally was what had survived: Spartan 4171 was still intact, as was the drill machine. They still had Hes-Thal. They still had a guide to lead them through the lost land.

He began to test his motive system, and then to stand. They were still in the valley. The fires had contracted back to individual wrecks, each one a white stain on his heat vision. He switched to standard sight. The image jumped, scattered into fragments, and then settled. The black bones of heat-distorted hulls flickered at the heart of the fires. His targeting array remained off-line, but he counted the fires with a glance. The count matched the enemy strength. No survivors. As it should be.

He turned where he stood, and looked at the surviving machines of the Cyllaros. None of them were unmarked by battle. Jarvak's Sicaran had been washed by flame, and soot skinned its hull. He noted Gortun's absence, and deduced that one of the heaps of wreckage must be his brother in iron. It was unfortunate, but merely one factor in their reduced strength. They would be low on ammunition, and this far from the Sightless Warren there was no way to resupply. No matter, they had to continue. He wondered if the other search groups sent by the primarch had begun to die like this, not in one moment, but eaten away bit by bit.

The Cyllaros waited, silent, measuring his strength, judging if he had weakened enough to let the damage drag him into failure.

'Navigator,' he said.

*'I see and hear,'* said Hes-Thal.

'Does the path lead as it did?'

*'The path leads where it has always led.'*

Hrend cut the vox without reply, and took a step forward, then another and another. Pain followed each movement, but he did not stumble. After three paces the pain was a simple fact. The rest of the war machines opened their circle, and followed him as he walked through the fires and towards the pass across the mountains.

THE ALARMS BEGAN to shout as the platform rose up the shaft. Argonis snapped around to look at Sota-Nul.

'What–'

'Full security alert in progress. Cause unknown.'

'We are blown.'

'Possibly. That is not a certainty.'

The platform clanged to a halt. The strips illuminating the shaft cut out.

'And now?' growled Argonis, pulling back to a corner, gun up, head twisting to track entry points.

'Our detection is looking more probable.'

Taldak stirred on the floor. Argonis glanced at him, and up at Prophesius. He began to form a command.

Hatches blew out in the shaft above. Smoke billowed in. Heavy figures dropped onto the platform. Argonis's eyes lit with target markers. His finger held still on the trigger, will overriding instinct. Sota-Nul whirled, hissing, arcs of blue power spitting from her.

'No!' shouted Argonis.

The deck rang under the impact of armoured boots. He saw the shapes of slab shields and the smear of red light from the eyes behind them. A buzzing fizz filled the air, and Sota-Nul slammed to the floor, sparks and cords of electricity flickering over her as she tried to rise. Argonis recognised the sound and effect of a graviton gun. He did not lower his weapon, but he did not move either. At his back Prophesius was scratching out words on his tablet, but Argonis did not turn his gaze to see what the astropath was writing.

Armoured figures and a wall of shields surrounded him, the muzzles of the guns slotted through each held steady on his chest. Sudden silence filled the lift shaft, broken only by the buzz of active power armour. The low light and still clinging smoke hid the details of the encircling warriors, but the way they had moved and the details of their posture spoke to who and what they were; the elite shield troops of the Iron Warriors.

'Lower the weapon, emissary,' said a heavy voice from behind the ring of Iron Warriors. It was Volk. Argonis could hear the flatness in the words. Some called the Iron Warriors callous, and he supposed that from a point of view they were, but he had fought with them, and seen the root of that quality. It was not pride, or because of stunted self-worth, it was simply that they would not let anything stand between them and what they needed to do.

He lowered his weapon. The shield wall surged forward. They pulled the bolter from his hands, the sword from his waist, and the pistol from his thigh. Not once did he have space to move, and three guns covered him at all times: thorough, precise, just as you would expect from the IV Legion. Once they were done they stepped back, so that Volk could step forward. He was helmed, but his hands were empty.

'I am the emissary of your Warmaster,' growled Argonis.

Volk just stared at him. Argonis fancied that there was more than anger in that stare. The Iron Warrior began to turn away.

'What are the Black Oculus?' called Argonis. Volk froze. 'The unlogged missions to the surface, what are they looking for?' Volk turned his glowing red gaze back. Behind him Sota-Nul twitched on the floor, limbs sparking as they tried to move. 'You have hidden things from me. You have hidden them from the Warmaster. Why are you here, old friend?'

'Take them,' said Volk at last, and the ranks of Iron Warriors closed around Argonis like a fist.

✚ ✚ ✚

THE KILL-TEAM CAME for Iaeo three days after she watched the Iron Warriors take Argonis. She was in a sump shaft which ran between levels of the shelter, draining extraneous moisture down to filter tanks in the deep earth. As wide as two battle tanks, it was a black void of mould and damp, dank air. Access to the shaft was by heavy inspection hatches, which could only be reached by crawling through passages. Rusting metal cleats dotted the inside of the shaft. Iaeo hung from the side of the shaft from two of the cleats, muscles locked, the pain of the exertion deleted from her awareness. She had been hanging in the dark for two hours when the attack began.

The first sign of the attack was the sound of the photon flash grenade arming as it fell from above. She snapped her head up and around, in time for the world to become a blinding white. Her eyes responded an instant before her mind processed it. Her irises contracted to nothing, blanking out the blinding light. Even then a frozen ghost-scar hung on her retina.

*Data: Photon flash, timed detonation to descent.*

Her eyes opened to see five figures running down the sides of the shaft above her. Black rope lines trailed above them. Her recovering eyes caught the lines of hard, compact armour, vision visors and gun barrels.

She sprang from the wall. Something hit the rockcrete where her head had been. Dust and glittering metal globules scattered from the impact.

*Data: Stalker-pattern rounds, secondary gas propellant, mercury-filled heads.*

She hit the opposite wall of the shaft and kicked away. The armoured figures fired. The sound of their guns was a stuttered purr. She caught a projecting cleat, then flipped back over as rounds exploded in silver clouds around her. She could see the attackers clearly now. They were Space Marines, but their armour was the compact, unpowered armour used by Legion recon units. They fired without pause, driving her down, the beaters driving her towards the executioners. It was a clever tactic, well executed, and with gravity on its side.

She flipped from the wall and dropped into the darkness. Above her the five shooters cut their rope lines as one and dropped after her. Anti-grav units lit with a ringing hum. That was good, she had predicted correctly.

Air rushed past her, the dark beneath roaring as it came up to meet her. After a hundred metres she splayed her limbs. Membranes of synskin between her arms, body and legs caught the air, and she snapped to stillness. The lead warrior falling after her reacted too slowly. His bulk slammed into her but she was ready. Her limbs ripped around him. Her hand came up under his chin. The digi-needler spat a sliver up under his jaw. A spray of rounds burst silently in front of her. Above and around her the falling figures were cutting their fall, anti-grav fields hissing in the damp air.

*Data: Recon configured troops of the Legiones Astartes commonly carry secondary armaments on the right thigh and/or holstered across the chest.*

Her hand found the power knife strapped to the dead warrior. She activated it in the sheath and ripped it out and upwards, carving through armour, flesh and bone.

She jumped from the dead warrior a second before a stalker round hit where she had been. The round blew the back of his head out. The fizzing power blade in her right hand cast shadows around her as she fell. Below her she heard a sound like a sharp breath, and knew that she had been right again. A second team were waiting beneath her.

*Data: Flamer unit ignition sound.*

She dropped the grenades, and snapped her synskin membranes out again, tucked her knees and flipped over as the air caught her. Stalker rounds thudded after her. In her left hand she held a bandolier of grenades she had taken from the dead warrior. She had pulled the pins in timed sequence before she had jumped from the corpse. The warrior she had killed had carried four grenades: two photon flashes, two fragmentation charges. She dropped the two flashes and a single frag down the shaft. The other frag she had left on the corpse that was still spinning in slowed gravity above.

On cue the world flashed to white beneath her. A second later she heard the simultaneous roars of frag denotations above and below her. Shrapnel rang off the rockcrete walls. She heard the secondary thump of a flame fuel cell exploding, and the air around her became a sea of fire. The edge of the blast waves hit her from both sides. She really was falling now, uncontrolled, tumbling over as she tried to reason out which way was up.

Her brain did what it always did in times of extreme stress. It went cold.

On reflection, things had occurred within predicted parameters. The Alpha Legion attack had been superbly orchestrated. If she had not been waiting for it, it might have succeeded. For a second she wondered if it had been within acceptable risk/reward parameters. Increased risk taking was another known consequence of prolonged, unbounded deployment. But it came back to the oldest of paradoxes: what other choice had she had?

The problem was information, or rather its lack. Iaeo's mind drank information and its thirst was never quenched. There was always more information to consume. Even confined to a featureless, white room – the textures of walls and the angles of surfaces could spawn endless datasets. One of the first stages of initiation in the Vanus Temple was to be drowned in data. Presented with an endless source of data, initiates would gorge themselves to the point of seizure. The lesson in that experience was about selection. Data on its own was just chaos without form. Selection and exclusion gave data shape, gave it use. Iaeo knew this, but her hunger was not just for *more* data, but for very specific information.

What were the Alpha Legion doing, and what did they know?

Those questions were now the unknown edges of her calculations. Without answers she could not extend her projections. Without answers she could not sense the potential of any of her actions.

She now knew something of what the Iron Warriors were doing and what they were hiding, but that data only became useful if she knew who else knew that secret.

So she had begun a separate operation to get an answer from the Alpha Legion, and she had used the only lure she could: herself.

She opened her eyes and found that the shaft above her was still alight. Liquid fire clung to the shaft walls. A second later the shaft walls disappeared, and she was falling towards a black mirror of water under the roof of a rock cavern. She cut her speed before she hit the water. As the water closed over her she heard the voices of the surviving members of the team sent to kill her.

'She is still active.'

'Too much noise, we have to pull out, now.'

Three of the kill-team had survived. An acceptable number, more than enough to carry the net-flies that already clung to them under the edges of armour, and in the folds of weapon pouches.

'Send a signal, termination failed.'

'She is good,' said one of them, a bitter edge of admiration in her voice.

'Yes,' said the other. 'Too good.'

As she sank deeper into the sump water, Iaeo smiled.

*Governor Militant Dellasarius died as the fire tide guttered in the skies of his world. He had been old before he had come to Tallarn, and had grown two decades older before the Iron Warriors killed the world that was his to protect. The Great Crusade had taken his strength, hollowing his cheeks, and pulling his liver-spotted skin tight over his skull. When he moved it was with the click of augmetic support, and he breathed with the hiss of pumps. In the moulded muscle of his armour he looked like a corpse left to shrivel and dry on the battlefield. He was not a kind man. The Great Crusade had not needed kind men. He was a warrior, and while the loyalists on Tallarn were a patchwork of factions and power, he was the keystone that held them together.*

*Perhaps it was because in the first months after the bombs fell he had spoken not of survival, but of striking back, of vengeance. Perhaps it was simply force of will. Perhaps it was because he was there, and people needed someone to follow. No matter the cause, he had become the father of the raiding war, and then the broker between the reinforcements that came later.*

*From the fortress of the Rachab, Dellasarius had pulled together the* scattered regiments, households, maniples of Titans, and warbands of the Legiones Astartes and created forces that had marched together. His voice and gaze cowed generals, persuaded Legion captains and arch magi to put aside their vision of victory, and accept his. If he slept, none of his aides saw it. He haunted the Rachab's central strategium through every cycle of day and night. Data-slates, and scrolls of logistical reports and battle plans followed him in drifts.

Not all agreed with him. Many believed that his strategies would do nothing but bleed the loyalists of strength. There were even some who voiced that opinion, and some that argued it to his face. But that did not matter. What were a few rogue voices amongst so many that were happy to agree, or at least stay silent? None could doubt his conviction, and against the man that the Tallarn-born called 'Ishak-nul', their 'promise of vengeance', what could they do?

Everywhere he went a company of guards followed. All were Tallarn-born. All ordinary people before the death of their world had remade them. They watched their master, following him like tattered ghosts clad in patchwork colours of a dozen regimental fatigues, When asked why he favoured these ragged citizens-turned-soldiers, he replied that he owed them vengeance for their world, and that he trusted them to make sure that he lived to see that vengeance fulfilled.

On the morning before the Inferno Tide washed the skies he declared that he would journey south to the Crescent Shelter. He had made such journeys twice before, never announcing them until an hour before he would move. His Tallarn-born company would go with him, their war machines bracketing his Baneblade. On each previous occasion he had arrived at his destination.

The true dawn was breaking over the mist-veiled land. The fire tide lingered as an oily tint to the light which streaked through the fog. Running in tight formation Dellasarius's convoy was moving at combat speed over a series of ridges to the north of the plains of Khedive. Just as the Governor Militant's Baneblade crested a rise the Vanquisher riding directly in front of it slowed suddenly, rotated its turret and fired a shell into the Baneblade. The distance was no more than forty metres, and the shell struck the Baneblade's belly armour just as it showed above the ridge line. The shell stabbed into the hull and hit the central ammo hoppers. The turret blew off. The Vanquisher lasted five more seconds before the guns of its comrades killed it in turn.

As the news passed through the loyalists, one question followed in its wake: how could this happen?

And the truth that settled in the growing panic was that no one knew.

# TEN

**Suspicion**
**Storm ghosts**
**Kill-space immersion**

'WHY ARE YOU here?'

Kord kept his eyes steady on the questioner. She had identified herself as Brigadier-Elite Sussabarka, and the chromed pins of her uniform echoed that claim. Her face was as lean as it was hard, narrowing from cropped dark hair to a pointed chin, by way of dark eyes and a thin mouth. He had spent most of his life in and around the men and women who fought the Emperor's wars and defended his conquests; he had seen officers, soldiers and warriors of every stripe, and felt he could judge the nature of another in a few minutes. It had not taken that long with Brigadier-Elite Sussabarka; he had her typed as soon as she had stepped through his cell door: hard, clever, not to be underestimated.

Kord let out a breath and brought his hands up to run them across his mouth. The chains rattled from the manacles circling his wrists. The cell was small, a single cot crammed into a box of rockcrete, and sealed behind a heavy plasteel door. It had been... he was not sure how long it had been since he had climbed from *War Anvil* to a waiting circle of gun muzzles. They had fed him and let him sleep before starting this; at least for that he was relieved if not grateful.

He looked up at the brigadier, whose eyes were steady on his face. Menoetius stood just behind her. The Iron Hand's armour filled the cramped space with a buzz like active engines and electricity. He had said nothing since the pair had entered, but just watched and listened. Of the two Kord found the Space Marine's silence and stillness by far the most disturbing. He looked back at Sussabarka.

'We were attacked somewhere to the south. We lost most of our–'

'I did not ask how you are here. I asked why.'

'We were not an extended patrol.'

'You are Colonel Silas Kord, commander of the reborn Seventy-First, latterly of the Seventy-First Tallarn?' Her expression added the words 'mongrel, and scrap regiment' without her needing to say them. 'Operating out of the Crescent Shelter complex?'

'Yes,' he said.

'Then why, colonel, are you nearly a thousand kilometres from the Crescent Shelter? And why were your units recorded as lost over eight weeks ago?' She said the words softly, stepping forward, so that she could lean down to speak to him close to his face. 'The Tallarn Seventy-First was deployed on a standard extended sweep patrol. It should have been back under earth and all of its crew tucked up forty-eight hours later, but none of them came back. No signals received, nothing. Another patrol found the wreck of an Executioner from the Seventy-First a week later. I had to monopolise some of our very limited signal capacity to confirm this. So that leads us back to the question of why you are here.'

She kept her head close to him, as if waiting to catch a whisper. Kord said nothing for a moment. He remembered the *Crow Call* peeling away from them when he had given the choice of following, or returning to the shelter. So none of them lived, not even those who had refused to follow him. He refocused his thoughts on the present. The brigadier wanted answers. He could not fault that need, even if he did not like her. The truth, though, was something that he was sure would not help take the chains from his wrists.

'We strayed off course, couldn't find our way back. Then we got hit, and we headed here because we heard there was a shelter.'

'A shelter?' She stood up, the disbelief in her voice and on her face too sharp to be feigned. 'You know what this is, don't you?' He shrugged, and glanced back at Menoetius. The Space Marine did not seem to respond. 'It is the Rachab, the Buried Mountain, stronghold of the Governor Militant, and the last place that a missing unit from the surface should stumble over. If we lose this battle, this will be the last place to fall. Making sure of that is my duty. Six days ago the Governor Militant was assassinated out in the world above by people who were supposed to be above suspicion. So, you see, Colonel Kord,' she crouched down, and leaned back in so that he could smell the recaff on her breath. 'I do not like nomads stumbling onto our doorstep with lies on their tongues.'

'We simply came for shelter.'

She smiled, a crooked slash of teeth under her gun-barrel eyes.

'I spoke to a colonel on the Crescent Command Staff. A man called Fask. The only reason he could plausibly think for someone called Kord being this far off his mark was if he were chasing some theory about a ghost patrol and patterns of enemy action. He said that if that was what had brought Kord here and cost him all but two machines of his command, that it would be kind to shoot him now.' She folded the smile back into a hard line. 'But that is only if you are who you say you are, and not... something else. Either way I do not like your answers.'

Kord dipped his head, took a breath, and rubbed his thumbs against his eyelids. Coloured smudges bloomed in the brief blackness. When he looked up Sussabarka was looking down at him, expectation held in her stare

'We were attacked to the south...' he said. The brigadier let out a sigh, and gave a small shake of her head then turned, and rapped on the door. It opened and Kord saw the guard standing on the other side of the threshold. The brigadier took a step through, turned and looked back at Kord.

'I do not need to hear the truth, even if you decide to tell it to me,' she said. 'Whether you are a spy, or just a renegade, the answer will be the same. You will have time to think about that. All the time there is in fact.' She stepped out of the cell. A moment later Menoetius followed. Just before the door sealed again, Kord saw the Iron Hand look back at him, a look that he could not begin to read in the flint-grey eyes.

'Arm,' he commanded.

The guns of the Cyllaros armed. Hrend felt it as soon as he said it, a hot blurred feeling spreading through him. For an eye-blink he thought he felt the rounds snap into breeches, and charges into focus chambers, in every weapon in every remaining machine. He tried to ignore the feeling. They spread out slowly. Hrend walked forward.

Sand and dust rattled against his iron skin. Above him the dust storm rose from the dun-coloured ground to the azure sky. Seen with clear sight it was a rolling cliff the colour of rust and snow. Flashes of lightning scored through its core. Hrend could feel the charge within it itching his sensors.

'You see them?' he asked.

'*Yes*,' Jarvak replied.

The dust and scoured rocks shifted like snow beneath his tread. The wind was rising. Snakes of dust were sliding across the ground. He kept his gaze on the storm wall. His weapons were ready. They had been ready from the moment he had seen the ghosts in the storm. At first he had thought they were simply shadows in the storm, scattered images created by the churning dust. Then one had briefly solidified into the shape of a tank, its silhouette swallowed as soon as it had appeared. Then he had seen more, each one a different size and in a different place, but every time he saw them they were closer.

'*I have no sensor readings.*'

'*We should fire.*'

'Hold.' He spoke the word as much for himself as the others. His world narrowed to the threat markers tracking the oncoming shapes. His weapon systems felt warm. He shifted. The fingers of his fists clacked shut and opened. He did not register the movement. The guns that were part of him were aching. 'Hold,' he said again.

'*It could be an entire army group,*' said a voice he could not identify. It did not matter. All that mattered was the building pain around the muzzles of his guns.

'*All the more reason not to shoot.*' That was Jarvak. At least he thought… He forced a thought to form in his mind.

'Signal them,' he growled.

'*Unknown units identify yourselves.*' The ghost shapes grew in the rolling wall of dust, shapes hardening into hulls of war machines, into gun barrels, and tracks.

'Do we fire?'

'Hold.' The heat was bleeding through him.

'Do we fire?'

Fire… Fire… Fire… The word echoed and rolled through him, like a drumbeat, like a heartbeat that had become his.

Fire…

The metal of his bones was aching. There was lightning under his skin. He was nothing. He was half a being, an empty skin hung like a banner in a dry wind.

Fire… We only live… in fire…

*And above him a black sun hung in the half-dream of his thoughts, scattering light that cast no shadow. It grew, swelling, and bloating, and he had to fire, had to allow the shadow of destruction to become part of the world. The black sun swallowed him and he was…*

Standing before the memory of Perturabo.

'You will be given a… guide, to lead you, and your cadre will go with you, but you will be alone.' The hard edge had returned to Perturabo's voice, and his eyes had seemed to sink back into the stillness of his face. 'There are eyes within our allies that watch us, and look for weakness in us. They are all around us, never blinking, never sleeping.' The primarch turned and began to move away as one the Iron Circle moved to enclose him. 'They cannot know of this. Even those that go with you should know only what they need. No other, even those within the Legion, may know what you do for me.'

'*I will find it, my master.*'

'*Others looked. Others failed.*'

'*I will not fail.*'

'*Unknown units identify yourselves.*' Jarvak's challenge rang across the vox. The image of his father was gone. The black sun was gone. He felt nothing, the embrace of his metal body cold without sensation. For an instant he felt loss. The dust wind was streaking past, swallowing the edges of everything in sight. The cliff-face of the storm was above, its crest flickering with dry lightning. The ghosts advancing with the storm were no longer ghosts, they were war machines of the Legiones Astartes. Three machines rolled forward as though riding with the wind, a Venator, a Sicaran and the slope-fronted slab of a Land Raider. Their armour was metallic blue, the edges of their armour plates rubbed to bright metal. Etched serpents reared across their plates. Numerals and archaic letters ran in neat rows down white bands painted along their flanks. Hrend did not recognise the unit markings or even the organisational structure they conformed to. But he recognised who they were.

They were scions of the last born: Alpha Legion.

The three Alpha Legion vehicles halted. Hrend switched to infra-sight in time to see that their weapons were hot, held at full charge.

'*Harrow Group Arcadus, Twentieth Legion.*' The voice came over the vox, filled with a pop and snarl of distortion. '*We see you, brothers.*'

'*Signal identifiers confirm,*' said Jarvak. Hrend said nothing, watching as heat bled into the surrounding air from the Alpha Legion tanks. The wind gusted and the ochre swirl of dust enveloped them. The sky above was gone, and with it the sun.

'How are you here?' he asked at last.

'*May I not ask the same question first, ancient?*' came the reply, the voice smooth and confident.

'I am not of the ancients,' he replied.

'*My apologies. I am Thetacron. Who do I address?*'

'How are you here?' he repeated.

Hes-Thal's sight had guided them on through desolation after the battle of the pass. They had not seen even the signs of the dead for a very long time. In his sight the targeting runes blinked between red and amber above the three Alpha Legion machines, the words of Perturabo rising from memory.

*There are eyes within our allies that watch us, and look for weakness in us. They are all around us, never blinking, never sleeping.*

'We hit an enemy patrol on the other side of this depression,' said the voice which had named itself Thetacron. Casual arrogance dripped from his tones. 'We are moving back across towards a hold position.'

'You move with the storm?' asked Jarvak.

'We are the storm.'

Hrend pivoted his head. Data from his sensors flickered as they tried to claw detail from the swirl of charged dust.

'You can navigate through it?'

'Of course,' Thetacron replied, paused, then carried on. 'From the damage I can see on your machines, you must have taken casualties. We also are below strength. Where are you bound?'

A line of lightning cracked above them, turning the ochre swirl to sheet white.

Hrend could feel the tension in the situation itching against his instincts.

'South,' he said.

'With the storm wind,' said Thetacron. 'We share a path. We will join with you.'

'Master?' Jarvak's voice cut through the vox, low, insistent.

'If you wish to keep moving through the storm we can guide you.'

The moment lengthened, and the wind tugged sheets of dust across them.

'That is acceptable,' he said.

'Master…'

'Good,' said Thetacron. 'You are the greater strength, you have our command. Who is it that we have the honour of following?'

'I am Hrend,' he said.

ARGONIS'S PRISON WAS a cube of plasteel, without seam or rivet. He had entered through a single door as thick as tank armour, and had heard a cascade of locks turn when it closed. Air seeped in and out from holes around the door no wider than a child's finger. They had taken his armour, of course, and left him with a robe of grey fabric. Water and nutrition paste came through tubes mounted on the door, though he could have lived without both for many months. The door had remained shut since he had entered, and he had no reason to suppose that it would open again. They were watching him though. A pict-lens and sensor blister sat behind a crystal dome at the centre of the ceiling.

He supposed that this state of isolation might have caused panic, or the mind to begin to eat itself with uncontrolled emotion. For Argonis, his mind became focused, his emotions stilled.

The mysteries that had made him allowed no other response. He had failed, but while that weighed on his thoughts it was secondary. First and foremost he had to plan, had to find a way of turning this situation. That there was hope of doing so did not matter. Hope was one thing that he did not need to live.

They had not killed him. Deceiving the Warmaster was one thing, killing his emissary was another. The fact that they had resisted crossing that line implied that this was not treachery in the simple sense. If Perturabo had intended to move against Horus in the future, killing his representative would have been a simple thing. Holding him prisoner held more risk, but also opened the implication that Perturabo wanted to keep what he was doing secret from the Warmaster now. There were many possibilities as to why that might be, but one stood out more clearly than all the rest as Argonis considered them.

*They have not succeeded in whatever their true purpose on Tallarn is, and if the Warmaster knew that purpose he might stop them before it was complete.*

What that purpose was remained unknown, a shape suggested by the few details that Sota-Nul had told him before they were taken.

*Black Oculus, ghost patrols, path seekers...* the words resonated with implication but without clear conclusion. He thought of the words that Maloghurst had spoken to him before he had left the *Vengeful Spirit.*

*Horus had not been present, but his throne with its empty chair had loomed in Argonis's awareness as though his gene-father had been sitting there, silent, his eyes turned away in reproach.*

*'Find out what they are doing,' Maloghurst had said, looking down at him from beside the empty throne.*

*'Cannot we just ask?' Argonis had kept his voice respectful, but he had pointedly not bowed his head to the Equerry. He might speak for the primarch, but he was not Horus, and Argonis had been one of Abaddon's chieftains for more than enough time to find making obeisance to Maloghurst a line that he would not cross, even now.*

*'We can ask, but there are answers and answers.'*

*'The Lord of Iron has always been stalwart in his backing for the Warmaster.'*

*'He has, but we live in times when presumption is as dangerous as cowardice.' Maloghurst left the word hanging at the tail of his words. Argonis felt the muscles tick in his jaws. 'Besides, this engagement of his is sucking in and spending forces at a rate which must be justified. It is a hungry battle he is fighting, and we are fighting a war in which we cannot let such strength be spent blindly.'*

*'What do you suspect?'*

*'Suspect?' A rattling smile had been in that word. 'I suspect nothing. I fear everything. That is my great virtue. Find out what they are doing there, and why.'*

*'If the reason is simple?'*

*'Then impress on them that this battle cannot last for all time.'*

*Argonis had wanted to shake his head. It was not that he was being sent on a mission that was so clearly a punishment concealed in an honour, it was that it felt dirty, tainted by subterfuge. After all that had happened, all the bonds of brotherhood severed, and the blood on all their hands, such a sense perhaps should not have mattered to him. It did matter to him, though. It mattered a great deal.*

*Maloghurst had watched him with wet, pale eyes while the instincts of honour and obedience warred behind Argonis's face.*

*'This is the Warmaster's will?' he asked at last.*

*'To the letter and word.'*

'And if there is… something else, some reason that is not simple?'

'Bring them to heel,' said Maloghurst.

Argonis had been able to hide the disbelief on his face. How was he supposed to bring a system-killing force, led by a primarch, to heel?

Maloghurst had heard both the disbelief and the question in Argonis's silence, and his eyes had sparkled cold, as he raised a hand and a pair of figures had drifted from the shadows. They had come to a halt beside Maloghurst: a black-robed spectre, and a green-robed man with a head locked in iron. Maloghurst had raised his other hand. Between his armoured fingers he held a key with twisted teeth.

'You will not go alone,' he had said.

Argonis thought of the key, taken along with his weapons and armour. Sota-Nul and Prophesius too, taken and imprisoned, or so he presumed. He would need them both, if he was to complete the mission his primarch had given him. It was not in his nature to accept the possibility of failure, but as the time had passed in the cell he had felt its presence growing in his awareness.

'This is a chance, Argonis,' Maloghurst had said, as he had handed him the standard of the Eye of Horus. 'A chance for forgiveness, or oblivion. Which will it be?'

IAEO BLINKED. IT was the closest she came to rest now.

Rest, what even was that? She had suppressed so many of the physical elements of severe fatigue that both exhaustion and rest existed only as concepts, terms to apply or not. She was fairly sure that the taste of blood in her mouth related to the presence of one, and the absence of the other, but she was not going to examine that data.

She could not rest, not now. She barely moved except to shift location, and she had taken the risk of not doing that several times now. There was just too much to process, too many lines of manipulation, of observed effect, and recalculation. She could not step away from it for even a second.

Half of the battle-scape of Tallarn breathed in and out of her subconscious. She had taps into the Iron Warriors communications, into the Alpha Legion's communications, she saw her enemies and they did not see her. She had even re-tasked a portion of the Iron Warriors communication system to leech data and signals from the loyalists. It was the finest data harvest she had created. With a blink she could see the operative called Jalen, with another blink she could read the reports of Jalen's operatives. There were holes, true, but what was art without imperfection? She had heard that once she was sure, but she could not remember where. She had suppressed a lot of extraneous memories recently. It did not matter, the point still stood.

It was beautiful. A few simple bare facts. A mission sent here, a location signal there, a report here, all circling ignorance like water draining into a hole. Fear, and defiance, and hope. People were supposed to be unpredictable, but they were not, they really were not. If you could see what they knew, their responses became like the directions of ships under sail.

Something wet rolled down from her nose in the physical world she was ignoring. It touched her lips. It tasted the same as the blood already in her mouth.

She had been wrong. Not wrong in her calculations, but wrong in her mission objective. It had been too narrow, too direct, too tame. The possibility she had sensed when Argonis and his witch discovered the Black Oculus Navigators was no longer a possibility. It was the primary target, and it was achievable, the calculations confirmed it.

She wondered if any being on the system knew the truth, besides her. Perturabo of course, but even he did not see as she did. Not now. This was her battle now. Her song.

She narrowed her awareness, focusing down on a few spurs of possibility. It just needed a shift, a little panic, a little desperation.

And there, shining like a silver fish cutting through dark water, was a beginning.

It was a simple signal. The layers of ciphers encoding it had baffled the Iron Warriors, but Iaeo had broken it by simply taking the key encoding from the Alpha Legion.

'*Iron Warriors sweep force under command of Hrend moving north towards Media Depression.*' A location code was embedded with the words.

She smiled, and the movement nudged a bead of still-liquid blood onto her tongue. The signal had yet to reach the Alpha Legion, and now it never would. She formed the signal which would, slowly taking her time over each phrase.

'*Iron Warriors sweep force under command of Hrend lost. Advise use of Imperial assets to intercept. Strong indications that they are closing the artefact. Advise use of all means to isolate and terminate this force.*'

She paused after she composed the signal. It would be the last to come from the force trailing Hrend and his machines. Even if they sent more they would never be heard. This was it, their last word.

She nodded to herself, and loosed the signal. She would have to shift location soon. She could see Jalen now, could predict him and his attempts to shut her down, but part of her still remembered that she needed to be alive to function. She would move, she would, but not yet. She wanted to watch for a little longer.

# PART THREE
# TERMINATION

Discord and desperation almost ended the Battle of Tallarn. The Governor Militant's death cracked the old fractures in the loyalists wide. Though Dellasarius had not been their leader he had been a pivot around which the battle moved, a stone that even the wildest currents of dissent had to flow around. Now he was gone, and every officer, hetman, demi-admiral, commander and captain saw the future differently. Some wanted to withdraw forces from the planet entirely, and make the battle one fought in the void alone. Others wanted to attack the Sightless Warren immediately, others argued for a return to the hit-and-run tactics of the battle's early phases.

The leaders of some factions did not even venture an opinion on a combined strategy. They simply began to take action. Myrmidax Kravitas Beta-Prime left the surface, their landing craft swarming up into the high atmosphere to create footholds in the charred remains of dead ships and gutted weapon platforms. A ragged company of war machines took to the world above, and began attacking any other machines they came across. Mesucon, Siridar Count of House Megron, formed a banner of fifteen Knights and struck to the southern polar marches in search of enemies. And more went their own ways, either to a battlefield of their own making, or to a grave made by their wilfulness. And the arguments raged on, echoing in the command chambers of the fortress shelters and across the vox connecting them. For some the conviction that they were right drove them to argue, for others the fears inside led them to see death and failure in every alternative put in front of them.

One man ended the discord. He was called Gorn. He had come to Tallarn with the rank of general, but for years had nothing to command. Caught on Tallarn when Horus's rebellion ignited he had waited as the war ignored him. Then the Iron Warriors had come and given him a war. In the days which followed the bombardment Gorn had been amongst the first to contact other shelters, and to begin to coordinate a response. His name was known by all, as was his reputation. A hard man, they said. Hard to like, and harder not to respect. He had taken to the surface thirty times, returning each time with at least one personal machine kill. A breech failure in one of those sorties had gouged scars across his jaw and down his neck. He had said nothing throughout the long hours of argument. The best accounts agree that he broke that silence with three words.

'Horus will win.'

At first few heard him, and those that did discarded his words. Later, there would be as many different accounts of what happened next as there were war machines on Tallarn. A few say he drew his weapon. Some even say he killed the next three people who spoke.

'Horus will win,' he shouted.

Silence echoed after those words and, after a lone minute of shock, he spoke into that silence.

'We will fail. Tallarn will fall. Traitors and rebels will pour through this gate to Terra, and Horus will win this war. He will win, and his victory will begin because here, on this world, we failed. That is certainty. That is undoubtable truth. If we allow it to be. We end this here. We have that power, we simply have lacked the will.'

When challenged on how victory could now be achieved, Gorn is said to have pointed up to the shelter's ceiling and beyond that to the sky of the land above.

'The heavens are clear. We bring all of our strength to the surface, all of it, no matter the cost. We drown this world in iron. We force the Lord of Iron to meet us up there in the open.'

'Why would he do such a thing?' a voice asked

'Because once he sees what we are doing he will see a chance to break us utterly. He will see a chance for victory, and a chance of defeat if he does not.'

Objections came, declarations of madness, of foolish bravado, of the logistical elements which would mean that armies of that size could not be controlled effectively, how there would not be enough supplies to keep them in the field for more than a few days… and the muttered dismissals and words of disbelief swelled.

Then one voice asked a different question.

'Where?' asked someone. 'Where would you make this battle?'

And, as though they had suddenly been captivated by the dream of an end, the commanders of Tallarn waited for Gorn to answer.

Gorn indicated the great flat expanse at the heart of Tallarn's northern continent.

'Khedive,' he said. 'On the plains of Khedive.'

# ELEVEN

### Belief
### Cthonian truth
### Error

THE TIME PASSED in the dimming and brightening of the cell's only light. Kord slept, and ate, and let his dreams take him. He saw Jurn again, saw the hinterlands around the coast cities, the fields waving in the summer wind. He saw old friends, and heard old words of hurt and love that he had forgotten. He saw his father, gone to the dirt long before Kord had taken the silk ribbons of service and gone to be a soldier. And when he woke the dreams clung to his thoughts like words blown into the present from the past. He began to live for the dreams, but to dread the waking. He counted each time he slept until the numbers frayed in his mind, and the point seemed to be lost. He wondered what had become of the rest of his crew, if they too turned through the circle of sleep and waking just as he did. He wondered what future he had led them to.

Then, in a gap between dreaming, the door to the cell opened. Kord looked up expecting to see a guard. The face of a demi-god looked back at him. Menoetius stepped through the door, and it locked behind him.

'I wish to speak to you,' said the Iron Hand.

'Then speak,' replied Kord, not breaking eye contact, not showing fear, even though it was crawling through his guts.

'You have met our kind before.'

'Yes, I fought on Oscanis with some of your kin.'

'I have not heard of that war.'

'Most wars are unknown to someone.'

'Why were you out on the world above? I ask this, not the Brigadier-Elite.'

'But you are here by her authority.'

'By my own.'

'She commands here though?'

'If you have seen us in war you know that we are our own authority.'

'I have, and I know that warriors of the Tenth Legion rarely ask questions to learn answers.'

'Then why do we ask questions?'

'To confirm knowledge.'

Menoetius nodded slowly.

'You were following an Iron Warriors formation across the edge of the Khedive. The enemy was light strength, alone, and without deep support. A hunter patrol your commanders call them. But they were not hunters. They were something else.'

'Seekers.'

'That is what you believe?'

'Yes.'

'Why?'

'Do you remember where you were born, Menoetius?' Kord thought he saw the shadow of a frown on the Iron Hands Commander's face. 'I do. I remember the house where I grew up. I remember the smell of the food my grandfather cooked. I remember the red and blue cups I played with before I could speak. I remember leaving it. I remember the doors of the landing craft closing on the light of my last morning. I remember realising that everything I had known would only be a memory from then on. I knew what I was doing. I knew that I would not go back. It was a choice. A sacrifice.'

'You believed in something greater.' Menoetius nodded.

'I believed that I could be part of something greater, that what I would do, and everything that would happen, mattered… That everything has a purpose.'

'And you still believe that?'

'Yes,' said Kord. 'I still believe that there is a reason for everything even if we cannot see it. I have to believe that.'

'Why?'

'Otherwise there is nothing but chance laughing at us.'

'You killed those under your command,' said Menoetius, his voice the flat hammer of stated truth. 'You allowed what you believe to draw you on, and if you felt any doubts, you put them aside, and so you led them to death.'

Kord felt the muscle harden in his jaw, the heavy warmth as blood flushed to his muscles. He returned the stare.

'Yes,' he replied.

Menoetius nodded, and something in the grey skin of his face changed. Kord had the strange feeling that the Iron Hand Commander's had just passed some kind of judgement.

'But you do not ask for forgiveness. You do not think you were wrong?'

Kord dropped his gaze for the first time. He thought of the ambush, of the sound of shrapnel ringing from *War Anvil*'s hull. He thought of Augustus Fask's red, fat face.

'No,' he said at last, looking back at Menoetius. 'No I was, and am, right. There is a reason all this is happening, and no one wants to see it.'

Menoetius blinked, slowly, and then nodded again.

'Those that followed you died because of failures. Some of those failures are yours, some of them their own. Life exists because of strength, the strength to move from the present into the future. Life ends when strength fails. You did what you knew you had to. You followed what you knew was right. They failed as much as you. Their death does not make what you believe false.'

Kord did not know what to say. It was the most he had ever heard an Iron Hand legionary say. There was something else as well, a feeling that Menoetius was not talking about him at all.

'How did you come here, Menoetius?' He was not sure why he asked, just that it was the right question to ask.

'From Isstvan.'

Kord nodded.

'Thank you for the conversation.'

Menoetius frowned for the first time. 'This was not a conversation. I simply wished you to understand what will happen now.'

He stood, and turned for the door. Kord did not move. Menoetius knocked on the door and it opened. He looked back at Kord.

'Come with me.'

Kord hesitated, and then rose and stepped towards the door. He could see the guard on the other side of the open door, his hand hesitating as it reached for his weapon. Menoetius's hand barely seemed to move. Stillness filled the outer chamber.

'This is not your duty,' said the Iron Hand Commander to the guard, his voice low. Kord felt the instinct to run shiver down his limbs. 'This man passes from here as I pass. Do you understand?' The guard nodded slowly. 'You will comply.' The guard nodded again. Menoetius let his hand drop from where it had rested on the man's arm. He turned away and walked from the chamber into the corridor beyond. After a second Kord followed. When he glanced back he saw that the guard was still shaking.

'Where are you taking me?' he asked. Menoetius growled, or perhaps it was a low laugh.

'To find the truth,' he said.

Hrend walked with the storm. Around him the Iron Warriors and Alpha Legion machines kept in close formation. The rattle of dust stole the sound of tracks and engines. Within the storm there was no day, no night, just the crackle of signals holding them together as they pushed on. Questions walked with Hrend, voices that asked him what he was doing, and all the while the call of the black sun rose and fell in him like a tide.

Thetacron and the other Alpha Legion machines said next to nothing. Once they had advised Hrend to call a halt in the lee of a crag of rock, saying that the storm would not let them continue for now. Hrend had agreed, and they had clustered together, a string of wind-scoured iron and azure blue. An hour later the dust gloom had become a strobing cauldron of lightning. Great dry booms of thunder shook the ground and air. It had lasted for a full day, and even when it had passed the storm remained. Hrend imagined the storm front circling the land, gathering dust and strength like a serpent eating its own tail. Once the lightning tide passed they had carried on, pressing on in silence through a never-ending veil.

With every step the black sun seemed closer. He did not sleep any more, but the dreams chased him without pause. He dreamed of Olympia. He dreamed of the world within the Eye of Terror. He dreamed of burning, of his flesh becoming slime inside his armour. He should have died then. He should have died again, up in the valley beneath the pass, with the snow of a dead world as his shroud. Yet he lived, and tried not to think how the damage to his frame had seemed to heal like flesh, how he could sometimes feel the wind blow over him, even though his skin was nothing but plasteel and ceramite. He thought he could hear laughter in the rattle of dust against metal.

When the first men had brought iron from the fire, and put an edge to the first blade, they had created this strength. And it was a strength that could not exist without its twin. What was a blade without the blood it drew? What was armour without the blow that rang upon it? They were strong, and he was strong, and that strength would not be allowed to fail. It would live as only iron could live: in blood.

'*Master,*' Jarvak broke his thoughts. '*The Navigator has–*'

'Change the frequency,' growled Hrend. Just beside him, close enough to touch, the serpent-etched hull of the Alpha Legion Land Raider kept pace with him. The vox rattled as it jumped between channels.

'*The Navigator has begun to speak.*'

'He has spoken before.'
'He speaks without pause.'
'What is he saying?'
'He says the gate of the gods draws near.' Hrend felt cold flicker through limbs he no longer had. 'He says that the black sun rises.'
'We follow where he leads,' said Hrend.
'What of our... allies?'
'They must know nothing.'
Beside him the Alpha Legion machines swept on in silence.

THE LIGHTS IN Argonis's cell cut out. The spiral of thoughts in his head vanished. He came to full readiness, muscles poised, every sense open. For a handful of seconds there was silence. Then he heard a sound, low, vibrating from far away even before it passed through the steel and into his skull. The sound grew louder and louder, and went silent. He heard feet clang on metal flooring, just outside. Then something heavy fell against the door, and rattled down its surface. He yanked himself back into the cell as the locks within the door clattered open, and it swung outwards.

He was ready, crouched low on the floor below the eyeline of someone standing in the doorway.

'Come with me, emissary,' said Jalen. 'There is not much time.'

Argonis lifted Jalen from his feet, and slammed him into the door frame. The human gagged, hands rising on instinct to the fingers around his throat.

'Be still,' growled Argonis, as he glanced into the corridor beyond. An Iron Warrior lay beneath the door, hands still gripping a bolt-gun. Smoke filled the space beyond, coiling in the silent flashes of alert lights. He reached down, and pulled the bolter from the Iron Warrior's grip. He took a slow breath. The scent and taste of the air spoke of weapon fire, of melta-charge detonations and overloaded wiring. There was something else too, a tingle of sweet sugar scent on the edge of his senses. He looked down at the supine Iron Warrior, and at the man pinned by his hand to the wall. Jalen looked back at him, his eyes cold and without fear.

'One twitch of witchcraft, and you die,' he said.

'Why would I do that, when I have gone to such trouble to free you? And what makes you think I did all this alone?'

An armoured figure stepped out of the smoke haze. He wore metallic blue battleplate and had a volkite charger levelled at Argonis. His eyes were cold green lenses in a beaked helm. He looked relaxed, as though he had just wandered onto the scene, as if he were almost bored by it. Argonis had seen that air before, and knew that to consider it weakness would be a fatal mistake.

Argonis nodded. The blue-armoured warrior did not shift his aim. Argonis let go of Jalen. There was nothing else to do. For the next few minutes he did not care why the Alpha Legion was here. All that mattered was getting clear of the cell. A strict hierarchy of needs applied to his next actions. He had a weapon, but he needed armour, his own by preference, then he needed the tech-witch, and most importantly he needed Prophesius. After that he would find a way to Perturabo.

'The others?' snapped Argonis.

'Down the passage, fifty metres left, then twenty metres right. Doors should release but only for the next four minutes. Route was clear as of sixty-one seconds ago.'

Argonis folded out of the door, and began to move down the smoke-filled corridor, keeping low and hugging the walls. Jalen and the Alpha Legion warrior followed, their movements fast and fluid.

He reached Sota-Nul's cell first, and pulled open the door. The figure he saw sketched in the silent pulse of the alert lights was a floating ball of coiled metal limbs and chromed snakes. A pair of what might have been atrophied legs was tucked up against her torso like the bone and skin limbs of a stillborn chick. A blister of optic lenses protruded from the top of the mass. Red light glowed in her many eyes. Chains of lightning held her in place above a humming box of black metal.

He looked at the machine and put three bolt rounds into it. The lightning chains collapsed as the box exploded. Sota-Nul began to fall, and then halted in mid-air. Flesh-metal tentacles unfolded around her.

Argonis turned away.

'Follow,' he said, and began to move again.

Prophesius was unchained in a bare cell, the thrumming dome of a null field above him. Argonis shot out the field projector and the null dome vanished into ozone and smoke. Jalen flinched as the masked astropath stepped forward.

Argonis turned to Jalen.

'Equipment,' he said.

'Fifteen metres left, there is a cache. The door is disabled.' He paused, licked his lips, and a tendril of tattooed scales formed at the corner of his mouth. 'You need to move fast, emissary.'

'What is your plan from here?'

'If you intend to reach Perturabo, you need to get to the *Sickle Blade*. It will be fuelled and prepared for launch.'

'Just like that?'

'A great deal has gone into this operation since you summoned me.'

Argonis's gaze hardened.

'I did not summon you.'

Jalen's face had gone still, his eyes flickering over Argonis's face.

'The signal came through with the activation ciphers given to Horus, and from Horus to you.'

'One of us is lying, and what reason would I have to lie?'

Argonis heard the microscopic noise as the Alpha Legion warrior behind him shifted.

'No,' said Jalen shaking his head. 'There is another possibility...'

'Another possibility?' said Argonis carefully. His bolter was still in his hand, held low at his side. 'What other possibility could there be?'

Argonis turned. The movement was casual, as though he were looking around at the others in the room.

He fired his gun into the thigh of the warrior behind him as he turned. The warrior slammed back, leg armour shattering. Argonis grabbed him as he fell and hugged his head into the boltgun's muzzle. The burst of rounds sawed into the legionnaire's faceplate and tore his head apart. Argonis dropped the corpse, turned, and brought his gun up. Genuine shock split Jalen's face. Clusters of malformed tattoo patterns bloomed and withered there.

'Prophesius,' he said quietly, and the astropath stepped closer. The air took on a storm-pressure edge. Jalen's normally calm eyes flicked up to Prophesius's iron face.

'You lied to us,' said Argonis. 'You lied to us from the start. You have been here since the Iron Warriors were here, amongst them, watching them, leeching secrets. You knew what was happening on this world. Lies layered under lies. How could you be what you are, and not?'

'I…' began Jalen.

'And why did you free us? What are we, a weapon to be used now because something has gone wrong?'

'You sent a signal…'

'Black Oculus, tell me what you know of that.'

'We…' the man was fighting to keep calm. Argonis could feel Prophesius's presence at his shoulder, hot and sharp against his skin. He could see the astropath's iron mask reflected in Jalen's eyes.

'Prophesius,' Argonis said carefully. 'Take it from him.'

The astropath extended a hand, green silk falling back from skeletal fingers tipped with the silver stylus spikes. Frost flashed up Argonis's arm from where he held Jalen's neck. He felt a stab of pain, in his mind. But he was ready for it, and it was weak.

Prophesius's fingers were extending slowly towards Jalen's open eyes.

'You have to stop them,' hissed Jalen. 'They almost have it. We cannot stop them, not now.'

The tips of Prophesius's fingers were a hair's-width from the smooth surface above Jalen's pupil.

'What is this battle for? What are they here for? Why are you here?'

'For a weapon, a weapon of primordial destruction.' Jalen nodded carefully. 'A weapon left here when there were still gods to war in the heavens. That is why my masters came here, and why Perturabo is here now.'

'If you say you were doing this for the Warmaster, I will watch as your eyes are pulled out.'

'We serve Alpharius, and Alpharius is loyal.'

Argonis looked at the man for a long moment then nodded slowly.

'So you *were* lying from the start,' said Argonis.

Argonis brought his boltgun up and fired: one round into each of the eyes, one into the heart.

He paused, looking down at the scattered meat and red liquid which had been the man. After a second he turned away, wiped the blood from his face.

'An unexpected tactical choice,' hissed Sota-Nul.

'If the liar has no tongue then he will tell no more lies.'

'An aphorism I am not familiar with.'

'It is from Cthonia.'

Argonis stepped to the door. If Jalen had not lied about the immediate situation then they now had less than two minutes before the Iron Warriors began to respond to the breakout. He began to run; he needed to reach his armour, and then they needed to get out.

'What is your intention?' asked Sota-Nul.

'We are going to follow Jalen's plan. We are going to get to the Lord of Iron, and we are going to do the Warmaster's will. We are going to call him to heel.'

IAEO WATCHED JALEN die, and shifted a set of variables to fixed values. She felt her face twitch. She was smiling. A sign of pleasure, but she was not conscious of why. Strange, very strange... The operative's death had been almost certain given Argonis's personality structure and the information available to him. He had time to piece together a few basic strings of logic. The Alpha Legion was here, they were concerned with the discovery of secrets, and now they had freed him. He knew that they knew more than they had told him. The response from a warrior conditioned, trained and seasoned in the Sons of Horus was obvious.

She replayed a recording of the execution. Fast and brutal, a killing straight from the gang warrens of Cthonia. The tri-shot obliteration technique was interesting. The descriptions she had read had not conveyed the speed, or mess. Yes, mess, that was the correct phrase. Brain, and blood, and bone, all sprayed across the walls, floor and ceiling. For his part, Jalen had also had little choice. The Alpha Legion had spent a long time trying to contain the Iron Warriors activities on Tallarn, and now he believed that they were about to achieve their true goal. The escalating battle on the plains of Khedive was significant, but to Jalen it was a side show; he believed that they were about to lose a prize they had worked for years to secure. So he had freed Argonis and told him part of the truth in the hope that Argonis would find a way to shut the Iron Warriors down.

Desperation. Such a clean tool when applied. Now she just needed to make sure that...

Something twitched at the edge of her awareness. Her first instinct was to override it. She had been deep in the data/problem/kill-space for a long time now, and had blocked out all but the most basic awareness of her body and environment.

She flicked between net-fly views covering her hiding place. Nothing. There was nothing there.

She went back to the flow of projections.

Stinging cold enveloped her. Needles of pain stabbed into her skull. She felt her teeth clamp together, tasted blood as she bit her tongue. She tried to move, but her limbs were cold and cramped, and invisible fingers of ice were holding her still. A wall of displaced air slammed into her. The duct she was curled in came apart. She fell, limbs still locked in a ball, and hit a metal grate ten metres below her. Bones broke in her back, legs and arms. Her mind fought to divide what was going on into data, and failed. The pain was profound, stronger even than her modified body could cope with, too strong to ignore.

A boot lashed into the base of her back, and she felt something rupture. Hands ripped the digi-needlers from her fingers. The joints popped and detonated fresh pain in her arms.

*Data: Enemy has knowledge of–*

Another kick, this time across her face, ripping the visor from her eyes. Her data projections and thought lines were falling apart, replaced by a vivid awareness that she was bleeding inside, that she could feel splinters of bone in her muscles.

'Come now,' said a smooth and reasonable voice. 'This is just the way this meeting must be, mamzel. You are very capable, and that ability demands respect. See what you are experiencing now as our mark of respect.' She heard steps moving towards her. The metal grating she was lying on shook slightly with each footfall. There was another sound nearby: the soft inhalation/exhalation cycle of one… no, two other people. Hands touched her face. She tried to snap her arms up, to grab, to strike. She could not. Her limbs simply would not move. The fingers felt warm, the tips smooth as they prised her eyelids open.

Light flooded her eyes. She looked up. Huge turbines turned far above. Ducts criss-crossed the air in between. A ragged hole split the underside of a duct ten metres above where she lay. She recognised the effect of adhesive-tipped krak grenades. Beneath her a gantry of gridded metal spanned a rockcrete crevasse. Blackness hid the bottom of the drop. A face moved into view. It was not a smiling face, nor a cruel one, but it was the last face she had expected to see again.

'I know you did not kill him, but I have a suspicion that I should thank you for the death of my brother,' said Jalen.

*Only later would it be called a battle. The need of history to codify, divide and label would eventually mark the start of the Battle of Khedive as beginning two hours before dawn broke over the storm-lashed basin. It would say that its first shots were the torpedoes fired from loyalist* Strike Force Indomitable. *Seen in the cold light of retrospect that moment is as suitable a beginning as any other.*

It began, like so many offensives before it, in the heavens. The Inferno Tide had scoured the lower orbits of Tallarn of ships and defences, but in the high spheres the Iron Warriors still held sway. A circlet of weapon platforms and warships had been set above the Sightless Warren since its creation, guarding its approaches from the void, and watching over the approaches to its northern hemisphere. The Iron Warriors, never needing to set war to poetry, called this cluster Outer Defence 1.

A spill of torpedoes converged on the clustered Iron Warriors ships and stations. Most had been shot days before by ships far from Tallarn's orbits. Their rockets set on delayed triggers, and they had glided close to their targets on momentum alone. By the time their engines lit, it was too late for the Iron Warriors to destroy them. Building-sized munitions slid *through void shields, struck armour, and detonated. Explosives, melta-cores, graviton generators, plasma charges and quake warheads strung the sky with fresh stars. The Iron Warriors frigate* Blood Tempered *died as a string of five torpedoes caught it in a perfect line across its back. The debris and force of its death blew the shields off its sister ships in a flickered blink of white light.*

Strike Force Indomitable *emerged, gliding along high orbits from behind the face of Tallarn. Twelve warships came in the first wave. They were not the heaviest ships the loyalists had in the system, but they were the fastest and most heavily armed. They had a single task: to kick open the door to the planet's northern hemisphere. They began to fire as soon as the first torpedoes found their marks.*

*Beams of las-fire laced the dark. Rushes of plasma formed comets as they boiled across the black gulf. Walls of shellfire spat from vast gun mouths. Kaleidoscope light boiled through the Iron Warriors ships. High orbital platforms split, burned, and began to tumble down the hungering gravity well into Tallarn's embrace. As the first signals shouted from the dying and dead ships, the Iron Warriors ships in the rest of the system moved to respond. Squadrons scattered around the moons of Tallarn turned their prows towards the battle-sphere and burned their engines white.*

Strike Force Indomitable *cut their fire and thrust forwards into the sphere of ruin they had created. They lost three ships in the first moments, split open by guns of the surviving Iron Warriors defences. The rest kept on, dumping macro-cannon fire into every target they could see. Half remained on the thinner edge of space and ripped into the remaining Iron Warrior defences. The second half settled deeper into low orbit, and began to roll fire down onto surface targets. Each captain on each ship knew that a counter-attack would come, that the might of the Iron Warriors would descend to close the sky above the Khedive. That fact was irrelevant, though. They had bought the time they needed.*

# TWELVE

**Vortex**
**Treachery**
**Second head of the Hydra**

'YOU CANNOT DO this.' Brigadier-Elite Sussabarka stood across the door to the muster chamber. A squadron of ten soldiers in crimson-and-grey carapace stood at her side. Kord noticed that they had not raised or pointed their cable-fed lasguns, but he could read the poised readiness in their stances. They were steady, professional, willing to stand with their commander as she stood in the path of a warrior of the Legiones Astartes. They were also intelligent enough not to point a weapon at the Iron Hands legionary.

Menoetius stared at Sussabarka without moving. After a handful of seconds his stillness seemed to seep into the air. Even to Kord it felt like a threat. Sussabarka shifted but did not step back. Her face was a mask, her jaw and gaze set. Kord felt a twinge of admiration in the same instant that he dismissed her defiance as foolish; she would get herself killed if she held strong.

At least that would get her out of the way.

'Stand aside,' said Menoetius, his voice low, like the purr of a vast engine turning over. Kord glanced up at Menoetius. The hum of the legionary's armour was making his eyes ache. Sussabarka caught the gesture with a flick of her eyes, shook her head and began to reply.

'I command–'

'You do not command me.' Menoetius voice was flat, devoid of emotion, carrying nothing but a blunt truth. 'You are strong. You are loyal, and you perform what you see as your duty with the fullness of your spirit. But now you will stand aside.'

One of the crimson-and-grey-clad troopers began to raise his weapon. Sussabarka's hand slammed the trooper in the face, once, hard. He stumbled back, blood running bright from the flattened ruin of his nose. No one else moved. Menoetius had not even moved his eyes. Sussabarka nodded then moved from out of the doorway.

Menoetius bowed his head, slowly.

'My thanks,' he said, and stepped through the doorway into the bright vastness of the muster chamber beyond. Kord flicked a glance at the brigadier. She was looking at him, her face still a mask, but he could feel the disgust in the sharpness of her eyes. He shrugged at her, and stepped after Menoetius.

The muster chamber was larger than even those of the Sapphire or Crescent City Shelters. The ceiling was a distant blur beyond a smog layer turned to white by stab-lights. War machines covered the rockcrete floor, turning the path they walked on a labyrinth of acid- and dust-scoured metal and oiled tracks. People surged between the machines. He passed tank crews, their unsealed enviro-suits hanging around their waists like half-shed skins. Labour teams lugged shells, charge packs and thick ribbons of ammunition. Test-firing engines coughed into the air, and the smell of exhaust fumes scraped the back of his throat. He was walking through a full battle muster.

He looked up and saw two gods of metal staring back at him. The twin Warhounds crouched in scaffold cages, the robes of attendant tech-priests standing out against the mottled grey and yellow of the Titans' skins. The harsh white of welding beams and phosphor cutters strobed from their joints, and manes of sparks fell from their feral heads.

Kord held the gaze of the pair for a second, before turning and hurrying after Menoetius. He suddenly did not like this, not at all; it just did not fit together.

'Where are we going?' he hissed. 'What are you doing?'

'Do you ask those questions because you think they require different answers, or because you don't understand that in these circumstances they are the same thing?' The Space Marine half turned his head, so that the edge of his eye caught Kord. He did not stop walking. 'My counter-questions are rhetorical. You need not reply.' He looked ahead again, in time to change direction, leading them down a gully created by twin lines of siege tanks. Kord began to feel sweat prickling his skin as he tried to keep pace. Menoetius waited a dozen strides before speaking again. 'To answer your query, I am overriding the Brigadier-Elite's authority, freeing you, and setting us both on a course to complete the mission you began.'

Kord shook his head.

'You disagree?' said Menoetius. 'I intend to finish what you began. You can come with us, or you can go back to your cell.'

'This will not finish. There is no way for this to finish,' said Kord. A sudden weight had fallen on his thoughts. He was free, but that freedom was meaningless. It was all meaningless. Right or wrong, he had no way back. The only thing that had pulled him forward, step by step and breath by breath, was gone, and no matter that the Space Marine seemed to share his sight, it did not matter.

'Is your human conviction so weak?'

'I was right. I am right. But that does not mean that we won't die out there with nothing found.'

'All true, if you don't know where to look.'

'No, that does not make sense. Nothing I said could have made you believe me. I did not say enough to persuade her, and I could not have persuaded you.'

'You are correct. My heart was curious, and my mind followed. You did not persuade me.' Menoetius turned a corner and halted so swiftly that Kord almost fell as he followed. 'Your crews did.'

Faces turned towards him. Some he knew; Kogetsu, Shornal, Zade and Saul nodded and gave ragged salutes. There was wariness in their eyes, hollowness too. He wondered how much they were here because they were loyal to him, or if, after everything, they had nothing else. Origo turned and straightened from where he bent over maps, which lay across the top of an ammunition crate. The lead scout bent his head and tapped his knuckle to his mouth, in a gesture that many of the Tallarn-born used in place of a formal salute. His eyes were as dark and calm as ever.

Kord smiled back, and turned to look around the circle of faces. Menoetius was a pace behind his shoulder, and behind him in turn another Iron Hand warrior in scored black plate, face hidden by a slotted faceplate, head distorted by a bulge of optical lenses over the right eye. Both stood motionless, a pair of buzzing statues. After a pause Menoetius stepped forward. The brushed steel fingers of his hand unfolded, and tapped the surface of the map.

'We will go here,' he said. Kord's eyes skated across the lines and colours showing geographical features which now bore only secondary relation to the reality of Tallarn's surface. Hundreds of marks had been made on the page. In part it resembled the map that he had used himself to track sightings of enemy units and engagements, but that creation was a shadow of the data which covered the map's smooth surface. The portion indicated by Menoetius was a dense tangle of markers. Bounded by mountains and crossed by the paths of rivers, which would now be dried or slime-choked channels. 'Hacadia' read the lettering which ran under Menoetius's fingers.

'How have you done this?' he breathed, his eyes still roaming over the information inked across the flattened images of mountains, hills, and plateaus. 'This would take communication and engagement data from across our forces... I could never access such data.'

'But I could, and I have,' said Menoetius. Kord looked up into his gaze. Menoetius nodded once. 'I am the bearer. You are the eyes through which meaning is given.'

He looked back down at the map. It was there, so clear that he thought that if he blinked the map parchment, ammo crates and floor would vanish and just leave the bones of the truth there, laid bare in front of him.

'And what do you see?' he asked without looking up.

'A circle. An end,' said Menoetius. 'Do you not see it, colonel?'

'No,' breathed Kord. The coloured dots and lines were floating in his sight, the data next to them the shadows and planes of ragged curves that rippled out like the currents of water searching for a sink hole. He was right. He had always been right, and now he was seeing it: the image of a hidden reality that he had always known was there, just beyond his ability to see. 'No. I don't see a circle. I see a vortex.'

HREND'S FIST CAME up. If anyone had been watching from outside the pack of machines they would have seen a simple gesture, casual, fluid, like a hand raised in greeting. The meltagun armed and fired in an eye-blink of screaming air and white light. The back of the Alpha Legion Sicaran flashed white. The spear of energy stabbed through armour plates. The tank's turret twitched, like the head of a man feeling the kiss of the knife in his back. Its ammunition core exploded. The hull ripped in two. Hrend had already stopped firing, was already turning, fast as an uncoiling tiger. The blast wave roared over him. The heat soaked into him. His iron frame was his body. There was no split, no difference between him and the roaring hunger of the guns in his flesh.

The other Alpha Legion tank slewed around, guns tracking. A shell flared from the muzzle of its main cannon. Hrend could see it, could see the shell ripple through the air, as though everything had become a tableau stuttering from frame to frame: the white-and-red death flower of the Sicaran, the Alpha Legion Land Raider skidding to a halt, the two Venators positioned to their rear, Orun twisting at the waist to train his guns on the surviving Sicaran. Only a second before everything had been steady, predictable, the blue hulls of the Alpha Legion machines moving beside the grey of the Cyllaros battlegroup.

The Land Raider accelerated away, braked and skidded around. Its assault ramp opened before it halted. Armoured figures scattered from within. Plasma and melta fire streaked from their weapons. The Land Raider began to pull backwards. A purple beam of light burned the ground where the Land Raider had been. The dust wind was a strobing swirl. The Alpha Legion was running forwards, the wind stripping the lacquer from their armour as they moved. They would not live long. The wind would cut through the seals on their armour, and Tallarn's poisoned air would claim them. But until that happened they were still deadly.

Hrend swivelled, brought his hands up to fire. A beam of light struck him. He reeled. Hot white pain was everywhere. It was real, shockingly, overwhelmingly real. Shrieks of static blanked out the voices of his brothers, as though the storm wind had spilled into the vox.

And the black sun was there, like a hole cut in the storm.

'Live,' it whispered, a voice of silken promise, of breaking bones, of wind rattling through dry skulls and the call of carrion. '*Your shadow waits.*'

*No*, he wanted to say. *No...* but the memory of the blood was filling his mouth with iron. The eyes of the Apothecary were looking down into his. They were empty, twin eclipses in the brightness.

'What are you?'

'I... am... Iron...'

'Then live.'

He came forward, blindness falling from his sight. He fired, and fired again, missiles loosed from his back, the boltgun roared in his hands, and there were lights, the bright colour of molten ruin, the shriek of armour shattering, and he was kicking a figure from the ground making it fall like a smashed idol, and his fist was descending, and the sand and sky and stars beyond were screaming back.

He stopped, and the battlefield before him was quiet ruin. The song of iron wove around him, pulsing like the breaths he could no longer take.

*You are iron, child*, said the song. The Alpha Legion machines and troops were gone. Fire and ruin remained where they had been unmade. There were other twisted piles of metal and flame, but

Hrend did not think of them. The fact of them did not matter. What other purpose did it have but to destroy and end?

Something was moving on the ground. He focused, his eyes swimming with the promise of targeting runes. A figure was crawling along the ground towards one of the wrecks. It was burning, flames and fluid rolling over the dust-scoured blue of its armour. Hrend walked to it, looked down, felt the heat and pleading of the strength in his hands.

He kicked the crawling figure over. Green eye lenses looked up at him. Hands reached for weapons that were not there. Hrend placed his foot on the warrior's chest.

'It ends here for you,' he said in the vox.

*'Treachery...'* The voice that replied was a wet rasp. He could hear something broken and seeping in the word.

'You are not the only ones to know its value, son of Alpharius.'

*'You will die out here...'*

Hrend rotated his gaze up. The facts of the situation were slowly filtering into focus. Orun was there, close by, still alive, so was Jarvak and his machine. Crucially, the excavator also endured, its Venator escort clinging close. The storm was whipping the flames from the wrecks into bright spirals. Darkness was falling, the dust and dusk stealing all but the flame light.

He looked back down at the Alpha Legion warrior. He wondered if it was the one called Thetacron; he could not tell from the voice. He extended the smallest portion of force into the foot resting on the warrior's chest. The ceramite creaked with pressure.

'No one knows you are here. The dust storm swallows your signals as well as ours. No warning will reach your masters.'

He paused, and within the soft coldness of his being he felt the question rise into existence.

'How many of my brothers have you murdered out here?'

*'More...'* The warrior paused, heaving a cracked breath. *'More than you will ever know.'*

'How did you know what we came for? How did you know we would seek it?'

At first he thought it was the sound of choking on blood. Then he realised it was a laugh.

'We already knew it was here, Iron Warrior.'

Hrend heard the words, and felt the silence form in the space after its passing. It felt like a lie. It felt like a desperate act of spite, like the last blow of a warrior breed who could never accept that they were not in control, who could not admit that they were not the centre of everything. It felt like it might be truth. He felt the fingers of his fist clack open and shut.

Hrend removed his foot from the warrior.

'And now that you have failed, who else is going to stop us now?'

'We are many.'

'And we...' growled Hrend. 'We are iron.'

He stamped down once. The warrior's head exploded in a spray of shattered iron and pulped skull. Hrend watched the corpse twitch once, and then opened another vox channel.

'Navigator,' he growled, and the panting breath of Hes-Thal answered him. 'It is here, you are certain?'

Hrend had kept his eyes on the blood seeping from the headless corpse into the dust. Already viral agents in the air had begun to reduce the blood and flesh to black sludge.

'You see it, Ironclad,' hissed Hes-Thal. 'And it looks back.'

Hrend felt the instinct to nod. His iron body answered by shivering. He switched the vox to the channel linking him to the crew of the Spartan carrying the Navigator.

'Execute the Navigator,' he said. He did not wait to hear the confirmation. A second later he felt something which had been itching at the back of his skull cease.

'Here, on this ground you will begin.'

The excavator machine rumbled forward, and began to unfold. Stabiliser feet slammed into the ground. Its back hinged upwards, and armoured plates peeled back like corroded insect wings. The drill head slid down towards the ground, teeth rotating, earth scoops rolling backwards over its bulk. Hrend stepped back. Beams of scanning light touched the dry ground, pulsed, swept then vanished. The other machines were moving around the great machine, settling into a circle. The drill teeth began to blur. Hrend watched piston feeds tense, and then the drill head slammed down. Earth fountained into the air, caught on the wind and blended into the billowing cloud. The ground began to tremble. Around him the fires of battle were still burning.

He looked down. The black sun was there, at the back of his sight, a cold presence on his shoulder. The drill was keening as it cut into the skin of Tallarn. He remembered again the conversation with Perturabo, back at the beginning of his quest.

*'There is a weapon on this world, hidden in its heart, or buried in its skin,'* Perturabo had said. *'The eldar call it the Cursus of Alganar. It is an ancient thing, old before Terra gave birth to humanity. It is why we came here, it is why we are still here – a weapon to lay low angels.'* The metal sheen of the primarch's skin had dulled for a second, so that his face seemed dusted with ash. *'I want you to walk the surface of Tallarn, I want you to find it for me.'*

Hrend had felt himself pause, and then gave the only answer he could. *'I will do this.'*

Perturabo had begun to walk away without reply. He had been almost at the edge of the cavern when Hrend asked the question which had been drumming inside his head.

*'Lord.'* Perturabo had half turned, his automaton bodyguards halting with a ripple of overlapping shields. *'When we have it what will we do?'*

The primarch looked at Hrend for a long moment, though whether judging or considering he could not tell.

*'When we have it we will be what the universe forces us to be, and do what we must.'* He dipped his head, and the light had drained from the lines of his face, leaving canyons of shadow. *'We will destroy all those who stand against us.'*

The memory lingered at the edge of Hrend's thoughts as he watched the dust billowing onto the flame-touched wind. The fusion cutters on the drill head flared to brightness. Smoke and steam began to spill up, blending with the powdered earth. The drill cut deeper and Hrend felt Tallarn tremble.

☷ ☷ ☷

The Iron Warrior was right in front of Argonis. The red eye-slit was so close that he could see the ghosts of tactical data projected onto the other side of the crystal. He reacted without pause. The gladius came up in a smooth motion, its power field snapping active the instant before its tip punched through the eye-slit. The Iron Warrior's head blew apart in an explosion of lightning. Argonis grabbed the dead warrior's shoulder with his other hand, yanked the corpse through the door before he could fall and kept running.

The next door was coming up fast. Behind him Sota-Nul was hissing out sounds that sent sparks up his spine. They were counting on speed now, pure speed and aggression. The old way, the Cthonian way. The door snapped open in front of him. The space beyond spread outwards. Everything was the beat of alarms. He could hear the keening of aircraft engines. The ceiling above was peeling back to show the dust-smudged stars above. An oily shield flickered against the darkness beyond, holding back Tallarn's toxic air.

He kept moving, slowing his run to a determined stride, and clamped his weapons to his armour. He had passed this way before, when he had arrived. It had been filled with activity then, but nothing like this. Dozens of craft in black-and-yellow slashed metal were rising into the waiting dark. The noise was like the breath of iron gods. Gunships, strike fighters, bombers and landers rose from platforms on shimmering columns of anti-grav and jet thrust. They hovered in layers, waiting as those above them ascended into the night's sky. He knew what he was seeing: it was a full battle deployment.

He saw the *Sickle Blade*. The green and black of her fuselage a crow amongst the brushed metal of the Iron Warriors. Lights winked on the tips of her wings. A tracked servitor was uncoupling fuel lines from her belly. Part of him thanked the now dead Jalen for his preparation.

He quickened his pace. He felt eyes and sensor blisters turn towards him. The downwash glow of thrusters caught his sea-green and black-armour. High above, a wing of Lightning Crows breached the shield, and roared into the dark. He swung under the wing.

Further away, an Iron Warrior in a spider-limbed servo-rig paused and looked towards them. The tracked servitor was backing away. Its steel limbs snapped inspection plates shut, pulling pins from the weapon systems. Sota-Nul and Prophesius were climbing the rear ramp.

He reached the ladder hanging beneath the cockpit, gripped and swung up in a single movement. Mag-clamps latched onto the power pack on his back and pulled him into the cockpit. Neural connections fizzed live with a tingle of static. Displays within the cockpit began to scroll with data. The engines woke. Power thrummed through the frame. His hands were moving without his thinking. The canopy closed over him. He could see data from the hangar's launch control. Out beyond the armoured crystal of the canopy the Iron Warrior with the servo-rig was moving closer, picking up speed. Whatever luck or plan had got them this far, it was about to run out.

Red warning runes began to pulse in his view. He could see other figures running now. The space above the canopy was a flow of ascending aircraft. Figures with weaponry were moving across the cavern floor: heavy bolters, claviers, missile launchers. He blinked system control markers, overriding cut-outs as they flashed back warnings. The *Sickle Blade*'s weapon systems woke. The power in the engines was rising, vibrating through him. Machine voices began to shout in his ears, telling him to power the craft down, telling him that he was not cleared to launch. Iron Warriors were dropping into cover across the launch pad. Over the neural connection to the gunship he felt their rangefinders touch the *Sickle Blade*. They felt like cold needles.

He glanced upwards. The swarm of machines was still rising and rising. He looked down again. A voice was speaking in his helm, telling him to power his machine down.

'We are ready,' said Sota-Nul's voice in his ear. He nodded, keyed a control, and squeezed the firing trigger on the control column.

The *Sickle Blade* was a Storm Eagle. Tens of thousands of its breed served in the Great Crusade, and now in the civil war which had replaced it. But the *Sickle Blade* was more than a machine of war. She, and her ten sisters, had been born in the forges of Mars and given to the Sons of Horus as an honour gift. Masters had crafted each part of her. The gold feathers traced across her back and wings had been the work of one of the most gifted artisans, and the hand of the Fabricator General himself had woken her machine-spirit. She was a queen of her kind, and a queen made to fly through winds of fire and destruction.

The twinned heavy bolters in her chin spat fire. Explosions swallowed the Iron Warriors as Argonis untethered *Sickle Blade*'s thrusters. She lifted off the launch pad, still breathing fire. A beam of light flicked out from across the platform, skimming her left wing. Argonis pivoted the gunship in mid-air. The line of fire traced across the platform edge and sawed through the shooter. Brass casings cascaded from the gunship's cheeks.

Argonis's senses were a wall of target runes. The cavern floor was alive with frantic movement: more troops, more guns, less and less chance of survival. As soon as he had seen the Iron Warriors move to stop them, he had known that there was only one way out: havoc.

He turned his gaze on a fuel bowser, and blinked the target rune. The line of shells flicked sideways and touched the fuel canister. A sheet of flame spilled out in every direction, burning white, and rage-red. Argonis felt the *Sickle Blade* rock. His eyes flicked across the cavern floor, blinking between grounded gunships, munition stacks and fuel cells. Rockets loosened from *Sickle Blade*'s back. Fire clouds thumped into the air, racing upwards to brush the craft hovering above. One column of fire slammed into the belly of a strike fighter. The craft rose, twisted, flipped over and struck the cavern wall.

Argonis pushed power into the engines, and the *Sickle Blade* rose through the inferno. Beams of light and lines of shells cut the air beneath her. He paused for a second, holding the breath in his lungs as the power in the engines became a shackled scream. The *Sickle Blade* tilted its nose up, still floating above the sea of fire and smoke. Argonis saw the stacked aircraft above; some had halted while others still rose to the dark beyond. He unchained the engine's power and they shot upwards. G-force punched him in the gut. Inside his helm, he smiled. Iron Warriors craft were streaming past, and he was an arrow spinning through them, spiralling higher and higher. The atmospheric shield was around them and then past them, and they were shooting high into Tallarn's night.

CLONES, THOUGHT IAEO, as she stared up at Jalen.

'Perhaps,' he said, and shook his head. 'The hydra has many heads.'

She blinked, and facts came together in her pain-streaked thoughts.

'Yes,' he said again, as though in reply. 'I am in your thoughts.'

'One...' she fought the word from her lips, 'One... less head... now.'

Jalen's eyes hardened, and tattoos unfolded across his skin.

'I thought your kind was created not to feel emotional pleasure at anything but a completed kill.'

'You have no idea what I am.'

'You are an assassin of the Vanus Temple, an infocyte operating under an Unbound Condition.' He smiled, a pleased and cruel smile. 'You did not think that the temples were unknown to the Twentieth, did you? We are the Alpha. We were there while your masters were still killing for coin.'

*Data: Pride, the need for the defeated to acknowledge their superiority, a compulsive need for complexity and showmanship, all qualities of the Alpha Legion psychological pattern.*

'But you have been out here and active for quite a while, haven't you?' he asked. 'You're not really built for that are you? The conditioning is probably fraying by now. You probably have started making mistakes.'

*You have made an error, Iaeo.*
*You have made an error, Iaeo.*
*You have made an error, Iaeo.*

'Of course you have made an error...' Jalen's eyes narrowed. '...Iaeo, the current situation is that error manifested.'

She closed her eyes, and tried to will her limbs to move. Fresh pain was the only answer. She managed to roll onto her side. Blood began to dribble from the right-hand side of her mouth. She could see her visor lying on the metal grating just an arm-reach away. She also saw the two other people she had heard. They were Alpha Legionnaires, but they wore compact recon armour. One held a fat-barrelled needle rifle, the other a block-framed assault shotgun. Both had near identical faces. They were not looking at her, but holding guard with the relaxed carelessness of poised predators.

She tried to move her hand towards her visor. It moved a few centimetres, and then the ice needles hardened in her nerves and her hand froze.

'That's far enough,' said Jalen.

*How did I allow this to happen?* thought Iaeo.

'Because to err is human,' said Jalen, 'and no matter what your clade gave to you, that is still all you are.'

*No*, she thought. *No, that is not right.*

Projections exploded in her head from memory, uncoiling into awareness from where she had buried them in hidden parts of her brain. They were vast, beautiful chains of probability, and possibility, of data inputted and data changed and pushed back into the world to do its work.

Jalen was frowning now, tattooed scales twisting and shimmering. She could feel the fingers of his mind in her thoughts now, cold fingers scrabbling to follow the exploding network of the full termination projection that she had created.

She allowed a smile onto her face. It was not natural, she had to imitate it from memory, but it fitted the moment well enough.

*Thank you*, she thought, and saw in his eyes that he heard. *Thank you for being so predictable.*

And she showed him what she had done, the manipulations she had hidden from him in her mind. There was just enough time for his pupils to bloom wide before the Iron Warriors security detail blasted onto the gantry and the first shots split the air.

The machines of war came from across the northern reaches of Tallarn. First hundreds, then thousands, then more than a mortal mind could count. They poured out of the buried shelters, long rivers of tanks, flowing down broken roads, across hills and plains. Knights, Dreadnoughts and Titans walked with them, striding amongst the flow of armour like men wading through a deep river. All flowed down into the plateau which spread across the heart of Tallarn's northern continent. Bound by mountains, the Khedive was a great, flat dish of land which had swallowed the blood of many since the battle for Tallarn had begun. Now the full strength of the loyalists poured into it without cease.

The Crescent City shelter emptied every machine which could move onto the plain, surging to meet the transporters which dropped from orbit to spill more and more machines onto the fog-veiled dust. More and more began to arrive, as the vanguards of forces which had ridden for days began to converge. Many stretched for hundreds of kilometres back across the continent. On the plain of Khedive the gathering forces marshalled, ordering themselves and pushing outwards as more arrived. Vanguard forces of skimmers took the mountain passes above the plateau unopposed, and within hours the first formations of heavier machines were grinding towards them.

The rising sea of iron did not go unopposed.

At the edge of the northern polar cap three Iron Warriors strike flights hit a convoy heading south from the Cobalack Shelter. The front five kilometres of the convoy became a burning grave of machines. Minutes later three Iron Warriors war groups hit the paralysed line of tanks from the side. Their convoy was annihilated, its fate screamed across the sky in an orange curtain.

To the south, a scratch force of Iron Warriors, Cassidnal Armour, and Cyberneticae maniples met a column coming from Essina Shelter advancing down the remains of the Northern Arterial Highway. The two forces met front on. The long snakes of machines broke apart, spreading across the land to either side of the highway as they each sought to encircle their enemies.

An hour after the first loyalists took the passes above the Khedive, the Iron Warriors struck back. Bombers and gunships poured explosives down on the mountain tops. Rock shattered under the rolling drum of explosions and the heat of the firestorm. Avalanches of cooling rock slid from the peaks, and roared down their flanks. Thunderhawks and Storm Birds skimmed the detonation wave to drop armoured units into the passes. Those few of the loyalist vanguard units remaining fought on but it was not enough. The Iron Warriors held the passes between the rising sea of loyalists and the Sightless Warren.

In the strategiums of the Sightless Warren, the Iron Warriors watched their enemy gather and saw the greatest opportunity for victory and defeat unfold before them. If they thought which of the two possibilities was more likely, none of them voiced their opinion. They waited for word from Perturabo, still in the void aboard the Iron Blood. When that word came it was as direct as it was brutally simple.

'Strike now with all strength. Hold them to the plains. Choke them in dead iron.'

His sons heard their primarch and obeyed.

# THIRTEEN

**Storm centre
Cursus
Sickle Blade**

KORD STARED DOWN the sight. The oil-black shape of the Iron Hands Predator was to his left. Both it and *War Anvil* had come to a halt as soon as they had crested the last line of hills and seen what waited for them on the plains of Khedive.

The storm was a pale band across the dying land. Dark smudges rolled within it, like bruises forming then fading in minutes. Lightning speckled its height. He could see the winds whipping its edges into blurred gauze. It was a great beast of a storm. He could feel the hairs on his neck and arms rising. Sparks of static were pinging off the hull. And there was something else, something that clung to the colours, and even to the stale taste of the air in his breath mask.

He had never believed in gods or supernatural forces. He had seen psykers and the impossibility they could make possible, but that was nothing more than something he did not understand, a subset of the many things which made the stars burn and time pass. The universe was a cold, uncaring machine, and humanity had only the place it could carve out for itself. Goodness, evil, kindness and cruelty, it was simply a matter of selecting belief. That was it. There was nothing more.

But as he looked into the storm he felt as if he were looking at something that he could only express in words that came from the language of myths.

It felt like looking into the face of a god.

'A vortex you said,' said Menoetius, his voice seeming to harmonise with the static of the vox. 'I thought you were intending your words to be metaphorical.'

'The storm is spreading outwards and increasing in strength,' said Kord. 'This is an eater, bigger than I have ever heard tell of. Anything that goes in is unlikely to come out.'

'You spent the lives of almost all those under your command to come this far,' said Menoetius. 'You had the strength to spend their lives but not your own?'

Kord kept his eye on the wall of rolling dust. Sweat was stinging his eyes.

'Colonel, I saw something,' it was Origo, from the position just in front of Kord, his voice breaking through his thoughts. Kord felt the fear recede, and become an itch at the back of his skull. The gunner had turned to look back at him, eyes wide and bright behind the lenses of his suit. 'Had it on the infra-sight for a second then it went. But it was there. A machine.'

'For certain?' Kord asked.

'For certain.'

'We are going in,' he said into the vox then switched to speak to the rest of *War Anvil*'s crew. 'All positions stand by to advance. Weapons ready.'

'Colonel, the storm...' called one of the crew, but he was not listening enough to even recognise their voice.

'Advance,' he said, and a second later *War Anvil* obeyed his will.

The winds closed over them with fingers of air which slammed against the hull and rattled grit on the hatches. Within a minute they could not see anything with their normal eyes except a swirling layer of dust the colour of bruises. Images danced and collapsed on the auspex screen. The infra-sights showed nothing. Every few moments lightning would split the view through the sight. *War Anvil* rocked as it ground onwards. Kord was breathing slowly, feeling his heart hammer as he waited for something to appear on the scope.

THE DRILL WENT silent. Hrend felt the ground beneath his feet become still. He turned, suddenly aware that he had been drifting. Time had passed as the storm pulled at them. They were at its centre, he was certain, but even here they felt its touch. The shapes of the other machines were unmoving, with billowing dust shrouding them and then revealing their shapes again. The heat signatures of each were a low murmur of brightness in his heat-sight. The breath of the air was muted, hushed, waiting.

Hrend turned towards the excavator the great machine was awake, its engines still turning. Cables connecting it to its drill head disappeared down a wide hole angled into the ground. They looked slack, as though cut while under tension.

'What is the drill status?' asked Hrend.

'It is no longer functioning,' said the monotone servitor. 'Cause unknown.'

Hrend walked to the opening in the ground. The drill had cut down at an angle, creating a sloped passage, which slid to a cold darkness. The sides of the hole were rough glass, fused solid by fusion torches. The lights mounted on Hrend's shoulders lit with a thought. The hard, white light spilled down the glistening shaft. Far down something glinted, a hard edge of something reflective catching the light. The cables and feeds for the drill head lay on the floor, two lines plunging down, beckoning.

Hrend was about to turn when he heard something. He went still, and turned slowly back to the hole. The black disc of the shaft's depths filled his sight, its edges fraying the light he shone at it. He heard the sound again, distant but distinct: a whisper of a voice, a voice that should not be here. Inside the coffin of his body he felt his true body shiver. The wind gusted around him, dust scraping across his frame. The blank disc before him seemed to swell and push against the light. It did not look like dark pooling at the end of a tunnel now. It looked like a black sun.

He took a step down the tunnel. The glass layer crunched under his foot. He felt calm, cold even. The wind was spilling a gauze of dust down the tunnel. He took another step.

His footing slipped, and suddenly he was falling, glass screaming as metal scored into its surface. He tried to turn, but his sight was a crazed mass of warning runes.

He slammed to a halt. His sight fizzed for a second, then steadied.

He rose, the light from his carapace touching the rainbow sheen of the walls. He looked back up the shaft. The sky was a distant circle high above. He turned his gaze back to what had stopped his descent.

The drill head, or what remained of it, lay across the tunnel. A neat slice ended the blunt mass of the machine after a metre. It simply stopped after that, as if something had cleaved the front portion away. Hrend shifted and watched as the stab-light caught the bright edges of precisely cut metal. Hrend looked up at what lay just beyond the truncated drill.

A wall of black stone met the beams of light. It was part of a larger structure. Hrend could see that at a glance, the slight curvature of the stone told him that he was looking at a small part of a great, curved wall, perhaps even a circle, hidden beneath the ground like a buried crown. Its substance looked like no stone or crystal Hrend had ever seen. At first it seemed opaque, but as Hrend watched the light slid beneath the surface and kindled reflections within its depths.

It was then that he saw the carving on the surface. A face was looking out at him. It was not human. Wide eyes looked out from a slim face above a mouth filled with needle teeth. It might have been snarling. It might have been grinning. It might have been screaming.

He heard something behind him, a low sound, somewhere between a hiss and a laugh. He turned, and the light found only the glass of the passage walls. Hrend turned back to the wall of black stone. He froze. In his capsule of amniotic fluid his true body shivered uncontrollably.

The carved face had moved. Its lips had closed over its shark smile, and its head had turned, its gaze seeming to focus on a point just…

'Iron,' said a voice behind him. He twisted, arming his weapons.

A figure stepped from the blackness. Its presence seemed to strain at the boundaries of the machine that encased it. Black pit eyes looked at Hrend as it halted.

'Do you still wish to be iron?' asked the face of Perturabo.

THE SKIES OF Tallarn danced with light. Re-entry fires streaked the dark, hundreds of them, thousands of them. The stars hid behind the blink of low-orbit explosions. Iron was pouring out of the sky, landers, drop pods, gunships and attack craft falling from the heavens. Beneath them the nightside of Tallarn bubbled with explosions, sparkling as though scattered with liquid gold.

Argonis climbed, running the engines red, listening to warning chimes ring in his ears but not listening. He was hauling the *Sickle Blade* on a corkscrew path towards the point of light that was the *Iron Blood*.

Thinning atmosphere streamed past the *Sickle Blade*. Feathers of heat edged its wings. Space bloomed above Argonis, and the roar of passing air dropped away.

Alert chimes screamed from his helm. Threat warnings flashed at the edge of his eyes. He slammed the *Sickle Blade* into a tumble as lines of las-light scored the void behind it.

'Brother,' Volk's voice fizzed across the vox. '*Cut your engines.*'

Argonis glanced at the auspex. A trio of runes was closing on him, fast. Weapon lock warnings chimed in his ears. Ahead of him the marker of the *Iron Blood* was swelling in his sight. Screens of ships and shoals of fighter craft blistered the void around it.

'You fire on me, you fire on the Warmaster,' said Argonis.

'*You have drawn our blood, you have broken our trust.*'

'There is no trust left in this war, brother.'

'You will not escape.'

'I do not intend to escape.'

'Whatever you intend, you will die here.'

'You did know your limitations, brother,' said Argonis, and cut the connection. Hostile weapon lock alerts screamed in his ear. He spun the *Sickle Blade*, shedding countermeasures in a fire-burst cloak. Bursts of las-fire licked the void. He was breathing hard, gravity slamming into him like hammer blows. He fired his thrusters, and the *Sickle Blade* tumbled.

'Missiles loose, and locked onto us,' said Sota-Nul's voice.

'I am aware,' he said. An explosion bloomed in the spinning night as a missile hit a decoy pod. He waited, feeling the G-force smear his flesh against the inside of his armour. The *Iron Blood* and its escorts were closing fast. There were a lot of ships in the spheres around Tallarn, the war in the void mirroring the escalating battle on the ground.

'Incoming ordnance,' called Sota-Nul, and building-sized torpedoes were suddenly burning past him. He spun through their thrust wake. The Iron Warriors were close behind, lacing the void with las-fire. Everything was getting very tight. Flying directly into a battle-sphere was not ideal, but did give Argonis certain advantages. A pursuing missile cluster hit one of the warheads and detonated. The torpedo corkscrewed off course, hit another warhead, and the void became a bright layer of boiling light.

The *Sickle Blade* rode ahead of the blast wave. Warships loomed ahead of them. Stitched planes of cannon fire spread from their flanks. Challenges and warnings filled Argonis's ears.

The trio of strike fighters broke from the inferno behind him, dragging banners of burning gas.

'Those ships have seen us.'

Argonis ignored the tech-witch, and flicked the vox to a multiple band, maximum power transmission.

'*Iron Blood* and escorts, this is Argonis, emissary of Warmaster Horus and bearer of his will. You will prepare for us to come aboard.'

A clod of burning debris spun in front of the *Sickle Blade*. Argonis rolled under it. Behind him the three strike fighters hugged close. Las-bolts streaked past.

'Cut your engines now,' said Volk over the vox.

Argonis flipped the *Sickle Blade* over, watched a target rune lock green on a strike fighter, and squeezed a firing trigger. The closest fighter became a burst of blue and white light. The *Sickle Blade* flipped back over and rolled away from its kill.

'Fall back, Volk,' said Argonis. 'You were never good enough to take me, and mercy does not suit me.'

A scattering of las-bolts answered.

Argonis switch back to the broad transmission, and spoke again.

'*Iron Blood*, this is the emissary of the Warmaster. I demand immediate audience with your primarch.'

Identification ciphers travelled with his words. No reply came. Behind him the two remaining strike fighters were closing and firing. The *Iron Blood* was a growing splinter of light against the stars, its shields fizzing as it ploughed through battle debris.

'In the name of Horus, you will comply.'

He could see the great gun batteries of both the flagship and its escorts, building-sized barrels yawning at him with the promise of certain obliteration.

*So far to come*, he thought, and the dance of light and explosions seemed to fade into a background. So far from the tunnels of Cthonia. So far from a near-starved youth with a mirror knife and a false smile. He was not sure if he would have chosen the decades of life he had lived. But then it seemed there was little choice in this life, and the first lesson of the gang wars he had learned was the only thing that still held true: we are born alone, and if we live it is alone, and in the end we die alone. His hands went still on the controls, and the *Sickle Blade*'s dance became a simple, straight line drawn towards its future.

Fire and darkness slid past him. He heard voices, but did not listen to them. He did not want this, he had never wanted any of it, but there had never been an alternative besides the swift, endless fall to oblivion. He thought of those he had grown up with, the gang warriors who had bled out into the dark. He thought of the brothers he had watched go down to Isstvan III not realising it was the last thing they would ever do. He thought of Horus, the warrior king who was his master, his primarch, but not his father. And he waited for the fire, and the silence beyond.

'*Emissary,*' the voice filled his head and grated down his spine. The las-fire had vanished from the void around him. The markers of the two remaining strike fighters moved into positions just beyond his wing tips. '*You wish my presence. So come to me,*' said the voice of Perturabo. In front of Argonis the guns of the *Iron Blood* turned away, and he saw doors open on a black and waiting space within, like teeth around a mouth.

THE IRON WARRIORS fired as they broke onto the gantry. Iaeo had an instant to recognise the scream of rotor cannons spinning up. Then the first line of bullets cut across the platform. Jalen dived to the side. Behind him the two Alpha Legionnaires were dropping and firing, the gun booming a counter-rhythm to the scream of the cannons.

*Data: Estimated force of Iron Warriors deployed fifteen.*

She could see them out of the corner of her eye, heavy silhouettes of armour, slab shields and glowing gun barrels. They were advancing down the gantry, shaking it with synchronised strides. She had brought them here. A timed signal aimed precisely to bring an Iron Warriors detail here at this moment. Without Argonis's breakout it would not have worked. She had brought target and termination together, just as intended.

The Alpha Legion warriors were calling to each other, short harsh stubs of decisions and commands. Jalen was flat on the grating. She saw one of the Alpha Legion warriors begin to move forward towards the pinned man. A second rotor cannon opened up and cut the warrior in half before he had taken a stride.

Jalen turned his head where he lay. She was looking right into his eyes. She felt something move in her mind, an echo of disbelief and fury. The tattoos of serpents and lizards were squirming under his eyes. She still could not move, but she thought of nodding, and knew that he felt the gesture.

The Iron Warriors' fire shifted. Jalen began to rise. A round pinged from the floor grating, and blew out his knee in a shower of bone and blood. He stumbled, tattooed face twisting in pain. He pushed himself up. A line of rotor cannon fire ripped him in two.

*Data: Two of three triplet operatives, designate name Jalen, eliminated.*

The numbness pinning her limbs released. There was a lot of pain to cope with. She tensed her muscles. Splintered bones cut into them. Fresh pain. Hard rounds ripped through the gantry, shaking it, shredding it. The Iron Warriors had formed a shield wall thirty paces away. The rotor cannon fire stopped. The last Alpha Legion warrior was still alive but had retreated, trying to reach a point where he could exit the kill zone. She saw movement behind the shield wall, and two narrow gaps opened in its front. The muzzles of heavy flamers thrust through the gaps, pilot lights bright against scorched metal.

She rolled to her left, her hand finding and grasping her visor. The torn edge of the gantry framed a drop to darkness. She paused for an eye-blink, hearing the rising pressure of the flamer hoses, seeing the black gulf below.

The end was so close now, all the lines of possibility drawing to a point, to a resolution. The projections said that most likely things would proceed without her now. Causality had developed its own, irreversible momentum.

Most likely… an imprecise phrase, the kind of phrase that would have earned her punishment and scorn from her mentor. But she was beyond exhausted, and the old master was a long time dead.

The flamers fired. She rolled over the edge of the gantry, blackness rising to meet her as flames filled the air above.

*Fire, smoke, and the roar of shattering metal filled the vast bowl of the Khedive. The mountains and hills running its circumference cupped over three million square kilometres of land. Wide enough that the sun would rise on one edge hours before its first rays would touch the other, it had been an ocean of swaying grass before the virus bombing. Terraced orchards had marched up the lower slopes of the surrounding mountains. In the high years of the Great Crusade, armies had gathered on the plains beneath, vast, system-cracking forces laid out in gridded order across areas so large that time marks changed twice between the outer edges of the muster.*

*Armies filled it again, and the sky above roared with the engines of warplanes and landing craft. But the order of the past was as much a memory as the sway of grass and the smell of fruit blossom blowing from the mountains.*

*The Khedive had become a nest of battles. There was not one engagement, there were hundreds, coiling together, spawning and eating each other by the second. By night the plain rippled with detonations and explosions, turning the fog-laced air to bloody red and strobing orange.*

*By day the smoke thickened the fog to hide the sun behind black veils. Titans strode through the murk, firing at targets beyond the horizon. Within hours a new, ever-changing topography of wreckage had swallowed the shape of the earth beneath. Tangles of dead machines formed forests of black metal beneath the slumped bodies of Knights. Plasma storms raged for hours in places where the greatest war machines fell. Spirals of glowing energy howled as they sucked the wind inside them.*

*Into this cauldron both sides poured more and more of their strength. Columns of loyalist forces from distant shelters continued to arrive. Many had spent much of their fuel and air just to reach the battle site, and failed within hours of joining. Many rolled from the southern passes only to die within seconds of touching the plateau. Fighters spun through the smoke as they hunted the landers that still dropped from the orbiting ships.*

*To the eyes of those looking down their gun sights, or at the screens of their auspexes, there seemed to be no order, just the unending roar of explosions and the flash of detonation. They were not fighting to a plan, they were just fighting what was in front of them. To other eyes, though, eyes that watched from high above and far away, there was a pattern, written in the shift of numbers, losses and ground held. It said that victory could go to either side, but that whoever lost the Khedive would not be able to hold Tallarn.*

# FOURTEEN

**Iron from within**
**Metatron**
**Termination complete**

War Anvil was firing blind. Every gun was roaring, the sound of the storm drowning in the rolling crash of guns. He could hear the voice of Menoetius, of Origo, and the rest, each one calling out words which shattered as the hull rang and rang like a struck anvil.

They had found the Iron Warriors.

The auspex showed the heat blooms of multiple machines. Heavy calibre rounds began to strike the front of *War Anvil*. The main gun fired, and the breech slammed back. The smoking casing rang as it fell into the space beneath. A second late the demolisher fired. Kord was half aware of a red target mark vanishing from the auspex.

*A kill*, he thought, but his eyes were pulling back to the sight block. The world outside was a swirl of dust and storm wind split by lightning and gunfire. He could see something though, something blunt and vast, covered by cables, its bulk stabilised by piston feet. He recognised it: a macro drill, its back tilted up. He could see the wind sweeping the top off heaped earth. A thrill of elation snapped through him. This was it, this was the answer. The

Iron Warriors were not looking for something on the surface but beneath the earth of Tallarn.

He watched, tracking the silent drill machine, even as Menoetius's Predator cut across his sight, firing on the move, stabbing at machines which were blurs behind the storm curtain. They were receiving fire, but he could tell they were winning. How could they not? He had been right, he had–

The beam snapped out from the storm and skimmed the top of *War Anvil*'s right track. Kord felt the heat of the beam's touch through the hull. The other track kept turning. The machine slewed around.

The bottom edge of its running track hit a pile of debris and pitched it over. For a long, terrible second, Kord felt *War Anvil*'s weight shift like a ship riding a wave. Then the tank tipped onto its side, rocked, and went still. Kord's head hit the sight mount in front of him, and the world went grey. The engine drive kept turning the left tracks. He could feel blood on the inside of his suit's hood. He could still hear the roar and boom of battle outside.

Something moved close to him, and he twisted to see Origo holding the side of his head. There was blood on the inside of his left eyepiece just under where his hand was pressed. The replacement gunner twisted around as Kord moved, and his hand snapped out, gripping Kord's own hand. There was still strength in the grasp, a lot of strength. Kord instinctively pulled his hand back but Origo held on.

'Call for help,' he said, his voice a rasp over the internal vox. 'Call them, call anyone and they will know, they will come for us.'

The engine drive finally cut out, and now there was just the muffled clamour of battle beyond the hull.

Kord shook his hand free of Origo's grasp and the gunner curled back, still holding his head. Kord found the key for the squadron-wide vox.

'Menoetius,' he called.

'*Two targets still active, colonel.*'

'We are–'

'Your situation is evident, colonel. It will be addressed after the engagement.' Menoetius's voice was ice cold, and unmovable.

Kord's head was whirling with pain, numbness and delayed panic whirling.

'Call, they will hear,' said Origo again, his hand still pressed to the bloody side of his head. His voice sounded distant, almost slurred. 'They will come. My brothers are dead. I am the last but they will come. We have found it. Tell them. They will come.'

Kord looked at the gunner. There was something odd in the man's voice, a simultaneous note of desperation and certainty. He sounded like he was not really talking to Kord. He thought of the blood smeared on the inside of the man's eyepieces where his head had smashed into the main gun mount. Damage, concussion, delirium, but in one thing he was right. Kord twisted and strained until his fingers found the main vox controls, and switched it to broad transmit with maximum power on every loyalist frequency. The storm wind was rising rattling dust on *War Anvil*'s belly, the sound rising to blend with the noises of battle. He hesitated, adrenaline making his hands shake.

Was there any point? Would his words reach through the storm? Would anyone come if they heard?

'To anyone that can hear, this is Colonel Kord of the Tallarn Seventy-First. We are damaged, unable to move. Current location grid 093780 in the Hacadia Flats. Please respond.'

'MASTER?' SPOKE HREND, but did not move. His sight was popping with static, runes and data fizzing into and out of existence.

'You have succeeded, my son. You have succeeded where all others have failed. You have walked the paths which others have walked, but for you, they have led you here.'

'What is this?'

'This is destiny. This is a chance that will never come again, not for you, not for your brothers or your father.'

'You are not my master. You are not Perturabo.'

Hrend raised his remaining arm, fingers snapping wide,

meltagun… cold and dead in his grasp. The creature which was not Perturabo, but which wore his face, smiled.

'No I am not. We are your shadow, Iron Warrior, but that is not why we are here.'

'This discussion is over,' growled Hrend. He activated his vox-link, formed a transmission to Jarvak on the surface. The signal did not even start.

The creature shook its head slowly.

Pain burrowed through Hrend, as one by one each of his neural connections began to burn. The pistons on his legs began to bleed pressure, cogwork and servos unwinding. He slid to the floor like a great, metal puppet with its strings cut.

Light continued to stream from his carapace-mounted lights, sheeting upwards, catching the angles of his fallen shape and casting them against the roof and walls. The figure of Perturabo cast no shadow, but bled into the gloom at its edges. It looked down on him, and cocked its head to one side as though observing phenomena it had not encountered before.

'We are here to offer you a choice, Ironclad.'

Hrend could feel the metallic bulk of the Dreadnought frame all around him. He could not move, even the ghost sensations of his severed arm were gone.

'What are you?' His voice scratched from his speaker grille.

'You know what we are,' said Perturabo's voice. 'We have met many times. We were there in the birth of your Legion and your brother Legions. We were there as you bloodied the stars. When you felt your first surge of martial pride, we felt it with you. When you bled, we were in the blood that stained the ground. When you felt the wounds to your honour, and dreamed of iron, we were both the wound and the dream.'

The figure's shape blurred, its substance and shape becoming dust and smoke. Other faces rose from the cloud: a face of cold hard lines beneath a shock of white hair, a face smiling in sympathy and mockery, a face which radiated control from its feral lines.

On they went, sliding from one onto another until they were a blur, until they were one.

And through the carousel of shape and shadow he saw new faces rise, faces of hounds cast of fire and brass, faces of pale flesh with razor-cut smiles, faces lost beneath clumps of tumours and veils of boils, faces that held other faces within them. He felt the heat of the fires of Isstvan V again. He could feel fingers he no longer had burning to black twigs, and eyes boil again in the empty sockets of his skull.

A sudden burst of red and orange light spiralled down the tunnel walls. The creature moved aside, so that Hrend could see the disc of light that was the tunnel's mouth. The angry glow grew and stuttered, and he heard the roar of gunfire, the scream of energy splitting armour. His vox activated. Noise screamed into his mind. He recognised the voices: Jarvak, Orun, the crews of his cadre, the crews who had been strong enough to reach here. They were dying.

'This is not an end,' said the creature. 'This is a crossroads.'

'We will destroy you.'

The creature wore Perturabo's face again to smile.

'You cannot destroy what will be,' said the creature. 'You can only choose.'

The shadows began to crawl away as furnace light swelled through the dark. Hrend's metal body began to glow with heat. Fire was pouring inside his iron coffin. He was burning away. The fluid around him boiled. His flesh sloughed from his bones. Black blisters formed across his sight as the last moisture in his corpse became smoke. He could still see, but the world was not as it had been.

'See, Ironclad,' purred the creature. 'See what you can be.'

Then he realised that he was standing, that his own limbs were unfolding beneath him. He was a glowing, molten god, his skin the cracked black skin of cooling lava. He felt his thoughts cut free of all concerns. He was a line running through time, a summation. He had been there when the first fortress fell. He had lived as the shell fell through from a clear sky onto a town that would cease to be. He had broken the skin of worlds, and roared his existence in the voice of the firestorm. There was only one beat and measure to this life and that was the heartbeat of the firing gun and the noise of bones breaking under the fall of hammers. He was not flesh. He was not blood, or fragile bone. He was obliteration, and he stood beneath the fire shroud of worlds.

The vision dissolved but still he stood. His armour was fading to red and black heat. He could feel it. He could feel it as though it were the heat of his own burning blood. He looked down. His arms were there, glistening, wet, like blood and muscle. Shackled power and heat coiled in his hands. He let out a breath. Smoke and steam hissed into the air. He raised his head, with a rattle of cogs and crack of bones.

'Your Legion will be as you,' said the creature. 'They can live, you can live. You can all be more than you dreamed. This is the truth of iron. Iron within and without, iron in the veins, iron screaming to the sky. It is the truth you have reached for all your life. Through pain, and death, and the drum of guns, you have walked here. You can be more than this. You can rise from it.'

He could see it, he could feel it: a Legion of iron and death, burning the stars, cowed by none and broken by nothing. It was what they were always supposed to be, what they should have been. Decimation, dishonour and betrayal would mean nothing.

'Call to your Legion, Sollos,' the voice sounded like a song hissed through a skull's teeth. 'Call to your Perturabo. Call to your brothers. Bring them here. Bring them to the gate of the gods.'

He felt his thoughts reach for the vox, and he knew that all he needed to do was to speak, and his call would reach through the storm above, and bring his father to the weapon he had murdered a world for.

And then he remembered the light of the ghost world beneath a black sun, and the shrieks of the Emperor's Children. The true face of his father, shrunken, but still strong, looked at him out of the core of his being.

'No,' said Hrend, his voice shaking as it fought to rise above the echoes of battle spilling down the shaft from above. He could feel the heat of his body pulling at his thoughts, could hear the thud of shells coughed into flight, and hear the scream of melting metal. The song of destruction called to him. It was him. It was the voice of his shadow.

'No,' his voice growled out, rising in power with every word forced out. 'You will not take our strength. You will not make us slaves to darkness.'

The creature laughed, and the laugh became the shaking ground and the roar of explosions. Hrend felt the furnace heat drain from his remade body. He tried to take a step towards the creature. The force sent cracks racing across his body. The fire at the core of him was dimming.

The creature shook its head, and stepped back towards the exposed patch of black stone.

'To refuse is still a choice. This end already stalks your Legion. You have already given yourselves. This is the Gateway to the Gods, the place of change, the door between past and present. The Eye of Terror is not amongst distant stars, son of iron. It is within you. It is here. The choice is not if, Ironclad. It is when.' The light of an explosion blinked down the passage. The creature was gone. A face of empty eyes and razor teeth stared at Hrend from the black wall of stone. It smiled in the stuttered blink of explosion light. 'So, my son, do you still wish to be iron?'

'Iron...' he hissed in a voice of dying static. He reached into the furnace within him, into the stinking core of obliteration, and pulled. 'Iron comes from within.'

The atoms of his being scattered outwards in a blinding white shock of heat. The earth flashed to vapour in a sphere around where he had stood. Burning gas raced up the mouth of the tunnel, and blew from the surface, in a single, brilliant, spike of fury. The shockwave spilled outwards. The wreckage and still-burning remains of vehicles shook where they lay, and then began to tilt downwards as a gulf opened beneath them. Dust and debris poured down into the expanding crater. The machines tumbled downwards, drowning in the earth spilling after them.

And then silence fell.

The dust plume hung in the air, the storm already pulling apart its substance. Beneath it the wind was already dragging fresh dust over the shallow crater, a vast hand wiping it away as though it had never existed.

On the edge of the desolation the hull of a tank lay on its side, like a fallen grave marker.

'You have drawn blood amongst my warriors, emissary,' Perturabo's voice rose over the roar of engines, as Argonis jumped down from the *Sickle Blade*'s cockpit. The hangar bay was a mass of stilled activity. Rocket engines were keening, war machines hung in the cradles beneath landers: all ready to fall on Tallarn. Perturabo stood before the brushed steel bulk of a huge tank, ringed by his Iron Circle automata. His augmented bulk swelled and contracted as though in time with great slow breaths. A slit-fronted helm covered his face, and he stared at Argonis with eyes of cold, blue light.

'You have concealed the truth from your Warmaster,' said Argonis, forcing strength into his voice. Behind him he heard Sota-Nul and Prophesius come to stand behind him. The Lord of Iron's gaze did not shift. He was still, but Argonis could feel pressure in that stillness, like a storm surge held back behind a dam.

'I have done what I needed to,' said Perturabo. 'As I have always done.'

Argonis shook his head.

'It no longer matters, it is over, lord. You will withdraw from this place.'

'You do not know what you say.'

'I do.' Argonis glanced at the waiting craft, and thought of the battle in the void he had seen around Tallarn, and of the glittering carpet of explosions on its surface.

'This is not a battle fought for strategic gain. It is a battle for...'

'For a weapon against betrayal.'

'A weapon hidden from those you serve?'

'We serve no one,' snarled Perturabo, and the words sent ice through Argonis.

'The Warmaster—'

'He was my brother before he was Warmaster.' Perturabo shook his head. 'I do this for him, for all of us.'

Argonis shook his head.

'You will withdraw. This battle is over.'

'We cannot do that.' Argonis turned to see Forrix step from behind a Thunderhawk. The First Captain aimed a volkite charger at Argonis. With him stood a line of dull-armoured Terminators. All of their weapons pointed at him, and Argonis could feel the death promised by the black circle of each barrel. 'We must finish this,' said Forrix.

'It is over!' Argonis shouted.

'That order is not yours to give,' said Forrix. Argonis looked back to Perturabo.

'You claim loyalty—'

'You will not speak to me of loyalty. I have given loyalty many times over, loyalty counted in lives and blood.'

'I speak as the Warmaster.'

Argonis did not even see Perturabo move, but suddenly the primarch was looming above him. The deck rang with the echo of his steps.

'You are not my brother,' growled Perturabo. 'Your voice is not his.'

'No,' said Argonis, fighting the instinct to turn away, to flee. 'No, it is not, but I bear the Warmaster's voice with me.'

He stepped back, his hand pulling a crooked key from where it hung around his neck. Prophesius stepped forward, as though called. Time seemed to have become syrup. The sounds of the chamber around muted. Colours dimmed, and faded to grey. Argonis felt his skin prickle as he reached out to fit the key into the back of Prophesius's mask.

'What is… it?' he had asked Maloghurst.

*'A creation of the Davinite priests. It was once an astropath. Now they call it a metatron, a conduit for voices, a caster of shadows from one place to another, no matter how distant. It is named Prophesius.'*

*'Why is it masked?'*

*Maloghurst had smiled before answering.*

The key slotted into the mask. Argonis felt his arm jerk, as though he had just touched a power cable. He could taste cinnamon and ozone. He turned the key. For an instant nothing happened. Then there was a click, then another, and another, and another, rattling together, like a chorus of unwinding springs and turning cogs. The back of the mask split apart. Prophesius's hands were shaking, fingers gripping the air. The wax tablet dropped from its grasp, melting as it fell. Shrill cries filled Argonis's ears as he stepped back. Forrix flinched, his aim dropping. Every living creature on the deck reeled. All except Perturabo.

The mask fell from Prophesius's head. Beneath there was a lump of pale flesh, and a wide, toothless mouth.

For a second the unmasked Prophesius just stood, its mouth flapping bonelessly. Then the mouth opened wide. And opened. And opened. A single, silent word came from within. Argonis felt it ring in the back of his skull, and vibrate in his bones. Glowing ashes and snow were falling in the air, and the word went on and on until it reached somewhere that was not here, but was just a shadow away. Smoke and ash vomited from Prophesius's mouth. The black cloud billowed, clotted, hardened, became something harder than smoke, yet thinner than light.

An armoured figure stood before them. The pelt and head of a huge wolf covered his shoulders. His clawed hand rested on the head of the mace that lay at his foot. Argonis bent his knees without being aware of the command passing from his thoughts.

Above him the shadow of Horus looked down at the Lord of Iron.

'Perturabo,' said Horus, and his voice was the hunger of flames and the crack of breaking ice.

Perturabo did not move.

'Brother,' he said, his voice steady.

'No,' said Horus, and his shadow form seemed to grow, light draining into the holes that were his eyes. 'No, not brother. I am your Warmaster, Perturabo, and I have watched from beside my emissary. I have seen what you have hidden from me.'

'Horus...' began Perturabo, but Horus's voice cracked out like a lash of thunder.

'You have deceived *me*. You have sought power, and kept it hidden from *me*. You have spent *my* forces for your own ends.'

The thundercloud presence of Horus grew larger, looming high, so that it looked down like the cloud of an explosion above a dead city. Argonis felt pressure building in his skull.

Beneath Horus's eyes Perturabo remained, a vast figure made small, yet still unbowed.

'Everything I have done has been for the Imperium we will build. Brother, you cannot be blind to serpents within us. I have seen the true face of our allies. I have felt the knife of their treachery. We must hold our own blade above their necks, or we will be unmade. It is almost in my grasp.' He seemed to shiver. 'Please, my brother, listen to me now. Trust me now.'

The silence grew in the growing crackle of the storm charge. Then Horus's shadow shook its head.

'You have strayed, Perturabo,' he raised his hand, 'and now you will hear my will.' The shadow of Horus seemed to shrink, to become harder. Argonis could barely keep his eyes open. He could feel the spit boiling on his tongue. He saw the shadow of talons reach towards Perturabo.

'Kneel,' said Horus.

IAEO FELL TO the waiting dark. Air rushed past her, pulling strings of blood from her body. She was dying. There was no escaping that fact. It was not even a projection, it was a fact: too much physical damage to live, and that was ignoring what the fall promised at its end. Her mind had responded by working faster, like a candle burning bright and clear before it went out.

And in the stopped-clock world of her fall, she heard the last strands of her creation resolve.

She heard the order to begin a tactical withdrawal roll through Perturabo's forces.

She heard the Alpha Legion signal channels buzz with confusion.

She heard the click of her last handful of seconds fall into the past.

It had been a long journey, a long way from the beginning of the mission to this end. All the projections had ended, all the variables had resolved. All apart from one. One final strand of unfixed possibility.

She cut away the sound of all the signals and the influx of data, until a single vox signal remained. The voice it carried rattled with static, but it was clear.

'To anyone that can hear, this is Colonel Kord of the Tallarn Seventy-First. We are damaged, unable to move. Current location grid 093780 in the Hacadia Flats. Please respond.'

No response came. Several communication arrays on both sides had caught it, but she alone heard Kord's voice. Filters and cut-outs meant that it would only reach the ears of others if she allowed it.

It had been the most tenuous part of the kill-projection, using Kord's obsession, feeding it, positioning him to ensure that Hrend's force never returned. It had worked though, and now they were a last unresolved factor.

'To anyone that can hear, this is Colonel Kord of the Tallarn Seventy-First. Please respond.'

If no one else heard the signal then *War Anvil* would become just another machine lost to Tallarn.

'If you can hear, please respond.'

They would survive for a while, but with Perturabo's forces withdrawing no one would go looking for them, and the loyalists would never hear their cries for help. No one would find what they had found.

'Please respond.'

They would end in silence when their air ran out.

'Please...'

A dust storm would come and cover them over, and their machine would become their tomb.

'...respond.'

She cut the signal.

Two seconds later her fall ended. Her last thoughts echoed in the now empty space of her mind.

*Termination complete. No errors.*

*Six days after it began, the Battle of Khedive ended. It ended not with fire, but with a slow, exhausted fading of fury. Thousands of tanks pulled back, like a storm tide ebbing down a flotsam-strewn shore. Wounded Knights and Titans limped from the jungle of heaped machines to stand at the plain's edge. Thousands died in the hours after the battle faded, their air and fuel finally running out, their crews dying in choking silence. Grey rain fell from the smoke-bloated clouds onto the fires that still burned on the wreckage-crusted plain.*

*Twelve hours later the Iron Warriors began to withdraw from the surface altogether. Within three weeks Tallarn was all but silent.*

*One week later General Gorn and his command cadre set foot inside the Sightless Warren.*

*Four weeks later, when no trace of the Iron Warriors or their allies could be found, a signal was sent to all loyalist forces on the planet, and transmitted by astrotelepathy far beyond the system.*

Imperium victor, *it read.* Tallarn stands.

# ACKNOWLEDGEMENTS

Some books have a battalion strength of people, other than the author, who need to be thanked – people who in ways great and small help the person with the pen do their thing. In the case of *Ironclad* there were two who stood at my shoulders as I wrote it. The first is my wife, Liz, who keeps me sane(ish), and tells me when something is good and when something could be better. The second person is Laurie Goulding, my editor, sounding board, and authoriser of wild ideas. If you enjoy *Ironclad*, and ever have the opportunity, thank these two. Trust me, without them it would not exist.

## ABOUT THE AUTHOR

**John French** has written several Horus Heresy stories including the novellas *Tallarn: Executioner* and *The Crimson Fist*, the novel *Tallarn: Ironclad*, and the audio dramas *Templar* and *Warmaster*. He is the author of the Ahriman series, which includes the novels *Ahriman: Exile*, *Ahriman: Sorcerer* and *Ahriman: Unchanged*, plus a number of related short stories collected in *Ahriman: Exodus*, including 'The Dead Oracle' and 'Hand of Dust'. Additionally for the Warhammer 40,000 universe he has written the Space Marine Battles novella *Fateweaver*, plus many short stories. He lives and works in Nottingham, UK.

## THE HORUS HERESY®

### Chris Wraight
# THE PATH OF HEAVEN
#### Riding out from the storm

Jaghatai Khan and the White Scars Legion
fight to clear the way to Terra

## READ IT FIRST
EXCLUSIVE PRODUCTS | EARLY RELEASES | FREE DELIVERY
blacklibrary.com